Forged in Love

Books by Mary Connealy

WYOMING SUNRISE
BOOK 1

Forged in Love

MARY CONNEALY

BETHANYHOUSE

a division of Baker Publishing Group
Minneapolis, Minnesota

Published by Bethany House Publishers
Minneapolis, Minnesota
www.bethanyhouse.com

Bethany House Publishers is a division of
Baker Publishing Group, Grand Rapids, Michigan

Printed in the United States of America

Library of Congress Cataloging-in-Publication Data
Names: Connealy, Mary, author.
Title: Forged in love / Mary Connealy.
Description: Minneapolis, Minnesota : Bethany House Publishers, a division of
    Baker Publishing Group, [2023] | Series: Wyoming sunrise ; 1
Identifiers: LCCN 2022037865 | ISBN 9780764241130 (paperback) | ISBN
    9780764241390 (casebound) | ISBN 9781493440702 (ebook)
Subjects: LCGFT: Romance fiction. | Western fiction. | Novels.
Classification: LCC PS3603.O544 F67 2023 | DDC 813/.6—dc23/eng/20220808
LC record available at https://lccn.loc.gov/2022037865

Scripture quotations are from the King James Version of the Bible.

Cover design by James Hall

Historical town photography by Gary J. Weathers / Getty
Cover model photography by Rekha Garton / Arcangel
Clothing imagery by Joanna Czogala / Arcangel

Author is represented by the Natasha Kern Literary Agency.

Baker Publishing Group publications use paper produced from sustainable forestry practices and post-consumer waste whenever possible.

23 24 25 26 27 28 29   7 6 5 4 3 2 1

This book is dedicated to Quinn,
my new granddaughter.
Beautiful and sweet and so welcome. True,
she's only one month old while I'm typing this,
but I sense that she is brilliant and
talented in many ways.

Welcome to the family, precious little girl.

1

A bullet slammed into the side of the stagecoach carrying Mariah Stover, her pa, and her older brother.

"Robbers!" The driver's voice roared in the hot Wyoming summer as the crack of a whip lashed, driving the horses faster. "Everyone, fight or die!"

Mariah heard the man riding shotgun on top of the stage land on his belly and open fire from the roof.

Bullets peppered the coach.

Mariah sat between Pa and Theo, facing the horses. Pa, a Civil War veteran, snapped his Spencer repeating rifle into his hand and fired out the window in a steady, rolling blast.

Theo threw himself to the opposite seat, occupied by two men who looked terrified. He aimed, fired, and fired again with his Colt pistol. Pa's rifle echoed the pistol in a steady volley of gunfire.

Mariah dug for the pistol in her satchel and checked the load. She looked out the window to her right. No one there.

Her pa and brother were tough men used to Western ways, who knew that civilization was often left behind at the town's edge. You just had to hope the uncivilized wouldn't follow you right into town.

You protected yourself, or you died. The stagecoach driver had it right.

Pa fired out his window while Theo used the window beside the two others. Both men looked more city than country, and if either of them had a weapon, he didn't produce it. Instead, they just slid aside for Theo.

Mariah gripped a six-shooter. When Pa paused from firing his Spencer, the one he'd gotten in the war when he'd been a sharpshooter, Mariah shouted, "Lean forward while you reload."

Pa did so without looking or speaking, focusing completely on his rifle and trusting her to be tough, competent, and ready.

Mariah watched out the window and saw four men riding ever closer, blasting away. One of them went down, likely from the gunfire of the man on the roof.

She aimed and fired, aimed and fired, and kept going, trying to get the most out of her flying lead.

They were miles from town. No way to get help before these gunmen finished their fight, died trying, or were driven off.

"Get back!" Pa hollered.

Mariah needed to reload anyway, so she gave way to Pa's superior marksmanship.

A cry from overhead ended the gunfire from the shotgun rider. Mariah saw him plummet from the top of the stage. As the three remaining outlaws rode past him, two of them fired into his body.

Pa growled in disgust at the vicious killers. He opened fire again. Mariah had her gun ready to go when she saw someone coming up beside the window on her side. She whipped her head around in time to see the rider empty his pistol into the city boys until they were riddled with bullets.

Her hair came loose from its knot on the back of her head and blinded her for just a moment as she cried out in horror. Then she glared at the skinny blond man. An ugly scar cut across his left cheek and through both his upper and lower lips. She pressed her body against the door and leveled her gun just as she heard a snap from under the belly of the stagecoach—an axle giving way.

She opened fire on the gunman as the stage skidded sideways. Crimson bloomed on his left arm. He brought his gun up with a wicked smile that revealed one of his front teeth was missing right in line with the scar. Their eyes met. He aimed.

The stagecoach tilted wickedly toward Mariah's side and slammed into a boulder alongside the road. The gunman fell back to avoid the boulder. The stage hit so hard the door flung open, and Mariah fell out. She felt the weight of the stage smother her.

More guns fired. Pa's Spencer fell silent, then Theo's Colt stopped blasting.

A bullet hit her in the side. White fire blazed in her belly as the stagecoach settled hard on her.

The world went dark.

Mariah's eyes flickered open from where she was caged by . . . by something. Voices sounded from outside. She tried to cry out for help, but the weight on her chest was so heavy she couldn't draw a breath to manage it.

"They're all dead—just like always."

"What about the woman?" Whoever said that sounded on edge. "First woman we've ever killed. I don't like it. And the Stovers. What were they doing on this stage?"

"Like it or not, she's dead. Crushed under the stage, and I got a bullet in her just to be sure."

Mariah stopped trying to call for help.

"I'll get the strongbox."

A bullet blast made her flinch, which hurt everywhere. A third voice asked, "Is there a good haul?"

"No, only a couple hundred. When we stripped the bodies, we got a couple hundred more."

"I thought this stage had a payroll on it for Fort Bridger?"

"We got bad information, or they pulled a switch, sent the money by another route."

"Maybe they know there's a leak. Maybe he needs to die. I don't like talking outside our group."

"He don't know why I was asking. He don't know nothin'."

"He'll put it together when he hears about this robbery."

"The horses broke the traces and got away, too. We're too close to town. We've gotta clear out. When those horses go storming into town, a rescue party will come a-running."

"You sure everyone's dead?"

"You helped kill them, same as me."

"The Stovers were good folks. This is a bad business."

The stage was pressed to Mariah's face so that she saw the dark wood and nothing else. She couldn't move her arms or legs, could barely draw a breath. Her head was pinned and aching. The pain was dizzying, and it came from every part of her.

Her belly was the worst, but her chest felt like it'd been smashed out of shape. Her vision blurred as she fought for each shallow breath. Her whole body was crushed.

Finally, she heard horses galloping back the way the stagecoach had come.

As much as those men terrified her, being left alone was almost worst. Tears slid from the corners of her eyes as she thought of Pa and Theo.

Thought how it felt like she was already in a coffin.

Clint Roberts was loitering outside his diner, hoping to catch Mariah's attention, when he saw the stagecoach team charging into town. The stage he'd been watching for wasn't behind it. The thundering hooves and wildly out of control speed told of panicked horses. He could think nothing but the worst. "Sheriff, get out here!"

Clint sprinted for his horse, penned up in the corral behind the blacksmith shop. He'd already lost one family. It would kill him to lose another one. The Stovers certainly didn't count him as family, but he'd begun to count them.

He didn't ride in from his homestead every day—it was an easy walk. But today he'd hoped Mariah and her family would be back, and he'd wanted an excuse to stop in, get his horse, and say hello.

The sheriff burst out of the jailhouse, saw the stage horses, and raced for his own mount tied to the hitching post. Willie Minton, the town deputy, was only a pace behind. Other men were coming, too. They all knew the stage was in trouble. And the trouble might be ugly.

Clint was galloping before he reached the edge of town. The stage had been late, so he hoped that meant they'd been close to town.

Mariah. Mariah . . . Please, God, let her be all right.

He'd been waiting until he felt established before he approached her, or, better to admit, before he approached her flinty-eyed father. Maybe even better to admit, he'd been waiting until his heart healed enough to risk sharing it with someone again. As he galloped up the trail, he was sick to think he'd left it too late.

Had he failed Mariah just as he'd failed his family?

2

Mariah wasn't sure if she'd passed out or was just so dazed and under so much pressure from the stage that time meant little to her. She startled when she heard a voice.

"That's John and Theo." A voice she knew well.

"It's got to be the Deadeye Gang." Another familiar voice. Sheriff Joe Mast. A man she trusted. She tried to cry out, but she barely managed a wheeze. No one heard.

"Everyone's dead. Most robbers wear masks when they hold up a stage, take everything of value, and ride off without killing anyone," the sheriff went on, sounding furious and grief-stricken. "John and Theo were tough men. If they couldn't hold off those men with Sculler on the roof fighting, no one can. The stage line should have outriders."

"They did for a while, but no one's struck around here for a year." Mariah recognized Willie Minton's voice. "We thought they'd moved on. Who ever heard of outlaws taking a year between robberies?"

"Where's Mariah?" That first voice again. Clint Roberts, who owned the only diner in town. But he wouldn't normally ride with the sheriff. "I know Mariah rode out with her father. They were going to a funeral down in Laramie."

There were sounds of movement. Men striding all around.

"You don't think they'd take her, do you?" the sheriff asked.

Mariah wheezed. It was the only noise she could make, and it sounded about like a gust of wind.

"They've never done such a thing before," Deputy Minton said. "But have they ever killed a woman before?"

"Not too many women out here." The sheriff strode off to Mariah's left. "I've never heard of a woman being on a stage that got robbed by this bunch."

"Have they ever found such a beautiful woman as Mariah?" Clint thought she was beautiful. Not many did, as she worked alongside her pa and brother in the blacksmith shop and tended toward trousers, bulky leather aprons, and soot.

"Look down here." Clint's voice sharpened. "That's a corner of her skirt."

Footsteps pounded toward her. She wheezed again. This time, with them close and paying attention, it was enough.

"She's still alive," Clint said. "Sheriff, hitch the horses to the stage so we can lift it. I'll only need a few inches. Just enough to drag her out."

He crouched low and looked under the stage while there were more sounds of activity. "Mariah, we'll get this off you and get you to the doctor. Hang on."

Hang on? She didn't have much else to do.

She wanted to ask about Pa and Theo, but she knew enough and couldn't get a word out anyway.

Clint drew her out, his hands under her arms. Once Mariah was clear of the stage, he shouted to the men riding with him, "I've got her."

The stage dropped back to the ground with a crack.

He knelt beside her, checking for broken bones.

"You're bleeding." He was scared to death of what harm had been done.

"I hurt all over."

"I'm taking you to town." He slid his arms under her and lifted, knowing it hurt. Hating it.

The sheriff was at his side.

"I'll get her to the doctor," Clint said.

"Go on. We'll be along when we're able." The sheriff gave Mariah a worried look and didn't mention bringing in the bodies.

The bodies. Mariah's family. Clint wanted to blame himself for that, too. He knew this trail was dangerous. The stagecoach robberies had seemed to stop, but he could have ridden along. He could have gone out to meet the stage. One more gun. The sound of an incoming rider. It might've been enough to save everyone.

With the sheriff's help, Clint swung up onto his horse and kicked the little black mustang into a gallop. He didn't have the will to go slowly, even if it spared Mariah pain. She would hurt whether he went slow or fast.

He looked down to apologize and realized she had

fainted. Kicking the horse to go faster, he hoped it was only a faint.

Please, God. Please let her be all right.

Doc Preston took one look and went into action. "Get her in the back."

"Mariah." The doctor spoke quietly, grief already in his voice as Clint laid her down. "John and Theo were with her."

"Yes, both dead. Mariah was pinned under the stage and left for dead. Heaven knows what injuries she has from the weight of the stage."

The doctor focused on the worst bleeding. He got a wicked knife out and slit the front of her dress to reveal an ugly bullet furrow cutting along her belly just below her navel.

The doctor took a pad of bandages and pressed them to Mariah's stomach. "Hold this down hard while I get a needle and thread."

As the two of them worked together, Clint told all he knew about the stage. They'd been at it awhile when Nell came charging in, with eyes only for Mariah. "Let me help."

Sheriff Mast was a few minutes behind. He looked from Mariah to the doctor to Nell and, finally, to Clint. Gravely, he said, "I need to be alone with the doctor for a few minutes. Doc, can you spare these two?"

"Uh, well, yes."

"I'm not leaving her." Nell set her jaw as firm as granite.

"Neither am I," Clint said.

"Um . . . Nell, I guess you can stay. But, Clint, please go

on out. Let us talk in private. It's a matter of the crime. I'm not ready to talk to you about it yet."

Clint glared at the sheriff, and for a minute he wrestled with leaving. He wanted to tell the sheriff he wasn't man enough to make him leave, but something in the sheriff's expression convinced him this wasn't a request made lightly.

Clint jerked his chin down in a nod. "I left things undone at Le Grande. I'll be right across the street."

He stalked out. Leaving her felt like tearing his own skin.

The sheriff stepped into the kitchen of Le Grande as Clint hung up the last of his pots.

Clint had left the back door unlocked, hoping he'd get news about Mariah and wanting to make it easy for anyone to get to him.

What he saw in Sheriff Mast's eyes twisted his gut. "What's wrong?"

The sheriff lifted both his hands as if to stop Clint from speaking. Or to push away the words that had to be spoken.

"I'm sorry, Clint." The sheriff stared at the floor, unable, it seemed, to meet Clint's eyes. "Mariah didn't make it."

Sheriff Mast turned to face the door connecting the kitchen to the dining room. Clint thought he was leaving, and he leapt forward to grab the man's arm.

But the sheriff wasn't going anywhere. He just stood and stared at the floor.

"She wasn't that bad. What happened?"

"Doc thinks maybe a broken rib punctured her lung or her heart. Maybe a head injury. He isn't sure."

"No." Clint pushed past the sheriff and ran for the doctor's office.

"Clint, wait! No, come back here."

But Clint ran on, sprinting through his dining room and out onto the street.

Mariah, Mariah. Please, God. It can't be.

As he ran, he saw the undertaker, Jim Burke, outside the mortuary, building a box. He had a big stack of wood for all the coffins he needed to make.

Including Mariah's. No. No. No.

He was vaguely aware of children playing in the schoolyard and Pete Wainwright, Pine Valley's mayor, standing outside his general store.

He slammed through the door to the doctor's office. Doc Preston came out of the back room and firmly clicked the door shut behind him.

"Clint, go on home. You can't be in here."

"She wasn't hurt that bad. Are . . . are you sure?" How could a doctor not be sure? Stupid question, but Clint had to ask. "Let me see her."

"No, Clint. Nell's with her, and she doesn't want any company. Go on."

"I will not *go on*," Clint shouted. "What happened?"

The sheriff rushed in.

Clint turned and saw through the open door that Jim Burke had quit building, and Pete Wainwright had taken the wooden steps down to the street.

"Come away, Clint," the sheriff said.

"I will not leave here without seeing her. I won't." His voice rose with every word. "I can't." He felt the burn of tears in his eyes. He refused to let them fall. He hadn't cried since his family had died, with him nowhere near to help them.

Nell came out of the back room. She shut the door just as firmly as Doc Preston had.

She stood silently. Clint's chest heaved as he watched her. Nell was Mariah's friend. If Nell said he could see her, then he'd be allowed in with no fuss.

"I'm going to see her. I'll knock you out of the way if I have to, Doc. Nell, you can't stop me."

She didn't respond. She looked at the sheriff, who'd come up beside Clint. Clint braced himself to fight.

"We have to tell him," Nell said quietly. "I didn't know you had feelings for her, Clint."

"Don't try and stop me, Nell," he repeated, ignoring her comment about his feelings.

The doctor looked at the sheriff.

"I'll have your word that what we tell you goes no further than this room," Sheriff Mast said with intensity. "Then you'll leave and mourn Mariah fully and publicly."

Clint swiped his wrist across his eyes. "What are you talking about?"

"Come into the back." Nell opened the door and let Clint in. To see Mariah unconscious but breathing steadily. Not dead.

Grief faded, replaced by elation. And fury. Clint boiled over. "What—"

Soft hands gripped his arm, drawing him back from the mad ramblings of his mind. He looked down into Nell's blue eyes. Kind eyes. Not the eyes of a woman who wanted to hurt someone.

"We're saying she died."

Clint waited for more, but Nell held his gaze as if allowing him to take in her single sentence for an extended time.

And then he knew why. "So the Deadeye Gang won't come and kill her."

"She's marked for death," Nell said. "We talked it over, and we think she should be declared dead. We'll bury an empty coffin, then we'll spirit her out of town and send her far away. I'm afraid that's her only hope."

He was going to lose her. But better to lose a living woman than a dead one.

One was a victory and the other terrible defeat. For Mariah, there was no choice. For Clint . . . he ended up with a broken heart either way.

"Thank you for telling me." Clint touched Nell's hand. He knew loss wasn't new to her. Nell was a widow who'd left her old life behind for the frontier.

"I didn't do it because you were causing a scene and possibly drawing a crowd who'd find out the truth," Nell said.

"Then why?"

"Because hiding her is going to be hard and dangerous. I offered to hide her in the rooms over my shop until she's well enough to travel. But if there's any suspicion that she's not dead, my place is the next place they'd search after her own house. But they might not think to hunt through the rooms over the diner."

Clint had lived above the diner for a while, but now he had a cabin on his homestead. He could easily use those rooms to hide Mariah.

And stand guard much more discreetly. As he fully intended to do.

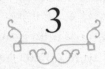

3

Mariah's eyes flickered open.

Nell Armstrong bent over her, looking down with a worried expression. Nell gasped and folded her hands together under her chin in what looked like an attitude of prayer.

"Becky, she's coming around," Nell called out.

Mariah tried to think clearly. "C-coming around?"

Then Becky Pruitt appeared on her left side, with Nell on her right.

Her two best friends in the world. In this very male world on the Wyoming frontier. Even with the vote for women's suffrage and the territory now proud of its stance on equality, a woman needed other women friends. They all three heartily approved of gaining the right to vote and a lot of other new freedoms. Still, a woman friend was precious.

Her friends were as different as two women could be and in most every way. Nell was delicate and feminine, blond with pale-blue eyes like Mariah, only Nell's hair was closer to white, Mariah's the color of honey. Nell wore pretty dresses in bright colors, often scattered with flowers and ruffles and lace. And skillfully made because Nell was a seamstress.

Becky, on the other hand, ran her own ranch, so *delicate* wasn't a word you'd use to describe her—for your own safety.

Becky's hair was a dark brown, which streaked in the summer sun. Her eyes were a pretty hazel color that turned green some days, brown others. They seemed to change to reflect the clothes Becky wore, or her background at the time, or her mood. She was darkly tanned and dressed in riding skirts and chaps, often with spurs, though Mariah hadn't noticed any jingling in the few minutes since she'd woken up. Rather than wear pretty shirtwaists to go with her very useful skirts, Becky leaned toward broadcloth, plain colors, but she had allowed Nell to make her clothes for her. Becky was a very busy woman.

Just now, a strong, wide smile spread across Becky's somber face. "We've been so worried about you. Clint Roberts carried you in unconscious. Nell came right over to the doctor's office and helped move you and has been sitting with you day and night ever since. She got word out to my ranch, and I've been here only a couple of times and then I snuck in."

"What happened? Where am I?"

"You're in an upstairs room over Clint's diner." Becky rested one of her strong hands with surprising gentleness on Mariah's shoulder. "They brought you here after the stagecoach robbery. You were shot, then trapped under the stagecoach. It rolled during the robbery and pinned you."

"St-stagecoach?" Mariah searched for anything that would clear her thoughts. "We went to Uncle Reggie's funeral. We traveled on the stage."

"The robbery, Mariah. Your stage was held up on your way home from Laramie. By the Deadeye Gang."

Mariah had heard of them. "They never leave anyone alive."

Nell wrapped her arms around Mariah, gently, but it hurt like mad.

A faint groan of pain had Nell pulling back.

Mariah had time to add and figure a bit. "Pa and Theo?"

Nell's eyes brimmed with tears as she shook her head. "They didn't survive. The only reason you did is because the stage rolled onto you and hid you from their guns. You have a bullet crease in your side where you were shot, but it cut across your belly and didn't embed inside you. It's going to hurt but you've just got a nasty cut. Doc Preston sewed it up. He thinks you have cracked ribs, and you have an awful knot on the back of your head. Maybe—"

"Pa and Theo didn't survive?" Mariah's thoughts rioted. Her heart started banging like her head. She felt the ribs. Her whole chest stabbed at her. She felt the bullet crease. Her arms and legs. Breathing hurt. Everything hurt.

But nothing hurt like thinking of Pa and Theo. "How long have I been unconscious?"

Becky took hold of Mariah's hand, a tight squeeze that pulled Mariah out of her dark, dreadful thoughts. "A week, Mariah. The stagecoach holdup was seven days ago. Your pa and Theo have been buried in the church cemetery. We couldn't delay the burial and . . ." Becky looked left and right, then behind her. And she leaned close to whisper, "We buried an empty coffin and carved your name on a wooden cross."

Mariah gasped, and pain cut across her chest, then reached lower in her belly. "What for? For heaven's sake, why?"

The horror of it might have knocked her down if she hadn't been lying flat already.

Becky looked at Nell. Mariah watched every expression that fluttered across both faces.

Then Nell leaned in close. "We did it because we're afraid the Deadeye Gang will come for you. They don't leave witnesses, remember? We need to spirit you out of town and send you far away, all the way out of the territory because the Deadeye Gang has hit nearly everywhere in Wyoming. You have to get far enough away that they'll never know you survived."

"I-I th-think being conscious doesn't agree with me."

And she let the black take her down to where she knew nothing.

Mariah woke up fully. She had a vague memory of being in and out of consciousness. Deadeye. Stagecoach. Pain. Pa! Theo!

In her muddled memories she believed that it was at this moment each time she'd slightly roused that she'd pass out again. She believed it because waves of dizziness crested in her mind until she wanted to fade away. Her heart ached with what she knew to be true. Her pa. Her brother. Strong, kind men. Tough, hardworking men. Dead.

And she'd crawled back into unconsciousness because the beating of her heart, shoving blood through her veins, burned with a fiery pain.

This time she couldn't escape.

She looked around the room and didn't recognize it. The doctor's office was brighter than this. The bed harder. Neither was she at home.

Where was she? Had she died, too? But she hurt too badly to be with Pa and Theo in heaven. For kind, Christian men such as they were could be nowhere else. And she fully intended to join them when it was her time.

But her time hadn't come.

Movement at the door caught her eye.

Clint Roberts.

Why was he here?

She studied him.

So different from her menfolk. Clint was tall like them, but he didn't work hard like her men did. Oh, that wasn't fair. He worked very hard. But as a cook rather than a blacksmith. Lithe and tidy, while Pa and Theo had bulging muscles and broad chests, and powerful personalities to match their powerful builds.

What she knew of Clint was that he was kind, yet that was the end of his resemblance to the Stover men. Clint had an easy smile and intelligent brown eyes that reminded her of the oak table Pa had built. Clint had dark hair that he kept very short. He owned the diner and was a fine, though somewhat odd, cook. She knew because she ate at his diner often. He called it a restaurant, though, not a diner. Le Grande Restaurante. Not grand, in fact. Mariah thought, everyone thought, that was how to say the word

Grande painted over his front door. But Clint pronounced it *grawnd*. Or something like that. He added strange *A* sounds onto the word *Restaurant*, too. Like *restaurawnt*. Most everyone in town just called the place *Clint's diner*.

And Clint was a good sport about it.

He often said he saw it as his goal in life to bring delicious food to the people of Pine Valley. Despite their preference for beefsteak and fried chicken.

His chicken soup was delicious. Why he called it *ko-ko vawn*, no one could understand. Mariah had a drink of cocoa once, and there was nothing chocolate about this dish. But no one in town denied it was spectacular chicken soup.

"Hi, Mariah. I'm glad to see you awake."

"Nell?"

Clint came to her side, sat in a chair that seemed positioned for this purpose, so she didn't have to turn her head, which she was just noticing hurt terribly.

"She just stepped out." Clint's voice was low and smooth, nothing like the Stover men with their loud voices, pitched to be heard over a clanging sledgehammer and a roaring forge.

"*Le Grawnd* is closed now. It's midafternoon. I told her I'd keep an eye on you for a few minutes."

"Where am I?"

"This is the room over the—" he paused, then grinned— "the room over the diner. I sometimes stay up here, but mostly I stay out at my homestead. We slipped you up here in the night. We agreed you should hide. Nell stays with you nights. I stay at her place to be close at hand."

"The Deadeye Gang. We thought they'd left the area

26

after the stagecoach line started sending outriders along. We'd've never gone to Uncle Reggie's funeral otherwise." Mariah shuddered when she thought of their ugly rule to never leave a witness alive. What Clint wasn't saying was that he was close at hand in case someone came gunning for her. Which they would do when they found out she'd survived.

"Yes. Doc Preston, the sheriff, and the deputy are the only ones, outside of Becky, Nell, and me, who know you're alive."

"After you buried an empty coffin."

His smile faded and he nodded. "I'm sorry, that must be such a dreadful thing for you, on top of the loss of your father and brother. Several men rode out with that posse when we brought you in. But we've spread the word everywhere that you died. I was let in on the secret only when it was clear we had to find a place to hide you. And I'd asked some hard questions of Doc Preston, because I didn't think you were hurt so badly. I saw the bullet wound and thought it was survivable. Doc consulted the sheriff and Nell. They agreed to tell me the truth to get me to shut up."

"So you got elected to hide me?"

Clint nodded. "We had to get you out of Doc's office. Becky lives too far out. Nell has only one bedroom. Besides, if for some reason someone didn't believe the lie that you'd died, they'd search your house first, and next Nell's apartment. I go over to her place late at night along the backs of the buildings, and she's living here with you. She's working up here and she needed something. Fabric or thread, I don't know. Probably more tanned leather. She's making a pair of chaps for someone."

A tired laugh escaped from Mariah. "She hates making chaps above all things."

Clint smiled. "So she mentioned . . . any number of times. But she does a good job of it. And there's a great need, unlike a need for bonnets and gingham dresses. Making chaps and trousers and men's shirts is her main job."

"She's learning to make boots." Mariah shook her head. She was grateful for Clint's easy conversation about Nell's sewing trials.

"Once she figures it out," Clint said, "she'll get really rich. Cranky, but rich."

Anything was better than thinking of a grave with her name on it, right next to Pa's and Theo's graves. And yet she couldn't think of anything else. "My pa. My brother . . ." Her voice broke and she couldn't go on.

Clint heard what she couldn't say. He took her hand, and she noticed it was soft. Her pa's hands were callused and rough. Strong man's hands. Theo's were the same, as were hers, Mariah, the blacksmith's apprentice. Pa had called her that. Always with his big, generous smile and deep pride. It was far beyond proper for her to work the forge, but Pa was a successful, busy man. Prosperous by Wyoming standards. He needed the extra set of hands and had even bought lighter-weight tools for her to use because the massive sledgehammers he used, well, she could manage them, but it took all her strength. She couldn't put in a full day using the heavier hammers.

And now Pa was gone. Everyone was gone.

"I'm sorry, Mariah. The stagecoach horses came galloping into town, dragging their traces. We knew something awful had happened, and every man available raced up the trail. Everyone was dead. Your pa and Theo included. Everyone but you. And now we're afraid you're in danger until we can arrest these men. Did you see them?"

And that's when, like a sweeping gale-force wind, it blew through Mariah that her mind was blank. For that stretch of time, she had no memory.

"I can't remember anything after the funeral. The day before we took the stage for home, I-I remember going to sleep in Aunt Augusta's house. But . . ." She dug deep, tried to recall that day until a sickening throb began pounding in her temples. She pressed the heels of her hands to her eyes, fighting back the pain. "But I don't remember anything about that day. I don't remember waking up. Boarding the stagecoach. Nothing about the holdup."

"Stop. You're hurting yourself." Clint reached for her hands and pulled them down to her lap. "Doc Preston said it's not uncommon to have no memory after some incident where a head injury is involved. Like it knocks the hours before right out of our minds."

She pulled herself out of her struggle for memory. She couldn't remember any man holding her hands before. And while, yes, Clint's were soft and mostly free of calluses, they were still strong. He held on as if he wouldn't let her sink into so much pain.

She quit racking her brain to remember. She'd try and find something of that day later.

Clint released his grip on her.

"Nell or Becky said something about my needing to escape? Leave town, even leave Wyoming? Run and hide before the Deadeye Gang realizes I survived?"

Somber and quiet, Clint said, "Yes. You need to get

away, and do it soon. They've never left a witness alive. Of course, they've never had one get away like you did. So they have no history of hunting down escaped witnesses."

"C-can we make it known that I can't remember? Can we get the word out? Then I wouldn't have to go anywhere."

Clint studied her for too long. "Right now, most everyone thinks you're dead. To try and stay here, we'd have to admit that was a ruse. Then we could push the memory-loss story. But it would be dangerous." With a hesitant hand, he rested one open palm on her shoulder. "Your family is gone, Mariah. What is there to hold you to this place?"

"Friends, memories, a home I own." A business she knew how to run. So a livelihood. She had no money beyond what Pa had stashed away.

"I wish you could stay." Clint took her hands again. "We can talk to the sheriff, see what he thinks. The way word travels in a small town, it wouldn't be difficult to let it be known you don't remember anything about the robbery."

She had no idea what he meant by *"I wish you could stay."* What did Clint's wishes have to do with her?

"It's nothing but the honest truth. We'll say you faked my death hoping I'd be able to identify the gang members, but now I'm fully alert and don't remember a thing. We'll make sure everyone knows the doctor says that's common."

Clint studied her, holding her hands. He faintly shook his head, such a tiny gesture she doubted he realized he was doing it. But she knew he was going to tell her she had to get away. Had to run.

She jerked her hands free. "I'm not asking for permission. I'm *telling* you this is how it's going to be. I'm good with a gun, and though I have a reasonable fear of this gang, I'm not going to run." She thought of Nell and Becky. Her best friends. Her only friends.

"I can take over as the town blacksmith." She couldn't leave the territory because nowhere outside of Wyoming would a woman be allowed to work as a blacksmith.

She'd take precautions. But she was staying.

Though he looked very doubtful, Clint said, "I'll tell the sheriff you've made up your mind, and we'll figure out how to help you stay safe."

A door beyond the bedroom opened and closed. "It's me, Clint."

He stood and backed quickly away from the bed. For a second Mariah thought he didn't want to be caught sitting so close to her. Then she saw the deadly serious expression on his face, and the gun in his hand.

"It's safe. Iron Maiden." Nell came in with her arms full of bulky leather.

She looked around from the doorway, saw Clint, and gave a firm nod of approval.

"What's Iron Maiden?" Mariah thought vaguely that maybe she'd heard those words somewhere before.

Nell turned toward Mariah, and her eyes lit up. "You're awake."

"Yes, just a few minutes ago she woke up." Clint holstered his gun. "And I think she's finally going to stay awake."

"Iron Maiden is our password," Nell said. "We've worried there's a chance the Deadeye Gang might figure out where you are and force me—or one of us—at gunpoint to come to your room to kill you." Nell's blunt words weren't

31

like her. As a rule, she was a soft-spoken, sweet-natured, very feminine woman. Not a blacksmith like Mariah or a cow wrangler like Becky. It was clear she was worried about the situation.

"She's told me she's staying." Clint came up beside Nell and took the bundle from her. "Where do you want this?"

Nell pointed at the top of a chest of drawers. Mariah also noted a table set somewhat in the middle of the room. It was loaded with thread and needles, an awl, and spindles of leather laces. Other things that told Mariah this was her bedroom, but also Nell's workroom.

Nell took the chair Clint had recently abandoned. She took Mariah's hands in an echo of how Clint had done a few moments before. Yet it was so completely different from Clint holding her hands, Mariah was a bit startled at the comparison.

"It's not safe."

Mariah settled into being stubborn and unreasonable. It was the only way she could think of to save her home.

She only hoped she was tough enough to also save her life.

4

Mariah stepped out of the diner onto Pine Valley's main street.

The first thing that struck her, and it almost always did, was the Cirque of the Towers. Spectacular mountain peaks that stood like guardians on the west side of town. Those towering mountains inspired her in a way so deep it always made her think of God.

A small lake between the town and the mountains reflected the peaks, doubling their impact and beauty.

The rest of Pine Valley was far less impressive.

Where she stood, showing herself for the first time since she'd been "buried," was called *main street*, but that was a highfalutin description of the frontier town. It had almost no women. A small school with a dozen students—half of them belonging to Parson Rolly Blodgett and his wife. There were one or two families out in the country who had young'uns. And new homesteaders showed up with some regularity.

They used the schoolhouse as a church, and Parson

Blodgett had homesteaded on the edge of Pine Valley, so he was part parson, part farmer, and served as the town's justice of the peace.

The challenges were legion for Parson Blodgett, because for all the modest amenities in Pine Valley, it supported a good-sized saloon. It was nearly the most prosperous business in town.

The saloon thrived, while the church was far more humble.

The sheriff was by her side, as was Clint. And Nell came hurrying up the street just as they had planned.

In the few seconds it took Nell to reach them, Mariah sent a prayer winging to God, asking Him for wisdom and protection. This was a reckless plan. But the thought of leaving this life, this town, her friends behind was too much.

She'd lost Pa and Theo. She'd almost lost her life. Now for safety's sake, she would have to give up her home, her friends, a life she understood . . . to the extent she understood anything.

Mariah considered herself a strong woman. You didn't slam a sledgehammer on a red-hot horseshoe for hours every day and not get strong as a result. She also knew firearms and knives. She was tougher than any woman she'd ever met and a whole lot of the men.

Somehow, when she pictured herself running and hiding rather than standing firm, she became a frightened, scurrying little rodent. A weakling and a coward.

Being afraid of the Deadeye Gang wasn't cowardice, it was wisdom, and she *was* afraid. But she'd face that fear from right here in Pine Valley.

As she revealed to her little corner of the world that she was alive, she rested her eyes on those mountains. They were part of the backbone of the Wind River Mountains. Part of the spine of Wyoming.

She'd draw strength from God, from the Cirque of the Towers, and from herself.

Henry Wainwright stepped out of his general store. "Miss Mariah, you're alive!"

Latta Blodgett was walking toward the store when she staggered into the wall. No small problem because Mrs. Blodgett was very great with child. "Mariah?"

Henry Wainwright jumped forward and caught her, though Mrs. Blodgett was a hardy woman. She'd've probably caught herself.

"M-M-Mariah? We held your funeral." Latta's voice wavered. Mariah braced herself for tears. But Latta was made of sterner stuff than that. Her chin came up, her eyes flashed with an emotion so strong, Mariah was a little afraid.

But no torrent of scolding came for putting Latta Blodgett through a funeral. Instead, she rushed forward to hug Mariah.

Mariah hugged the sweet lady back, even with her belly in the way. Quietly, she said, "It was decided before I regained consciousness that I wasn't safe from the Deadeye Gang, so Doc and Sheriff Mast pretended I'd died and buried an empty coffin. They've kept me hidden until I healed. But I'm up and healthy enough to watch out for myself now, so the hiding is over."

Mrs. Blodgett pulled back, nodding. "You have a care now."

Everyone in these parts had heard of the Deadeye Gang, who never left a witness above ground.

Nell arrived at Mariah's side a few seconds later. In only a slightly raised voice, she said, "Have you remembered anything?"

"No, Doc Preston said I never would." Doc had said she possibly never would, but Mariah wasn't letting that truth be told.

Becky galloped into town riding the magnificent palomino stallion with the creamy white mane she favored. She rode straight up main street to where Mariah stood outside Clint's diner, on the boardwalk that was several steps up from the packed-dirt street.

Henry Wainwright turned and said something to someone back in the store. He was three doors down from the diner. Mayor Pete, who owned the store with his brother, came hurrying to see for himself.

"Mariah," Becky said, who was in on spreading the news of Mariah's lost memory far and wide, "you're up and around. I'm so glad to see you. How's your memory?"

This had been staged to draw enough attention to Mariah and her lost recall of that day, which hopefully would help protect her.

"The whole day is a blank," she replied. "I can't even remember getting out of bed in the morning. Nor can I remember one moment of the stagecoach ride. Doc Preston said that it's not uncommon to forget the time before and after a bad head injury."

Both the Wainwrights heard every word. Someone stood just inside the door to the saloon one building down from the general store. Mariah saw only the person's silhouette, but she was sure that whoever it was, they'd heard. There were several men loitering on benches outside the saloon. Another man walked along the boardwalk, his heavy boots thudding like a drum.

Several other folks stepped out of their shops and homes. One of them James Burke, who'd buried her. He looked shocked.

A few called out, surprised to see her. She was the center of attention for a while before her story was told to everyone. She and Nell repeated her lack of memory several times.

Not everyone in town was there listening, yet in a small town, news spread like fire through a dried-up fir tree. Soon everyone would know, including, Mariah hoped fervently, any members of the Deadeye Gang who were nearby.

Becky dismounted in her sleek, catlike way. She was one of the finest horse trainers in the territory and ran a prosperous ranch with red, white-faced cattle she called Herefords. A different choice when so many others had herds of longhorns.

"I'll help you get settled back into your house." Becky came to her side and slid an arm around her waist. "Nell and I packed up your father and brother's things. We didn't dispose of them, just set them out of sight. You'll have all the time you need before you deal with that. I'm so sorry for your loss."

Mariah walked down three wooden stairs to the street. Nell and Becky walked on either side of her. Sheriff Mast and Clint followed behind. It was like having a group of bodyguards, and Mariah reckoned that was exactly as it was meant to be.

"Aren't you going to go home?"

Mariah looked at her friends. Mariah had lived in Pine Valley for ten years. Nell and her brother had come to town three years after Mariah. Becky had been born out here.

Nell was older than Mariah, nearly thirty, while Mariah, twenty-one—was just a year older than Becky.

Mariah and Becky were already friends when Nell moved to town. But they'd all three become close friends right away. Mariah was only a few dozen paces from her home. But instead of heading there, she headed for her family's blacksmith shop.

Becky said, "I think you should settle in at home for a day or two before you think about the smithy. You've been lying down more than standing up for over a week."

"Mariah, you're going to be surprised how quickly you get tired." Clint was trailing behind her.

The sheriff muttered something she couldn't quite hear, but she figured she knew what he said. Some version of, You're an idiot and you should run for your life.

"I'm sure you're right, all of you. I just . . . I just need to see the shop. Spend a few minutes thinking about Pa and Theo before I face our home, alone." She led the way into her pa's blacksmith shop. The barn-like building stood empty. No horses in the pens waiting to be shod. No fire in the forge. The tools all lined up in neat rows. Pa and Theo, along with Mariah, had set the building to rights before riding away from it for three days.

When Pa had gotten word his brother, who lived in

Laramie, had died, Pa had decided he wanted to go to the funeral. Mariah had known Pa's family when they'd lived in Dubuque, Iowa. Pa had grown up there after his family had moved from Illinois, then Pa had started his family there. A wagon train and the itchy desire to explore a new land had taken him here to Pine Valley, along with Ma, Theo, and Mariah.

The beautiful mountains had stopped him. He'd found his home. Mariah had never had a single doubt God had led him to this beautiful place and those magnificent mountains they called the Cirque of the Towers.

Now she stood quietly studying the empty barn, the cold forge, the resting bellows, the anvil used to shape the iron, the tongs and hammers, both in all shapes for different purposes. This was a world she knew. A world that would take all her strength to manage, but she could do it.

As she stood there, Henry came running in, breathing hard. "I saw you head over here, Miss Mariah. I hitched up my team and found a broken wagon wheel. Can you fix it? I need to make the run to . . ."

Mariah bit back a smile while Henry Wainwright told his story of urgent need. For a blacksmith, it was always an emergency. Pa had forged horseshoes and nails, pots and pans, wagon wheels, most anything to stay ahead—the walls were lined with them. But the heart of what made a blacksmith so sought after was the emergency work. A hole in your bucket. A horse threw a shoe. A broken wheel. And no one wanted to buy a new anything if they could avoid it.

"When do you need it?" But she knew the answer.

"Today. I was packing to leave right now, hoping to

get to South Pass City before dark. I'm mighty glad you survived unharmed, miss."

Mariah, unconscious for a week. Another week getting the worst of her headache to fade and her ribs to stop aching. Not exactly *unharmed*.

"I was wondering if the blacksmithing was over for Pine Valley. We'd surely be in trouble if it was, and I know your pa taught you the way of smithing work. I saw you often enough, shoeing a horse or repairing a wheel."

Repairing a wheel was not the hardest job she would have to do. But it required long hours at the forge and banging on red-hot iron with a stout sledgehammer, plus heavy lifting. She needed another day of rest, and then she'd start small.

"I'll tell you what, Mr. Wainwright." Mariah gestured toward the wall of the blacksmith shop. "Use one of those wheels."

"Oh, I'd prefer not to buy a new one."

Not having much money to spend, few people around Pine Valley preferred a new one. Yet Henry Wainwright was a reasonably prosperous man. He owned the general store with his brother Pete, and they took many trips running a supply wagon.

"I'm just up from my injuries and I don't have my strength back just yet. But if you'd take a new wheel and bring in the old one, I'll try to have it repaired by the time you return. Then we can trade wheels. If you put a lot of wear on the wheel you've borrowed, maybe we can come to some agreement about what that's worth to you, and I'd accept payment in supplies." Mariah well remembered that Pa had done a lot of bartering in his job, as cash money was usually tight. "Sorry, I don't have the strength for repairs today."

She was deadly serious about that, too. Just standing here, she felt her knees weakening. She needed to sit down or soon she'd fall down. "Take the new wheel or find another way to repair the old. I do apologize, but even now I'm heading home. The head injury from that stagecoach landing on me has wiped out my memory of the whole day. I am still fighting bruising headaches."

Mr. Wainwright had been standing outside his store. He'd come over and spoken to her outside the diner. He'd already heard this. But he saw everyone in town over a few weeks' time. He was a good man to spread the story of her missing memory.

He was grumbling but nodding when Mariah's knees buckled.

"Mariah!" Nell's sweet voice calling her name was the only word she recognized. Others shouted.

She never hit the ground, and when she blinked open her eyes, she saw Clint had caught her. It felt familiar somehow, though she couldn't say how. She'd certainly never been in his arms before this moment.

"I told you," Clint said while looking down at her, worried and cranky, "you need to go home."

"Everyone likes hearing 'I told you so.'"

Becky laughed. Nell gasped. Clint shook his head.

From behind her, Mr. Wainwright said, "I'll get the wheel off the wall and switch it with my old one."

Mariah rested her head against Clint's chest and snuck in a nap.

5

Mariah woke up to see Clint sitting in a chair. She saw the candle lighting the room and knew it was night. Then she recognized the room. It was her own.

"What are you doing in my room at night?"

There was a silence that went on far too long.

Finally, almost sheepishly, Clint said, "I'm staying in your house with you."

With a gasp so loud it was almost a scream, she lurched up in bed. Pain threatened to knock her flat on her back, but she grimly stayed sitting upright with her blankets clutched to her chest.

"You are not!" Another near scream.

Nell rushed into the room. She slammed the door open. She had on a nightgown and a robe over it, which she clutched to hold closed even though it was buttoned and tied. She gave Clint a rather frantic look as he turned to watch her come crashing in.

"You'd better step out, Clint."

"Wait! No, tell me what's going on." Mariah looked from one to the other.

Clint spoke first. "We can't let you stay here alone. Nell is here to guard you, but she's not much help."

Nell quit holding her perfectly secure robe closed and plopped her fists on her hips. "I'm tougher than I look."

"I believe you."

"You do?" Nell smiled and let her arms fall to her sides.

"Yep, but only because it would be next to impossible to be less tough than you look." Clint smiled.

Nell sniffed at him and lifted her chin.

Clint turned back to Mariah.

"Nell is staying here with you. I just came over, well after dark, and I was mighty careful not to be seen. To help with sentry duty."

Mariah's eyes narrowed. "If we're watching for danger, wouldn't it be better to stand by the door? Or position yourself so you can watch the front and back doors?"

"That's what Nell was doing. Most of the night she's been sitting in here. But I asked her if we could trade off. I was falling asleep downstairs, thought a change of scenery might keep me awake. And we're a little bit afraid those outlaws, if they come, might not come storming through the door. They might climb up on your porch and come right through the window. We're just not sure how best to guard you."

"My reputation and Nell's will be ruined if anyone finds out you spent the night here. You have to go home."

"I'll leave just before sunrise. Becky is coming in to take over."

"She's riding into town in the dark?"

43

"We should put the sheriff on a shift, too. We've all gotta sleep."

Mariah's stomach twisted to think how much danger they feared she was in.

"Will you both guard me all day, too?"

Clint rose from his chair. It was the first time she'd noticed he wore a holster with a pistol—a Smith & Wesson Model 3. The gun was so new, she wondered if it'd ever been fired. She knew they sold them in Wainwright's general store. Had Clint gone and bought a gun just today? Could he hit what he aimed at?

"It's almost morning. I'll go on back down and set up to watch there. Mariah, try and get a few more minutes of sleep. As soon as Becky shows up, I'll need to go start making omelets."

Mariah had known him and his cooking long enough to know he meant scrambled eggs.

Mariah turned on her side and it hurt everywhere. Shaking her head, she said, "I'm not going back to sleep. Do you think I can walk around today without collapsing?"

Nell gave her sweetest smile. Her blue eyes were dimmed by exhaustion but still held their usual kindness and sympathy. Her tidy blond hair was tucked into a rather bedraggled bun at the back of her head.

"Maybe take it really slow. And let's don't try and get the forge fired up quite yet."

"Sounds like a good idea."

"Why don't you plan on spending the day with me? I've got two pairs of chaps made during the night. Guarding you is going to make me rich."

Maybe what Mariah saw wasn't exhaustion so much as

44

a woman who wanted to make fine bonnets and dresses, tired to the bone of making western men's clothes with the single desired trait of being durable.

"That sounds like a good idea."

"I can't make my friends stand guard over me forever." She felt fear tightening her midsection. "What am I going to do?"

"Would you be interested in learning how to use an awl and poking holes in leather?" Nell tried to sound like it was a joke, and yet there was just the tiniest thread of begging to be heard. "No reason I can't guard you forever if I put you to work."

"I'm in. If I can work on the chaps while I'm sitting down."

Nell patted Mariah on the shoulder. "It's practically required that you sit down. Maybe when you're stronger, I can pay you back by working the bellows on the forge while you hammer iron into different shapes."

Mariah smiled to imagine delicate, feminine Nell coated by smoke and sweat working in her blacksmith shop. And she knew if she asked, Nell wouldn't mind at all.

6

Is it time to eat yet?" Mariah was finding out why Nell
didn't like making chaps. "My fingertips are raw from
punching holes in leather. And that's strange when
you consider my hands are callused all over. I swing a
hammer at hot iron for a living. But I'm not tough enough
to make chaps."

"Stop now before your fingers start bleeding. Mine did
as well the first time I made chaps." Glaring at her hands,
Nell held them up. Her fingers looked odd, dented.

"They're hard now, almost like I've got fingernails on
both sides of my fingers. And I use a thimble on four fingers. Still, I might end up scarred."

Mariah set her leather aside and rose, slowly, still prone
to dizziness. She gave herself time for her vision to clear.
"Let's go eat at the diner."

"I've got bread and a roast from yesterday. I can boil
some potatoes. We can eat that."

"Nope, I want to see what crazy thing Clint comes up
with this time."

Nell set everything aside. "Remember that delicious chicken soup?"

"Yep, what did he call it? Something chocolate."

"Not chocolate. Cocoa. But the rest escapes me."

They headed for the door. Clint had strange words to describe things, but no one could deny he made delicious food. The word popped into Mariah's head. "Cocoa van."

Mariah looked at Nell with a wrinkled forehead.

Nell shrugged one shoulder as she held the door open for Mariah. "Something like that. But there was nothing chocolate about it."

"Clint's always got some notion or other."

"We'll try and work you having no memory into any conversations we have while we eat. I'm hoping if there's no trouble for you, it'll mean the Deadeye Gang isn't coming after you. I don't know when we can start to trust in that, but someday we'll start to feel confident."

"We've brought it up to everyone who's come into your shop." They'd gotten orders for three more pairs of chaps this morning. "Why not entertain the folks at the diner, too?"

"How does your head feel?"

"It has a pulse in it sometimes, like my heart is between my ears pounding, especially when I first stand up. Not fun."

"Have you remembered anything at all about the day of the stage robbery?"

"No, and I've said the words 'The doctor says I'll never remember that day' so many times I'm starting to believe it."

They walked downstairs to the *Grawnd* Diner. Mariah

shook her head. It was embarrassing to think of it that way, but since Clint didn't seem to be embarrassed by the name, Mariah felt embarrassed on his behalf.

Rather than walk through Clint's kitchen, they went around to the front of the diner and then inside. They must've been a little early because there were just a few men there, one of them being Pete Wainwright. He and his brother Henry always took their meals here, and they took turns so someone could always keep the store open. Except Henry was on the road, so Pete must have locked up for a quick run to the diner.

The two men had dedicated their lives to keeping the good people of Pine Valley in flour and other useful items.

Clint came out of the back with a plate loaded with something red. Mariah wished she could identify it, but she'd given up guessing at things by sight. She'd just wait until Clint told her whatever odd thing he'd made and then thoroughly enjoy eating it. He'd been here two years now and had a nice homestead with cows and a nice-sized herd of pigs, also large flocks of chickens and, oddly, ducks. The man raised geese and turkeys, too. Those were things men hunted for. Mariah wondered if he'd build a really high fence and get his own herd of deer.

He had a big garden full of vegetables of a far greater variety than potatoes, onions, and carrots, though he had those, too.

And he almost always just made one thing for a meal. So, you either ate it or ate at home, since the diner was the only one of its kind to be found in all of Pine Valley.

He took the plate to Pete, set it neatly in front of him, then turned to Nell and Mariah.

"What's the meal today?" Nell was the very image of feminine good manners.

Mariah tried, but she could never quite be a proper lady like Nell.

"I'm trying something different today. I was trained in French cooking, but I'm overrun with tomatoes, so today it's Italian. I made chicken parmesan. I've also got crème brûlée for dessert, served with caffè français."

Mariah had to bite back a smile. She wasn't sure about the chicken, but the dessert was a regular here: delicious custard and coffee, foamy with milk. Which was unusual. Still, she wasn't sure why the man didn't just call it what it was.

"Can I have a *regular* cup of coffee with my chicken?" Mariah knew Clint had made concessions to please western tastes, and serving hot, black stout coffee was part of that.

"Of course. Right away."

The door to the Le Grande Restaurante, though hardly grand itself, opened behind Mariah. Becky walked in, her boots thudding, her spurs jingling as she approached their table. The diner had about ten tables, each with four chairs, and one long table where folks eating alone came in and sat together.

Becky smiled and rested one strong hand on Mariah's shoulder. "You look good. I stopped at Nell's shop first and then thought I'd find you here instead."

Nell stood and moved around so she was sitting next to Mariah instead of across from her. "Sit in my chair so you won't have your back to the room."

Mariah and Nell both knew Becky liked to be able to see who was coming.

Becky dropped onto the chair just as Clint came out. He was both cook and waiter, running the whole place on his own. He slid a full cup of coffee in front of Becky, knowing what she'd want.

"I'll have whatever you've made, Clint."

He grinned, nodded, and hurried back to the kitchen.

They were soon eating the chicken parmesan, which was an odd but tasty dish—chicken with some kind of tomato sauce and melted cheese. It reminded Mariah a little of the chili soup she made in the wintertime. She'd learned the recipe from Becky, who'd learned it from the Mexican who worked for a time as a bunkhouse cook at her Independence Day Ranch. But it wasn't Mexican. Clint had said Italian. Mariah wondered if Clint knew how to make chili. She might try and teach him.

She'd've never considered pouring the soup over a piece of fried chicken. Clint was always coming up with strange and delicious concoctions.

A steady crowd came in. Others left. Nell, at one point, got up and helped clear tables. Clint didn't ask for such help, but he'd accept it when he was working at a run.

Then the door opened again, and Mariah saw Becky stiffen. Her face suddenly expressionless.

Mariah saw Joshua Pruitt, Becky's pa, step inside with a group of his cowhands. They headed for the big table. Mariah noticed a few familiar faces, but the turnover at the Pruitt place was regular. It was said that Joshua Pruitt was a hard man to work for. And Becky had made it clear that her pa was a hard man to live with. When she'd inherited a goodly sum of money from her ma's parents—her ma was long dead—Becky had defied all conventions, bought her own ranch, and called it the Independence Day Ranch. Her brand was an ID, and folks around town, including Becky, called it the *Idee*. She'd hired her own cowhands and, with their help, built her own ranch house, a barn and corrals, then moved out of her father's place.

His protests since had been loud and long.

Mariah had known Becky from the time she was ten years old, and she'd known Pruitt's ranch, the Circle P Ranch, was a rugged place to live. Joshua hired hard men, and Becky hadn't liked living near most of them.

When she'd left, she hired her own crew, including a married couple who lived in the ranch house she'd built. She needed a woman's help because she never had time to cook and care for the house. But she also liked the respectability of not living alone with ten or more cowpokes. Her men lived in the bunkhouse, of course, but it would still be outrageous, even in a territory as modern-thinking as Wyoming.

Her hands, including the married couple, were a steady bunch. So far most of them stayed year in and year out.

Joshua's gaze swept the diner and landed on Becky. He smiled, but it was disgruntled. He had brown eyes, much darker than Becky's. He was a huge man, a couple of inches over six feet. Broad through the chest with thick, muscular arms. He'd always been known for his strength and for his mean streak. Some of that strength was now under a layer of fat, but Mariah knew he still had the mean in him. After two years, he'd accepted that his daughter wasn't moving home. But he didn't care for it. It always struck Mariah that the man liked having Becky under his thumb.

Joshua waved his men toward the big table and came over to Becky. One of his men tagged after him while the rest sat with a lot of scraping of chairs.

Clint was serving coffee before they were settled.

The man with Joshua was lanky and had overly long blond hair. He had a badly healed scar across his left cheek that cut at an angle from the corner of his eye through his upper and lower lips. She noticed a front tooth missing that lined up exactly with the scar, so whatever blow had scarred him had probably knocked out that tooth. His hair dangled in greasy twists from beneath his battered Stetson.

Joshua said to Becky, "I've hired a new hand. I thought I'd introduce you to Key Larson."

Key tugged on the brim of his hat. Then his ghostly cold blue eyes shifted to Mariah in a strangely penetrating way.

"Welcome to Pine Valley, Mr. Larson. It's nice to see you, Pa." Becky didn't sound like she meant either.

"Mariah Stover and Nell Armstrong," Joshua said and gestured to each woman in turn, "this is Key Larson."

"Howdy." Mariah nodded briefly, then reached for her steaming cup of coffee. She didn't like the way the man was looking at her and didn't want to encourage any familiarity.

"Hello, Mr. Larson," Nell said with perfect manners.

Larson's eyes shifted to Nell, then went right back to Mariah. "I think we've met, Miss Mariah."

Mariah noticed he favored his left arm. And she also knew she'd never have forgotten a man so badly scarred. And his pale, watchful blue eyes were unforgettable, no matter how hard she'd try to forget them.

"I've been laid up for the last two weeks. Before that I was in Laramie for a few days. Otherwise, I've been here in Pine Valley for a long time. I don't remember you from Laramie, and if you're new around here, I doubt we've met. I was injured on my trip home during a stagecoach robbery." She remembered she was supposed to work that in every chance she got. "I can't remember anything from that whole day. Did you see me in Laramie? Or here in Pine Valley after the accident? Maybe that's why I've forgotten. I apologize for that, but the doc says this is common to forget things after an injury to the head. It's permanent."

"No, I must be thinkin' of someone else. I weren't in Laramie. Sorry for the mix-up, miss." The man tugged on the brim of his hat again and joined the other hands at the table.

"What brings you to town, Pa?" Becky lived a short distance from town. She'd chosen the land to buy deliberately because she liked to be able to ride in for church services and to buy supplies, even to eat. Her pa was much farther out. Not so far he didn't come in whenever he wanted, but it was still a distance.

Joshua hesitated overlong, then shrugged. "Had errands. Slow day so I told the men I'd buy them a noon meal."

Clint was bringing plates to the table three at a time. One rested against his elbow and another in each hand. He set the plates down quick and smooth, then hurried back to the kitchen.

"Better go see what the greenhorn made this time." Joshua's smile had a mocking twist to it.

"It's delicious, Mr. Pruitt. I hope you enjoy it." Mariah

would wager that he'd eat every bite of his meal despite his sneering tone.

By the time Joshua swaggered over to his table, Clint had the whole table served, not including Joshua. Clint asked him if he was eating. Joshua said yes and sat down, and mere moments later, Clint set a plate in front of him.

For some odd reason, the phrase *pearls before swine* popped into Mariah's head.

That wasn't fair.

Becky and her pa didn't exactly see eye to eye on things, yet he was a successful rancher, just a gruff man who hired cowpokes Becky didn't feel safe around.

That didn't make Joshua Pruitt swine. Then she saw him plowing through his meal so fast that he couldn't possibly be chewing, and she wondered.

7

Mariah had dawdled long enough.

She'd been more or less unconscious for a week, and since she'd fully woken up, she'd dawdled for a week without working—not counting chaps. She had people clamoring for blacksmith work, although Henry Wainwright had been pleased enough with his new wheel, he'd quit pestering her for his old wheel to be replaced. She had serious doubts about repairing a wheel alone. It was heavy work, and Pa and Theo had always worked together.

There were others who needed work done, and not all of it was blacksmithing.

Her pa had also been the town farrier, shoeing horses. Theo had learned to be a cooper, making wooden pails and butter churns and such.

She'd have people hunt her up in Clint's diner and say their horse threw a shoe and needed her help. Their bucket was leaking, and they needed a new one.

A hinge was broken on the cellar door of one of the

area ranches. She had hinges on hand, but he wanted his repaired.

The saloon owner, Dave Westcott, wanted a new poker for his fireplace. The rumor was, his old one had broken during a fight when one of the Pruitt hands had tried to bash in the brains of another Pruitt hand. No one had been killed, and now Dave wanted a new fireplace poker.

It felt as if she were furnishing weapons, so she was in no hurry to make that.

She had those requests, along with a list of other things that needed to be repaired or replaced.

Three days ago, after a week of staying above the diner, she'd revealed herself as alive to the town. The excited murmuring about that had quieted down.

Nell was worried for her safety. Truth be told, Mariah was a little worried herself. But there'd been no threat against her.

She felt like she was at full strength. No aches or pains dragging at her. It was time to get back to work.

Her cabin sat beside the smithy with a corral between the two buildings, both anchoring the south end of Pine Valley. The diner was the nearest business in the row of main-street businesses. Her house was behind the diner.

She'd yet to be alone in her house. But now she left Nell's shop and went home to change into her work clothes. Stepping into the house alone for the first time since the holdup took her breath.

The silence was total. No Pa. No Theo.

She'd hurt and grieved ever since she'd been told they were dead. But now it hit her hard. Her family was gone. Pa was a man with a loud laugh and a good nature he often hid with gruffness. But he'd always been kindhearted. Since Ma had died birthing a baby out here in Wyoming, the baby dying with her, Pa had done his best with a girl child. She'd been old enough to stay well back from the hot forge, so he'd taken her along to work. She'd gone to school when it was in session, but not Theo. His plans were to be a blacksmith, and all he needed was to be able to do some simple arithmetic and read, both of which he'd been taught by Ma. Theo and Pa both agreed that was enough.

Mariah had gone all the way through eighth grade, then she'd put her foot down because Pa was working long hours at the smithy. Theo had taken over the farrier work and learned how to build wooden buckets and barrels, butter churns and washtubs. Whatever anyone needed.

They made decent money providing all this to the town and yet they couldn't get it all done. Mariah showed up one morning and demanded Pa quit his nonsense about sending her to school and instead put her to work.

And now here she stood in her house, so alone the silence was like a pulse. A pounding in her soul. Pa had been a good Christian man, and he'd raised Theo and Mariah the same. Mariah tried to find comfort in knowing the men she'd loved were right now with God in heaven. Maybe they'd been welcomed into Ma's open arms. The image comforted her quite a lot. But not enough to stop her tears.

She wept while she pulled on her clothes. It felt, as she dressed, like she was becoming someone else. Taking on the family legacy of forging iron in fire. Her crying eased as that internal iron cooled and hardened after the refining fire of her tears.

Her clothes were strictly practical. A black riding skirt

with the legs of the skirt cut narrow to keep her from having loose fabric around open flames. They weren't exactly britches, but they were as close as Pa would let her get away with. And Pa wasn't overly observant.

Her hands trembled as she buttoned up her dark blue shirtwaist—she only wore dark colors to do her blacksmithing. The soot from the coal fire'd ruin anything light. And of course sturdy boots. She twisted her honey-blond hair into a tight bun and anchored it with pins. Then she heard a hard knocking at her front door.

Fear leapt inside her. She hadn't realized she was quite so nervous.

She rushed downstairs, prepared to fight for her life, and found Clint standing outside her door. He looked cranky, but that didn't scare her. In fact, she was glad to see him.

"You're not ready to go back to work, for heaven's sake." He'd come over determined to make the woman rest a few days longer. It might be different if she was sewing dresses like Nell, who honestly rarely sewed a dress.

But blacksmithing? Ready to launch into a scolding, he saw she'd been crying, and without really planning it, he stepped inside and swung the door shut.

"What's wrong?"

Her eyes, puffy but dry, must've found more salt and water to spare because she burst into tears. "I-I'm just missing P-Pa." She threw her arms around him.

Clint caught hold and let her sob. He breathed soothing words that meant little as she wept in his arms. He felt the strength in her and the fear and the grief.

In all the stress of her healing and the fear of the Dead-eye Gang, he didn't know if she'd even begun to mourn her family.

And he knew how deep a cut that was. He held on and let her cry. His own eyes burned, for her but also for his own family and how terribly he missed them.

He let her cry until the trembling eased and her sobs became sniffles. He felt the dampness of his tear-soaked shirt and fished a handkerchief out of his back pocket and tucked it into her hands.

She swiped it across her eyes, then blew her nose. Then hiccupped. When he thought she was done, he saw a new tear run down the already-damp tracks on her face and knew she needed to get her mind off how alone she was.

"You should stop being a blacksmith—it's no job for a delicate little woman."

Mariah launched herself backward, but he held on tight. Her swollen, bloodshot eyes and tear-stained face turned to fury.

Clint laughed. "Gotcha."

Mariah grabbed him by the lapels of his shirt, then a smile quirked her lips and she started to laugh.

The laughter was tinged with hysteria, but it was real. She leaned forward again and rested her forehead against his chest. He wasn't that much taller than she was, but enough. Her laughter turned to giggles until finally she was all the way quiet.

He whispered, "I think you're the strongest, bravest woman I've ever known. And you can do anything."

She said into his soggy shirt, "Thank you, Clint. Today I'm going back to work."

He nodded. "I've got no right to an opinion, I suppose, but I'm really proud of you."

She lifted her head and smiled. The worst of the emotional storm over. There would be more of them.

She felt the calm win out over her grief. At least for now.

Grimly determined to do the work her father had trained her to do, she walked out of the house with Clint, and after a long look, they separated. Him to his diner. Her to the smithy. She walked past the corral that separated her house from the smithy. The blacksmith shop was a large building. Pa had started out building small, with the business up front and a couple of back rooms to live in until he'd had money enough for a cabin. Then once they were moved out of the smithy, he'd added onto the barn and corral to stable horses in need of new shoes. He'd also owned a couple of horses and rented them out on occasion. Mariah didn't see them anywhere and wondered what had become of them.

She didn't think they'd been here that day she'd first come to the smithy. The day Henry had asked for a wheel repair and Mariah had collapsed in Clint's arms, but she hadn't noticed.

The blacksmith doors stood open. Pa had left it like this when he'd traveled to Laramie in case anyone in town needed to use his tools or grab a wheel or a wooden bucket. Pa trusted the good folks of Pine Valley to pay when he returned, and he knew his business was vital to the town.

Right outside the doors, she noticed a pile of broken or bent metal needing repair. Besides this, she had a list of jobs she'd kept to hand. She had helped Pa get set up in the morning for years, so she knew her first job was to get a fire going in the forge.

The forge was built of brick from the ground up to about waist high. A flat area, already stacked with coal, nestled on top of the square foundation of the forge. Above the coal was a domed brick roof, open in the front and arched a couple of feet over the coal. This had a chimney to draw away smoke. From the ceiling hung a huge bellows with a rope hanging down.

She would let the fire catch fully, and when she wanted the iron red-hot, she'd put what metal she would work on into the flames and pull on the rope repeatedly to make the fire burn white-hot. Hot enough to bring iron to a temperature that could be pounded into shape.

But first the fire had to be kindled.

While she waited for the fire to grow hot, she donned a leather apron to keep her clothing from catching fire. Pa had fashioned for her a leather headscarf that she pulled over her head and tied under the bun she always wore. His and Theo's hair was short enough that he had a leather cap for the two of them, while he wanted her longer hair fully covered.

The scarf had always annoyed her, but right now, thinking of Pa and how he'd worried for her safety, tying it on reminded her only of his love.

Everything she wore was for practical reasons and safety. Sparks flew, and clothes and hair could catch fire. How she looked didn't matter to her.

She knew there were plenty of places where the thought of a woman blacksmith would be outrageous, and she would have been condemned for her masculine dress and the heavy, manly work with iron. But not here in Wyoming Territory. There'd already been a woman justice of the peace appointed over in South Pass City. There were women winning elections to many public offices and serving on juries. Here in Wyoming, no one would deny a woman the right to earn a living doing honest work. She loved this territory for that. And it was a part of why she risked staying here when it was possible she was in danger from the Deadeye Gang.

The fire was finally spreading through the coals. She decided to start her work with something simple, and the broken hinge would do just fine. She turned away from the forge to gather the cracked-up iron that had been left for her. She'd heat it up, then hammer the crack until it fused into one piece of solid iron.

As she bent to pick it up, the forge exploded with a deafening roar.

The force of it knocked her facedown in the dirt. Fire blasted right over her head. Smoke swirled and she inhaled it, breathing in air so hot she wondered if her lungs could catch fire.

The fire had shot out five feet. She saw the tongues of yellow-and-red fire flare out far enough, it was visible with her lying on her belly. It would have roasted her alive if she'd been standing upright in front of it. Yet, strangely, the fire was silent. She realized everything was silent.

She couldn't hear.

Slowly her ears began ringing, but there was no sound beyond that.

What had happened? She knew sometimes there was a buildup in the chimney and that could ignite.

Staying down, she gave the explosion all the time it needed to recede. After a few more seconds, she glanced over her shoulder. The flames had sucked back into the forge as quickly as they'd detonated.

She rolled onto her back and shoved herself backward toward the door. Scared it would blast again. What had caught fire like that? It was as if someone had poured kerosene onto the coals, or even dynamite.

Forges could blow up. Her pa had lectured her and Theo over it. She remembered that now when only through luck had she survived an ugly death.

The two weeks with no activity must have allowed the chimney's soot or the coal or something to get too dry or too wet. She'd come in here like a brainless calf without even considering that the forge might need the old coal, so neatly resting in place on the forge, cleared out or the chimney inspected.

She backed well away, almost out the door. But when she stopped, all she could do was stare at the harmless-looking fire. Inches from killing her, and yet now everything looked just fine. Her mind wasn't working right. Not now, and not before this had happened.

Clint came racing into the building. He must have heard the blast in the diner nearby, and he almost tripped over her as he rushed in. Skidding to a stop, he knelt at her side, breathing hard, his face ashen. His lips moved. She thought maybe he said, among other things, "Are you all right?"

He was inspecting her, looking for injuries.

"I can't hear." And then she could, a little. At least she faintly heard herself. The ringing eased a bit.

Clint rested both hands on her head and spoke slowly, not shouting. "Do you need a doctor?"

She heard his question but only faintly. She shook her head. She'd had about all she could stand of Doc Preston for the rest of her life. "Unless I'm on fire or bleeding from a wound to my heart, no doctor."

Clint eased a bit farther away, and she wondered if maybe she was shouting.

Clint frowned, then stood, and with gentle strength he lifted her to her feet, watching her so intently, she was surprised at how cherished it made her feel.

Her knees wobbled, but she thought it was mainly a reaction to the close call. His strong arm around her waist kept her upright.

Speaking normally, she hoped, she said, "The forge blew up. I didn't even think to clean out the old coal and put in fresh before I started work."

"Forges can blow up?" Clint sounded somewhat horrified. As if kitchens never blew up. Did kitchens blow up? She'd certainly seen some of the meals she'd tried to make catch fire.

He was listening, nodding, still focused completely on her. "Come over to the diner and sit a while. It's midmorning still. I've got coffee and dessert. Later, you can have some lunch."

8

He stopped talking, studying her. Then, without shouting, he asked, "Can you hear me?"

Mariah nodded. "Mostly, and I'm reading your lips."

He smiled. "I'll go get Nell to join you to eat if you want. Then if you can wait until after the noon meal, I'll close up and come back with you. I can help you clean out the forge. You'll have to tell me what to do, but I can help you set up to start again."

A smile bloomed on her face. She had expected nagging. Or him telling her she shouldn't have returned to work just yet.

Pa had loved her, Theo too, but they'd been blunt men who expected her to prove herself on every task.

Clint just believed she could do it and expected nothing else.

He seemed unusually interested in her smile. But then he'd been watching her closely, so why not watch that as well? And as she was reading his lips, she was focused on his smile, too.

And Nell would probably jump at the chance to stop working with leather for a while. To her annoyance, she'd found her customers were willing to wait however long it took to get the chaps. Unlike blacksmithing, apparently, there were no chap emergencies.

"All right. Yes, I want to sit for a while, then get back over there and clean out my forge. Thank you, Clint."

They walked out the door, Clint's arm still around her back. She stepped firmly away from him. Her legs held her up, and they walked toward the diner. "Why did you come? Was it loud?"

Her ears were still ringing so she knew it was loud. But that wasn't really her question. What she meant was, *Why did you come and no one else?*

"The breakfast rush was over, and I had a few minutes before starting on lunch. I decided to see how it was going over here and was most of the way here when the forge exploded."

"And no one else heard it?"

Clint looked at the empty street. Then looked at her. She was asking the obvious.

"But it was so loud. My ears are ringing. It must've been loud enough for—" Mariah stopped talking and threw her arms wide. "Oh, forget it."

She walked up the single step to the wooden sidewalk fronting the buildings alongside the diner. Clint made a quick move and reached past her to get the door for her.

Mariah entered an empty building. Clint helped to seat her by pulling out the chair, then sliding it in. Mariah had noticed him doing that before for his female customers. Strange habit.

Clint hurried to get her coffee. He soon returned and slid a slice of strange cake in front of her, full of things she couldn't quite identify.

"I'll go for Nell." Then Clint was gone. She was glad he hadn't asked her to pour coffee for anyone who happened by while he was out. She wasn't up to it.

Sipping the coffee, Mariah considered the forge. Had she ever seen a forge act like that before? She remembered the chimney in their shop catching fire once. Pa had shut down and spent three days cleaning all the built-up soot out of the chimney. She smiled fondly at the memory of her pa, coated in soot. Theo took a turn and was equally filthy.

Maybe it was her turn.

But it wasn't the chimney that had exploded. It was the fire. She'd heard pinecones could explode. And she'd seen a dead pine tree go up in flames so fast, it was as good as an explosion. Could coal do that? She was missing her pa right now more than ever. He knew everything about smithing. Her eyes burned to think of how alone she was in the world. She remembered her early morning bout of tears and wondered at how deeply she might grieve for her family. Tears trickled down her face. Fumbling in her pocket, she got out a large handkerchief and mopped at the tears. The white kerchief came away black.

It was the first she'd considered what she looked like. Rushing to the kitchen, her knees threatening to buckle again, she soaked the kerchief at Clint's hand pump beside the sink. She scrubbed her face, then scrubbed it again. Clint had soap there, and Mariah applied it liberally, scrubbing and rinsing. Clint still wasn't back so she quick rinsed out the cloth one last time and scrubbed some more. This time there was no sign of soot.

She thought of her pa again. How much he knew about blacksmithing and how humble her own knowledge was. As she returned to the table and her coffee cup, for the first time she doubted herself.

Under her injuries and sorrow, she'd never given a thought to quitting. Maybe she should. But then who would do the blacksmithing work in town?

She sipped her coffee. Clint's coffee really was unusually tasty. Everything he made was delicious. Maybe he needed someone to wash the dishes and wait on the customers. Of course, he was doing all that by himself already. She probably shouldn't impose herself on him further by asking for a job.

Maybe Nell could let her join in the sewing business. She was learning how to sew chaps.

As if thinking of her friend conjured her, Nell came rushing into the diner looking worried sick.

It made Mariah glad she'd washed her face.

Nell came to her side and sank into the chair beside her. "Someone tried to kill you?"

Mariah's head reared back. Clint, a few paces behind Nell, said, "I never told you that. No, the forge was just . . ."

Nell launched herself into Mariah's arms. Mariah caught her and was glad the chair was sturdy so they didn't go over backward.

"Now, Nell. Calm down. I'm fine. I had a scare for sure.

But the coal in the forge had dried out too much, I reckon. I'm fine, not a mark on me, not counting soot." But though she said the words just like she'd said them to Clint, for the first time a niggling little worm of fear curled in her belly.

An accident, she was sure. But still she wondered. And now she feared going back to work. It was a dreadful feeling. She didn't consider herself a nervous person. Working with white-hot iron required a steady hand. She sure didn't need to pile being fretful on top of her grief. And the town sure enough needed a blacksmith.

"I have to get on with my noon meal. There's plenty of coffee. If you need more, call out. I'll bring you a cup, Nell."

Nell stood as Clint headed for the kitchen. "I'll fetch it, Clint. You don't have to wait on us."

She trailed after Clint through the still-swinging door and returned a few seconds later with a steaming cup of coffee and her own piece of cake. Raising the cake, Nell said, "He made this while you were in Laramie, and it was such a huge success that he's adding it to the regular desserts. He calls it *carrot cake*."

Mariah, who'd been busy washing her face, had never gotten to her cake. Now she sliced a bit off with her fork and tasted it. Her eyes widened and she called out, "Clint! This is the best cake I've ever eaten."

He shoved the kitchen door open, smiled, and said, "Thank you. I made it back east but hadn't tried it out here. Raisins are sometimes hard to get, and I had to make my own cream cheese, which is sweetened for the frosting."

"It's delicious."

His smile widened. "Thanks." Then he vanished back into the kitchen.

The man made the most unusual food. Carrots in a cake? Cheese in frosting?

"Tell me what happened, Mariah."

So Mariah went through it for Nell. In much more detail than she had for Clint, what with her ears ringing and him being there to witness the aftermath. As she talked, her opinion firmed that it was carelessness on her part that was to blame.

"We've talked ourselves into being scared to death, Nell. I'm practically jumping when a cloud passes overhead. I've got to calm down. It's been two weeks since the holdup. A week mostly unconscious in Clint's rooms. A week at my cabin recovering from the aches and pains."

And blinding headaches and dizziness.

"If those robbers had wanted to harm me, they'd have done it by now. And since I'm up and around, anyone with one working ear should know I can't tell the sheriff anything. If they're so careful to leave no witnesses, then they aren't going to attack me in town, not in daylight hours."

"The forge explosion could be an attack that would be brushed off as an accident," Nell suggested.

As it had been.

The door swung open, and Doc Preston stepped in. "I hoped I'd find you here, Mariah. I've broken the metal hasp on my buckboard tailgate. I've got to give Martin Barritt a ride home in it at the end of the day. I heard you were working again."

Mariah took the last gulp of her coffee and finished her

carrot cake in a few swift bites. Not much would make her leave a single crumb behind.

"I can work on it right now, Doc." Mariah rose, gave Nell a pat on the shoulder, which was meant to reassure Nell but didn't do much to reassure Mariah. She tossed a few coins onto the table. "Tell Clint I'll be back for whatever he's making for lunch. It smells wonderful." She turned and followed Doc Preston out the door.

Mariah finally got some solid work done. No explosion this time.

Pumping the bellows, heating the iron to white-hot, banging on iron braced on the anvil to bend and shape it. She began to feel almost normal again.

She broke for a meal, which was Clint's *co-co van*. She sadly refrained from telling him all the folks eating out front called it chicken stew. It was, as the smell had promised, delicious. And of course not a sign of cocoa anywhere.

Clint came over to the smithy once his kitchen was clean and prepped for the next morning, and he spent the afternoon with her. She was surprised how much she enjoyed his company. And to keep him busy, she taught him how to make nails.

That was the first job Pa had taught her, and there seemed to be an endless demand for nails.

"I've got a pan in my kitchen that I've set aside, assuming it's ruined. I wonder if you could repair it. It's copper."

"I've worked with copper before. Somewhat different, and a pan for cooking would need to be perfectly smooth, so it's difficult. I'll give it a look."

The relaxed company and listening to Clint bang on the anvil helped her to leave the last of her nerves behind. There were no explosions, no threats, no menacing robbers.

Hopefully, her life was getting back to normal.

Well, no. Not normal. She'd never have what she considered her normal life back. Not without Pa and Theo.

9

"How late do you work?"

Mariah jerked as if he'd startled her.

Clint had thought she'd calmed down well through the afternoon, but maybe not.

Mariah glanced out the open door of the blacksmith shop. "It's got to be past suppertime. I lost track. I'm so far behind, and I . . . well, there's no hurry getting home, is there?"

The double doors of the barn, big enough for a wagon to be driven through, faced the north. The sun was slanted so far to the west, the shadows stretched at a sharp angle, almost sideways.

"So not usually this late, then?" He hated to speak of them, but it was wrong not to, wasn't it? "Not when your pa and Theo were here with you?"

Mariah's face was soaked in sweat on the hot August evening. And soot had colored her face. Clint looked at her—in her leather apron and leather headscarf, she was a mess—and saw her eyes fill with tears.

He set his hammer on the anvil and left the nail behind. He'd probably made a hundred of them this afternoon and tossed the finished product, one by one, into a wooden peck. He noticed two other peck-weight wooden kegs filled with nails. "How many nails do you need?" Clint's hands, one for hammering, the other to hold a pair of tongs clamped on each wickedly hot nail, were cramped and aching. He was going to have trouble flipping pancakes in the morning.

Mariah smiled, set aside her own set of tools, then took off her apron and scarf. Her honey-colored hair, too light to be called brown, too dark to truly be blond, was crushed to her skull, wet with sweat. The tears receded.

"Nails are what Pa started me out on. Very simple. And we have so many, I know, but it's not unusual for someone to come in and buy half a peck or even a whole one if they've got a big job to handle, so Pa liked to have plenty on hand."

She checked the keg he'd been filling. "Thank you. I appreciate the help. You can go now—you must be exhausted. You start so early in the morning."

Clint heard the hesitation in her voice, and he didn't blame her. "I expect that Nell's already at your house. She told me this morning when you ran out on my carrot cake, she'd settle in there after I was done with the noon meal."

"I did not run out on your carrot cake. I ate every morsel. It was delicious. Where did you learn to cook? And why do you call chicken stew *cocoa* or whatever you said?"

Clint smiled. He watched her bustle around the room, hanging up tools. Extinguishing the fire in the forge.

Everything neat and in its place. He was like that, too, with his kitchen, so he respected her tidy nature.

She stopped by a basin and washed her hands and face. Clint probably needed to do that, too.

"The recipe is from France. It's not cocoa. It's *coq* . . . which is French for chicken. *Au vin*. The *vin* is French for wine. So it's chicken braised in wine. Except I don't have any wine, so it's braised in a savory sauce I invented."

"In the end then, it's really chicken stew."

Clint considered how the man who'd taught him to cook would turn up his nose at that description. "I reckon it is."

"Like I said, it's delicious. Best chicken stew I've ever had."

"Thank you. Nell is planning on sleeping at your place for a while. I'm hoping there's no reason to fear someone will want to silence you, but if they ever did, coming to your home late at night would be a likely time to strike. Having two people there might help. Did you know Nell is good with a gun?"

Mariah came to his side then, halted suddenly, and looked at him with a furrowed brow. "No, I didn't know that. How did you find out such a thing?"

"I was worried about the two of you in there together. I can't figure out a way for me to stay, it's just unacceptable behavior."

"And you're supposed to stay out at your homestead, aren't you? Proving up on it requires you to sleep there."

"Yes, I spend time out there." Every day. To care for his animals and tend his garden and get food for the next day. He still had that to do today. But the homestead was just beyond town.

"I've got three more years before I prove up on the homestead. As a rule, I sleep out there and have the rooms over the diner for winter nights when I'm afraid I won't be able to get to work. Even then, though, I have to go out and do chores, feed the cattle and chickens and such. But I'm staying in town until I'm sure you're safe."

Clint patted her on the shoulder and wondered if she ever thought past his being a big old help and a good cook of strange food and instead saw the man who admired her. He'd been out here for two years now and had admired her from the first time he'd set eyes on her.

"I'm—I'm—" He stumbled over the words. He couldn't speak to her about his interest in her now. Not while she was mourning her family, struggling to run a business herself, and scared. But the time was coming soon when pretty and usually oh-so-tidy Mariah was going to have to notice Clint as more than a cook.

"You're what?"

Clint couldn't make himself speak to her of anything personal, so he blurted out, "I'm heading home to milk my cow and gather eggs. I'll do a few more chores after I walk you to your place. Then I'll come back to town to sleep."

"Eggs? Milk?" Mariah realized just how late she'd worked. "You still have to go home and do your night chores, don't you? Then more in the morning. That's what you usually spend your afternoons doing. You can't spend them guarding me."

"Did I or did I not make excellent nails for you today?"

Mariah grinned. "You're nearly a professional. Tomorrow, I can teach you how to make something more complicated. But we won't make such a long day of it."

She closed the distance between them. "I appreciate your hard work and how much more hard work you have left before your day is done. How about tomorrow, I finish up quite a bit earlier and maybe even go out with you and help you with your chores? I know how to milk a cow and gather eggs. I've seen that you have a huge garden and other livestock. If you stand guard over me for a few hours in the afternoon, I'll come along and you can guard me out at your place."

"Sounds like a good idea. I walk there—is that all right with you?"

"A walk will do me good. Maybe we can get Nell to come along."

Something faltered in his expression, which she couldn't quite understand. Mariah knew he got along well with Nell, but for some reason he wasn't fully pleased with her company. She had no idea why.

"Bringing Nell is fine with me. She can get away from her chaps, and you can all help me carry to town whatever I need to haul back to the diner for the next meal."

"You carry it all into town?"

Nodding, Clint said, "This is what I do out at my homestead. I didn't settle out there thinking to be a chef."

"A what?"

"Chef. It's a fancy word for cook."

"You know a fancy word for everything."

He shrugged one shoulder sheepishly. "I came out here

intending to settle a few acres of my own. To farm, raise cattle, a few horses. And chickens."

"You've done all of that."

"I have, but I didn't have much money. I'm not a good farmer. The few animals I had did well, but I couldn't seem to grow enough corn and hay to feed them."

"I think animals mostly graze on the grass that's growing out here. You don't need to plant corn and hay."

"Good to know. But a little late. I needed an income, especially since at first I didn't have any chickens and I was going hungry as much as my livestock were. The first year, I was looking at a cold, hungry winter. So cooking is what I know. I grew up working in my parents' restaurant in New York City. Then I got a job at a fancier restaurant for a while. But my family died, and I was left alone."

"I'm sorry your parents died."

"They were killed when a fire broke out in their diner. They still lived above the restaurant, and it burned to the ground with them inside. I had two sisters who died in that fire, one of them married. Everyone died."

Mariah stepped much closer to him and rested her hand on his arm. "Such a terrible grief. Your whole family at once." She felt like it could be a bond between them.

"I had no one left. I wanted out of the city. My boss at the restaurant was a tyrant. A fine chef who taught me a lot but was mean as a rattlesnake. And I had this dream gnawing at me to own a little piece of the earth. A little land all my own. And I needed . . ."

She didn't think he'd go on. "You needed what?"

"I-I needed to just be alone. To get past the guilt for abandoning my parents, my whole family, because I wanted something nicer than the diner they owned. I walked away from them, and they died. I'm a light sleeper, and I'd've gotten us out when the diner burned."

Mariah slid her hand up his arm and back down. "And I'd've saved my pa and Theo if I'd been faster with my rifle, and more accurate."

Their eyes locked in silent understanding. Finally, Clint went on, "I sold the lot my parents' restaurant was built on and I had a little saved up. Enough to afford a trip west. I threw in with a wagon train for a while, then rode a train some, even wandered on horseback. I didn't know where I was headed until I saw those towering rocks and knew I'd found my place in this world."

The Cirque of the Towers. Magnificent. Mariah smiled. "I feel safe when I look at them. As if we have giant watchmen always standing guard." But her father and brother hadn't been safe, so the watchmen idea was merely a fantasy.

"Then I got hungry being a farmer and opened my Le Grande Restaurante."

He said it that funny way. *Grawnd* Restaurant.

"And it's been a success. I've got the homestead humming along now, thanks to the money coming in from the diner. And I've got the diner humming along thanks to my garden and livestock. I'm a prosperous man, heading for proving up on my homestead. I've found my life."

He looked at her when he said it in a way that made her heart ache a little. Reminded her of how alone she was, and how kind he'd been.

Her hand tightened just slightly on his arm. Then he was closer . . . then she was.

They stood too close together for too long before her mind snapped back into her head. She dropped his arm as if it were a red-hot iron, stepped back, and turned away. Then, speaking to her toes, unable to meet his warm, kind eyes, she said, "I'd best get home."

Mariah reached for one door to swing it shut, and Clint reached for the other.

"Pa liked to leave the doors open so folks could drop things off. No one's ever made off with so much as a hammer or a pair of tongs. The town knows it needs a blacksmith. But he could lock it if he chose to. There's a chain on the front door and a heavy sliding bolt lock on the back. I'm sure this morning's explosion was an accident, but I will feel better about everything if I lock up."

Mariah pulled a chain through the door handles and fastened it with a padlock.

"I've got the diner locked up, too. I'll walk you home."

It was a nice walk. The day had been long and hot, but with the setting of the sun, the worst of the heat eased its cruel grip on Pine Valley. They were up at a fair altitude, though with that Cirque of the Towers standing guard over the north side of town, it didn't seem all that high. Still, it got cool most nights, which made sleeping comfortable.

"I'm glad you're staying, Mariah. For now, you should plan on me making nails with you every afternoon."

Mariah turned to him at the front door of her house. "Thank you, Clint. I got along when I worked over there alone, and I know you must be busy. But I felt better having you there. I really appreciate it."

Their eyes met. The moment lingered. The cool breeze,

the day turning to dusk, the hoot of the night owl. Even the foolishly off-key piano music coming from the saloon in the background. It was a sweet moment.

The door opened behind him and whacked Clint in the back. It was so sudden he stumbled forward and knocked into Mariah, who staggered back under the unexpected assault.

Nell poked her head out the door. "What's blocking this?" She looked at Clint.

"I was." He narrowed his eyes at Nell while rubbing the back of his head.

She arched her brows. "Oops, sorry. I saw you walking over and came to greet Mariah."

Clint shook his head. "Good night to you both."

He turned and strode toward the diner. When he heard the door to Mariah's house close, he glanced back, saw both women were gone, then headed for the trail he always walked to go to his homestead. He didn't want Mariah knowing how much work he had to do, because she'd feel bad for keeping him in her blacksmith shop all afternoon.

The piece of land he'd claimed was a fifteen-minute walk from Pine Valley. Though he had a horse, he didn't bother riding most days—unless he had a lot to haul. If so, he'd hitch the horse to his small wagon, load it, drive in, unload the wagon, then drive the rig back home and walk back to town. He had nowhere to keep his horse in town unless he boarded it at the smithy.

Mr. Stover used to board horses by the day. His blacksmith shop had several stalls in it and he had a corral, and sometimes he had a few horses to rent or sell. Though there were none in that corral now. Becky Pruitt had taken them to her ranch until Mariah was able to tend them.

Maybe he'd start keeping his horse there, at least some of the time. He made decent money at Le Grande Restaurante. He could afford to spend a bit. As hard as Mariah worked today, though, Clint was sure she would make a decent living.

Living being the important word.

If that gang didn't come for her.

He walked faster until he was nearly jogging, just to force himself not to turn back and stand guard over her all night. He rounded a small rocky outcropping with a copse of trees that seemed to grow out of the craggy rock formation. As he walked along, he heard rustling in the trees.

Looking to his right at the trees, he saw nothing. And the rustling, was it someone? Someone waiting for him to leave Mariah alone so they could attack.

Then a cat ran out of the trees. His cat, dashing for the barn as if it realized he might notice it wandering.

Heaving a sigh of relief, he tried to laugh at himself. But he couldn't quite manage it. It felt wrong to leave Mariah, even with Nell there.

Tomorrow he'd find a few minutes to talk to Nell and ask her again just how good she was with her gun. She didn't strike him as being all that salty.

He came around the rocks, and about the time he was out of sight of the town, he saw his house and barn. His corral and the vegetable shed. The chicken coop and pigsty.

He had a lot going on at his place, most all of it aimed at running his restaurant. And he took great satisfaction in what he could do with fresh food.

He was going easy on himself for the next few days because he was exhausted. And simple seemed to make the good folks in Pine Valley happy. So biscuits and sausage gravy for breakfast. In case he was still too sore to flip pancakes. Beef stew for lunch. But he'd call it *ragoût de boeuf* just to make his customers a little crazy. And what he made was better than a standard beef stew, for he had special spices and a few tricks beside. But fancy or not, it was beef stew. Smiling over the games he played as he tried in his own quiet way to educate the palates of the townsfolk he'd grown to like and admire, he headed straight for the door that slanted up from the ground. His root cellar. It wasn't going to be a day for the wagon.

He'd save time by planning simple meals, then get his supplies back to town, then get some sleep.

He loaded a gunnysack with potatoes, carrots, onions, and garlic. He added herbs to a smaller bag and unhooked a nice rump roast from where it hung, properly aged at last, from overhead in his cellar. He set them on the ground, then headed for the barn to milk the cow, gather eggs, and feed the livestock. He needed to have a look at the garden, too, and see what was ripe.

He'd be back in town in an hour.

And that'd put him far closer if Mariah proved to be in any danger. But still, much too far away. As he worked, he considered sleeping on the floor of his diner.

Grimly he thought of that "accidental" explosion and worked faster.

Key Larson eased his hand off his gun when Clint walked on.

He'd've hated to kill the diner cook. The man was talented, and Key was known for being hungry.

When Roberts reached his homestead without changing his mind about searching that clump of trees and rocks, Larson relaxed and turned back to study the house Mariah now lived in.

The boss had agreed she needed to die, but he wasn't as sure as usual. He was disgusted that they'd killed Joe and Theo Stover. Now, with two weeks gone and no sign that Mariah remembered a thing, the boss said she could only die if it looked like an accident.

Key could tell that the boss didn't have much of an appetite for killing a woman.

The first attempt to kill her today had failed.

But Key was good with sneaking. He'd found a way to make a living at it until he'd had to run from Denver and ended up out here.

So how to make it look like an accident? He had a few ideas, one in particular that just might be perfect.

But he'd seen that other woman, the pretty blond one, was staying in Mariah's house, and he didn't want to go in while she was there.

He stared at the house a long time, knowing he could slip around once they were both asleep. But one of them was downstairs moving around. For now, he'd have to wait. Soon, though, they'd relax and his chance would come.

Nell followed Mariah into the house, the two of them not speaking.

"You look exhausted." Nell was usually an unusually polite woman. So that stung. "I set up a tub of water for you to wash in your bedroom, Mariah. I've a clean nightgown laid out for you and a clean skirt and top for tomorrow, besides clean underpinnings."

"Thank you so much."

"There's a bar of soap, and if you want to wash your hair, holler and I'll pour the rinse water for you."

Mariah looked over her shoulder as she headed upstairs to her room.

"I'm so exhausted, I don't think I can stay awake long enough to dry it."

"Go ahead and bathe. Clint sent over leftovers from lunch."

"I'll be in and out of the water fast. I just realized that, along with being exhausted, I'm starving."

"See you in a few minutes."

Mariah swung the bedroom door shut.

Clint was back in town, toting three bags of supplies, a bucket of milk, and a basket of eggs. He was impatient with himself for bringing so much, but as he rushed along, he knew this was about what he brought every day.

He'd need to run home during the midmorning break and milk the cow again. He hadn't done it this morning, and she'd been cranky about it.

He didn't blame her.

Despite his heavy load, he was the next thing to running.

He ignored the rustling in the trees this time, which was to say he noticed it and hurried along, yet he didn't take time to worry overly.

He let himself in through the back door of the diner. As quietly as possible, he tiptoed into his kitchen, set things down without bothering to light the lantern, and headed upstairs to sleep light.

10

Clint considered himself a hard worker. But after watching Mariah at the smithy for the week since she'd gone back to the forge, he was a shirker.

It'd been three weeks since she'd been shot and she was at full strength now except, she complained, for her utterly blank memory of the day of the robbery.

She was up and came over from her house while he was just getting his stove fired up. No pancake batter mixed up. No fresh bread out of the oven. She left Nell sleeping at her house and came to the diner every morning.

He fried her up some eggs and bacon, served her biscuits and coffee, and he did it fast because she didn't seem inclined to wait. He could have fed her so much better, but it was fast or she'd go to work on an empty stomach, or so she declared.

She gobbled whatever he served her and then was gone.

This was a new Mariah. She had always been a helper when her Pa ran the place. He wondered if she mostly made nails, then looked at his blistered fingers. Now the work was all on her.

She was gone early, and by the end of the first week of staying with her in the afternoon, he'd learned she worked late, too. He'd thought she just lost track of time that first day, but the work came in with surprising speed. Someone always needing something repaired or replaced. It was always urgent. He hadn't given it that much thought, but he was learning she was the town cooper, too. She had wooden buckets and butter churns and kegs of various sizes to make.

She was the town farrier as well. That one worried him. It was strange to watch her pick up a horse's hoof and see the big animal rest on her. As if, deprived of a leg, it'd use Mariah's back for balance.

The rest of the blacksmith trade, though hot work, wasn't overly heavy, except for the making and repairing of wheels. That was a rugged business. As for those horses, she seemed able to handle it, though he wondered how long a farrier's back would hold out.

He was learning to help quite a bit. He wasn't really good at it, yet there were a lot of simple jobs she'd trained him to do.

And he'd talked Deputy Willie Minton into staying with her part of the time. Clint knew the sheriff and deputy had been in town when those horses came charging in, dragging the broken remnants of their traces. That meant they weren't members of the gang. Mostly he was suspicious of everyone. He'd come to know a few other men in town, too, and he figured he could trust them.

Willie was proving to be a decent hand helping her,

and privately, Clint wondered if Mariah should hire him permanently as an assistant. A deputy didn't make much, and near as Clint could tell, aiding the sheriff didn't take much of Willie's time.

Thankfully, Mariah had no more brushes with death.

Maybe the explosion that first day really was an accident.

Nell had moved home, though he often asked her to eat supper when he had leftovers for Mariah. Usually the two of them came to the diner to eat. He'd invited her tonight, and both Mariah and Nell had a key to his diner.

He rushed home in the afternoons to do his chores, usually leaving Mariah with Willie. He made a point to get back before the end of Mariah's workday. Willie would head home, and then Clint would get to work on whatever job Mariah had saved him. Today he was making hinges. There were no orders at the moment, but it was one of the items Mariah liked to have on hand in case they were needed.

Clint finished rounding the end of the hinge. Two of them, one screwed onto the door, one attached to the doorframe, would slide together, and a bolt would lock them in place and they'd hold a door up and let it swing. Clint had seen plenty of hinges, but he'd never really wondered about who made them.

Turns out it was the work of a blacksmith.

11

Mariah finished attaching the handle and set the wooden pail aside to be delivered to Henry Wainwright first thing in the morning.

She studied it with satisfaction, then filled it with water. All wooden buckets needed to be kept full of water. At first the water made the wood swell slightly and stopped any leaks. But then you could never let it dry out or the wood would shrink until the bucket was permanently ruined.

Setting the bucket down, she looked at Clint. "I'm ready to close up a little earlier than usual today."

He smiled. "Sounds good. I have some leftover chicken parmesan from lunch."

"That chicken with the tomato sauce?" Mariah pressed her hand to her belly. "I didn't realize how hungry I was until now."

"I told Nell there was enough for her. But it's a little late. She might've eaten hers already." He followed Mariah out the door and waited for her to lock it. After a little pause, he added, "It's so much better right out of the oven.

I'm almost embarrassed to serve it to you. Still delicious, though. It's at the diner, so we can eat there."

As they walked the short stretch of main street from the smithy along the row of buildings in Pine Valley, then around the back of the diner, Clint asked, "Are you still having the headaches?"

"They only bother me when I try and remember. If I'm tired and fall asleep fast, there's no trouble, but if I've got any energy left at the end of the day, I brew up that tea the doctor gave me, have a cup before I go to bed, then try and push myself to remember. When I do that with the medicine, well, I get a headache. Even so, it's manageable."

"The doctor said you'd probably never remember."

She nodded as she reached for the knob on Clint's back door.

He stretched past her and pulled the door open. It was unlocked, which meant Nell was there.

They'd barely stepped inside the narrow back entrance when Nell came rushing toward them, waving something in her hand.

"It came!"

"*The Revolution* came?" Mariah answered, just as excited. "Good. I can't wait to read it!"

Clint noticed the thing Nell was waving was a newspaper or something akin to it.

So there was news of a revolution? They'd just finished the Civil War. Who had America taken up arms against now?

Excited as they were, Clint was suddenly afraid he was going to have to fight alongside these women in a war. He hadn't figured on that when he'd started making nails.

91

"Have you read it yet?" Mariah didn't grab it, but she had a fight on her hands to resist. Then Nell shoved it into her hands, and Mariah's spirits lifted sky-high.

"I've read every word. Twice. And one article ten times. Mariah, you'll never guess—there's a speaker coming to Pine Valley."

Mariah gripped Nell's hand. "Who? Not . . . not one of the ladies who created this? Not Elizabeth Cady Stanton or Susan B. Anthony?"

"No, it's not a name I've heard of before, but there's a wonderful article about her in *The Revolution*."

"*The Revolution* is a newspaper? Thank God." Clint locked the door firmly, then slipped past them. "I'll get supper on."

He was gone before Mariah could explain about *The Revolution* and the National Woman Suffrage Association. It flickered through her head that since Wyoming had already given women the right to vote, there shouldn't be much fuss about a speaker who favored that. In fact, Mariah felt thrilled to find out there was still interest in Wyoming. She'd feared they might be forgotten as the pressure to allow women to vote moved on to other territories.

But a few would kick up a fuss, no doubt about it. Joshua Pruitt came to mind. Would Clint? She'd started to admire the man, but if he wouldn't support her on this topic, she'd feel the betrayal deeply.

Nell was here alone in Pine Valley. After her husband died, she'd moved to Wyoming with her brother. But the big lummox thought women voting was an embarrassment. Becky had left her father's home, at least in part because he was so ugly about women's suffrage. Oh, Joshua was a difficult man in many ways. Nell's brother, Bart, might have left, but he hadn't been nasty and insulting to Nell when she'd stayed behind. Joshua had been so unkind to Becky that there was only grim politeness between them now.

Meanwhile, Mariah, whose father hadn't held strong positive or negative views on women voting, had decided a daughter hard at work at a man's job ought to have some say in larger matters.

And now Mariah was alone, had no man to be her voice in the voting booth, and she felt she would vanish if she couldn't vote. It was the thing she loved most about Wyoming, next to those beautiful mountains on the west side of town.

She thumbed through the newspaper, all sixteen pages of it. She found the article about Josette Mussel coming to Pine Valley next summer. "I have to sit down," she announced.

To faint in response to a paper that was fighting for respect for women would be in poor taste. But the excitement was definitely making her knees wobble.

And to think Josette Mussel would be coming here, where no train passed.

And then, just as Mariah sank onto a chair at the table nearest the kitchen, with Nell settling in across from her, it hit her. "She might be attacked. She might have her stagecoach robbed like I did. *She might be killed.*"

"Let go of that paper." Nell's sharp slap on her hand brought her out of the panic, at least partway out. "You're tearing it." Nell rescued the newspaper and laid it on the table, smoothing it like fine silk fabric. And considering how Nell adored silk, that was no small thing.

"Is something wrong? Are you hurt?" Clint came rushing out of the kitchen so fast he skidded to a stop at their table.

"No." Nell narrowed her eyes at Mariah. "She was wrinkling the paper."

"It's more than that." Mariah turned to Clint and caught his forearm. "A speaker is coming to Pine Valley. It says here she'll be coming next summer. She'll be riding in on the stagecoach, the same road I came in on. We have to make sure she's safe."

Clint stared at her for a long minute. Then with a jerk of his chin, he said, "It's more than one woman. We need to figure out a way to make that stage safe for everyone. This isn't the Wild West anymore. There are laws out here. We'll work out a plan, and do it soon."

Clint paused and stared into the middle distance for a few moments. "The stage line ought to hire outriders for every route, start sending a strong contingent of them until the Deadeye Gang is stopped. We need U.S. Marshals involved in investigating. We should apply pressure to Fort Bridger to send out cavalry patrols. And they need to do it now, not wait until next summer."

He patted Mariah's hand in a way that seemed to say he was dead serious. She then regretted thinking the word *dead*, even if she hadn't said it out loud.

"I've got to tend my supper for now." Clint left. Coming from him, somehow his assurance that he'd help made her believe it could be done. It *would* be done.

Mariah left the rest of her panic behind, along with her worry over her knees. She was sure they would no longer wobble with excitement should she try to stand upright.

"I'm calm now." Mariah slammed a fist on the table. All right, maybe not completely calm. "Yes, we have to do something. And we will. Now let me see that paper again."

Nell grinned and held the paper close to herself. "I'll read you the article. It might set you off again, and I want to protect this."

"Is there just the one paper?"

Nell arched her brows. "There were five issues in the mail today. This is the most recent."

"And you've read them all?"

"No, I picked this one to read first to find the latest news. Then I got an order for five more pairs of chaps from Joshua Pruitt." Nell rolled her eyes, and Mariah knew hers matched the expression. "But I'll read them all, and so will you."

"For now, read me the article about Josette Mussel. Where is she from? Does she——?"

"Shh!" Nell slashed her hand sideways. "The article will tell you everything I know, and more."

Nell set to reading the article aloud. When Clint came in with two plates of delicious chicken with tomato sauce and cheese, he listened while Nell, who had indeed already eaten, read it again.

12

Mariah's head was buzzing from exhaustion by the time she set the newspaper aside and turned down her bedside lantern.

It crossed her mind to take her medicine, but surely it wouldn't be necessary tonight. She was plum tired. And today she'd begun to accept that her memory of the stagecoach robbery was gone forever.

She lay there with her eyes closed. Her brain buzzing faintly but pleasantly with exhaustion, and there she lay. Awake.

She'd been lying there with her eyes closed for what seemed like hours but was probably not even thirty minutes when she tossed her blankets aside and got up to find her medicine.

The medicine was a mixture of who-knew-what, which she kept in a canvas bag. And the mixture needed to be brewed up like tea. It took a few minutes, and not for the first time, Mariah considered just taking it every night.

She made her way down to the kitchen. The teakettle

had been pushed to the back of the still-warm stove. Mariah was only moments dragging it forward, measuring out her medicinal tea, and pouring water over it.

She let it steep the doctor-ordered ten minutes, then strained out the dried herbs and leaves the doctor had concocted into tea.

Mariah sipped. Yes, this was it. Bitter as always. And the right temperature to drink. Normally when she had a cup of hot tea, she liked to linger over it—read, visit with someone, or at the very least, warm her hands.

Not tonight. Not ever with this stuff. She wondered how Doc Preston had come up with this wretched witch's brew of a medicine. She resisted the urge to hold her nose as she gulped the medicine down in one long swallow before setting the cup aside.

Grateful to be done with it, she went back up to bed.

She slept and dreamed of a woman with eight children clinging to her while she gave a speech about women's rights. Then a stage tipped over on all eight of the children. There was shooting, a forge exploded, and then the dream meandered into Mariah wearing a pretty pink dress instead of fireproof aprons.

That last part was probably the least realistic part of her dream.

Key worked the lock.

It took him too long. Frowning, he bent closer, worked his picks around, found the tumbler inside the lock and got it moving.

Strange lock. Once inside, he studied it a little, saw it

was homemade, no standard type of lock bought at a general store. It stood to reason a blacksmith might be able to make his own lock and key.

Next time he'd be faster unlocking it.

Looking inside, he saw the back door opened right into the kitchen. With Mariah sleeping, he could have his run of the place.

He moved forward and spotted a bedroom right off the kitchen and a stairway leading to a second floor. Climbing the stairs, he saw a woman's bedroom and a man's, both smaller than the bedroom downstairs. Brother and sister probably slept upstairs, their pa downstairs in the bigger room. It stood to reason.

A smile quirked his lips.

The smile, of course, was because no pa, no brother. Not anymore. If Key had his way, there'd be no sister soon enough. No witnesses.

They'd tested her and it was clear she didn't remember much of nuthin'. Leastways she hadn't remembered anything yet. They could probably risk letting her live. But of all of them, he was the one she'd seen.

He had everything to lose.

The boss had said to wait. Pine Valley was a peaceful little place. Fact of the matter was, Key was a little surprised to find someone in this town who locked her doors.

He wandered the house, picking things up. He liked touching other people's things. Liked to imagine them later, touching things he'd handled. It was like leaving something of himself behind.

Not much in here. Never much to steal from poor people. It was part of why he'd taken up stagecoach robbery.

He wasn't sure what he was looking for, but he wasn't finding it.

A way to make her death look like an accident. But looking around the place, nothing came to mind that he could set up in advance.

Then he thought of the smithy. He'd tried there once and failed. It'd been wide open then, yet he knew she was locking it up now.

He felt that smile again because it didn't matter. Keys were his gift. His ma hadn't called her baby boy that. He'd earned the name.

Mariah jerked awake, not sure if wearing the dress was the nightmare or the dearest dream of her heart.

She remembered that she'd lost the only decent dress she owned when she had it cut off her after the stage was robbed. Or at least she thought it had been cut off her. Her only feminine dress. Black, fit for church on Sunday and funerals all in one.

Pa had never seen the sense of light-colored dresses. He claimed they got dirty too easy.

Which, indeed, they did.

Mariah lay there instead of leaping out of bed as she always did, rushing through a breakfast Clint barely had time to make for her and getting straight to work.

It occurred to her that this was the way she'd been living all her life, with the small change of her always cooking for Pa and Theo. Cooking fast. Once the men hurried off to get the day's work going, she'd clean up the kitchen and join them.

She thought of the usual hurry, the work always pressing to be done, and realized she wanted a new dress. A pink one.

Nell would love making her a dress. But it was so embarrassing to want a girly color, lace and ruffles. Mariah didn't know if she'd ever be able to show her face outside wearing such a thing.

Maybe a nice navy blue.

Shoving the covers aside, Mariah hurried into her black split skirt, her dark brown shirtwaist, and her boots, then rushed downstairs.

For once, rather than being in a hurry to get to work, she was sorely afraid she was running away just so she could avoid Nell and asking her for a ruffled dress. Knowing that for foolishness, she slowed down and went to the diner like she always did.

Because she'd lingered a bit, Clint met her at the table with biscuits and sausage gravy.

Nodding as he set the plate down, she said, "I may just be a bit slower about getting around in the morning. Your sausage gravy—in fact, all of your food—is worth waiting for."

A smile crinkled the corners of his eyes. "You always make short work of the eggs and bacon."

"I've never had a bad meal served in this place. It's a fine talent you have."

"I'll get coffee." He left the dining room and returned with the pot and two cups. "Can I join you? You're always done and gone so fast that I barely get to say good morning."

Mariah gestured to an empty chair. "I'll be glad for the company."

Settling in, Clint sipped his coffee while she ate at her usual brisk pace. It struck her as very polite to let her chew away without interrupting her.

When the last bit of biscuit was gone, she sighed, picked up her cup and took a long drink. "You make the best coffee I've ever had, too."

"Can I ask you a question about the suffragette who's coming?"

Mariah leaned forward. "Mrs. Mussel. Of course."

"Well, women's suffrage is women earning the right to vote, right?"

"Yes." She was so eager to talk about this, to educate him. So few men wanted to discuss women's rights.

"Don't you already have the right to vote? What is the point of her coming to Wyoming exactly? We're the standard for the country, aren't we?"

Her eagerness died like a forge without fuel. "Just last year our territorial legislature voted to repeal suffrage. The governor vetoed it, but the veto was overridden in one house, and the other house failed to override it by only one vote. Our rights are not secure at all. There are plenty of men who object to suffrage, and they don't like women serving in appointed offices or on juries either. Even now there's a move afoot to bar women from jury duty."

Clint nodded as she spoke, but he didn't seem to have any urgency about him.

"Do you know who Esther Morris is?" she asked.

"Sure, I've heard of her. She was justice of the peace in South Pass City."

"The ground she broke is still rough. It needs more work. In fact, Nell is writing to her today to make sure she knows about Mrs. Mussel coming here. South Pass City isn't that far. We hope she'll come here and listen to the speech and get to know Mrs. Mussel, and while she's at it, she might get to know Nell, Becky, and me. She's so inspiring."

Clint nodded silently for too long. "Don't you worry that she's been subjected to terrible gruesome crimes as a justice of the peace? She's had to listen to every sort of crime and who knows what kind of ugly language."

Mariah really had no fondness for ugly language and gruesome crimes. Pa and Theo had always been mindful of a lady being present.

"The trouble with shielding women from nasty words and violent crimes is that it makes us seem less than fully mature adults. By thinking of women as delicate and worthy of shelter, which sounds kind and decent, the truth is, we're being sheltered from adulthood."

Clint nodded again. "I see your point. And considering what you've gone through lately, trying to shelter you only puts you in danger. You have to be alert to be safe. And I don't think of you as a child, Mariah. I think you and your friends are intelligent, self-supporting, competent women. But to me, that's different from sitting through trials. It's one thing to face up to danger you can't avoid. It's another to seek it out like a justice of the peace would."

"It's not just Mrs. Morris, you know. Women are now allowed to sit on juries and run for office. They can be lawmen."

Clint visibly flinched but didn't say anything.

"I'm a woman working in a man's job, so nobody can say I'm overly delicate."

Clint set his coffee cup down and reached for her free hand. He turned it over and looked at her palm and the calluses on every finger. "You're strong, Mariah. No, you're not overly delicate."

She wondered if he'd say that if she had on a lacy pink dress.

"But that strength doesn't make you less of a beautiful woman."

Mariah's eyes rose from where their hands were joined. Her gaze locked with his. She felt his hand, warm on hers. She remembered the moment they'd shared in the smithy one night. A moment of closeness. A moment when it had flashed through her mind that she'd never been kissed.

A moment when she thought of herself as most definitely a woman.

She rather liked the idea of a moment like that happening again.

"Clint, thank you. I—"

A fist banged against Clint's diner door, and he dropped her hand as if it were boiling coffee . . . or a red-hot forge. Both worked with heat.

He leapt to his feet, rushed to the door, and fumbled a bit with the lock.

Which made her hide a smile.

And also want to escape.

13

While his back was turned, she set her daily payment for her meal on the table, rose, and, as soon as the first of his customers cleared the door, dashed outside.

"Mariah, wait!"

She moved on with a fast stride toward the smithy as if she hadn't heard him. But oh goodness she had. She'd heard *"Mariah, wait."* And she'd heard him call her a beautiful woman. It kindled something inside her that she hadn't known to be flammable.

Had anyone ever thought that before? She certainly couldn't remember Pa or Theo commenting on how she looked. And she'd never spent time with any other man, leastwise not without Pa present and a forge blazing before her.

She was glad her back was firmly to Clint as she strode toward the smithy, fishing the key out of her pocket that unlocked the padlock to set free the chain she had threaded through the door handles.

She noticed a metal basin and two pails tossed in a bit of a jumble, their holes visible in a single glance, right outside her door and to her left. She wondered who'd dropped them off. But it didn't matter. She'd fix them, and eventually someone would come fetch their basin and pails.

Deciding to get the forge fired up first, Mariah left the work where it lay and hurried inside to get started for the day. She had to force herself to pay close attention. She worked with red-hot iron after all. Paying attention was vital.

Yet it flickered through her mind that maybe not a pink dress, neither did it have to be dark blue. Maybe something in between with a few ruffles added discreetly.

A few beautiful ruffles.

Although maybe not. Not so soon after Pa and Theo had died. Feeling guilty for considering not honoring her father by wearing somber clothing, she piled coal in place and set it to burning. It was always a bit slow getting started. As she waited for the fire to catch fully, she gathered up what she needed for the day and checked to see if her wooden pail needed more water, which it did.

She donned her leather apron and covered her hair. When finally the forge was ready, she spent some time on a broken handle for an iron skillet Doc Preston had brought in a couple of days ago. The least she could do was get his job done right away since he'd saved her life.

That job done, she saw to a few other emergencies. Then she went to fetch the work someone had so generously— she snorted at the endless generosity of the folks around here—dumped on her. The two metal buckets lay on their sides. She grabbed them by the handles and held them in one hand. The basin was upside-down. She reached for it and lifted just as a rattle sounded from under it.

A sound she'd heard before. An unmistakable warning of danger.

A snake struck out at her and, only through pure luck, hit one of the buckets she held in her left hand.

Screaming, she staggered, then fell on her backside as the snake struck again. The snake aimed high and missed her on the ground. She rolled to her belly and clawed her way along. Fighting to get to her feet. The snake struck her boot hard enough that she heard its fangs scrape on the hard leather.

Every breath was a scream or a cry for help. Noise tore through the small town as she leapt to her feet. She was one pace away from it, then two, almost out of its range, before she stumbled and fell to her knees just as she felt the vicious pain of a strike on her arm. The snake sunk its venomous, needle-sharp teeth into the flesh of her arm. She slammed one of the buckets against her arm and knocked the snake loose.

A gunshot blasted the ground only inches from her. She whirled, backing away, putting distance between her and poison, even though it was too late.

The snake twisted and tumbled into a knot as the gun fired and fired again. She looked up to see Clint coming at a dead run. He reached for her with his free hand, the gun held in his other, its barrel still smoking. He hooked an arm across her back and another under her knees and he ran.

"Did it bite you?"

"Yes, got me in the arm. My left arm." Way too close to her heart.

Clint charged across the street as more people emerged from their businesses, reacting to the screaming, the gunfire, the pounding feet.

Clint slammed through the doctor's door. Doc Preston, who was in the back room, rushed out to meet them. The doctor was stout, with white hair and wire-rimmed glasses. But he was a strong man who never quit, no matter what was asked of him.

"Did she get shot?" Doc Preston asked.

The question shocked Mariah, but then she realized the truth was worse.

"Bit by a rattlesnake." Clint kept moving into the back room where he laid her on the table.

"It's my left arm."

"Tear her sleeve off. And hurry."

Clint nodded, moving so fast she didn't have time to think about helping. A knife appeared in his hand. The slice and rending tear of fabric being ripped away barely registered in the chaos of the doctor rushing away, then coming back with a strip of rawhide. Just as Clint cut the sleeve all the way off, the doctor wrapped the leather strip tight around her arm just above the bite, which was halfway between her shoulder and her elbow.

She turned to see the doctor pull a wickedly sharp, slim blade she'd heard called a scalpel out of a drawer beside the table where she lay. At that moment fear took hold, followed by pain. She felt the shock of how much hurt the bite had caused.

He came at her with that wickedly sharp knife. She had an idea of how a snakebite was treated.

"Hold her still," Doc Preston said.

A slash of the doctor's knife wrenched a scream out of her throat. She looked at her arm to see what the madman was doing.

At that very moment, Nell rushed into the doctor's office.

"What happened?" She rushed to Clint's side, closer to Mariah's head. She caught Mariah's right hand in hers.

"S-snakebite." The word caught in Mariah's throat, as she could barely say it aloud.

The doctor slashed again. Mariah screamed. Her mouth only worked for one thing right now. Her whole body thrashed involuntarily from the pain.

She couldn't seem to exercise any control over her muscles.

"Talk to her, Nell. Distract her. Clint, grab her left hand. Calm her down if you can. Slowing her heartbeat will help keep the poison from circulating."

Clint was holding her down mostly with the weight of his own body.

A hard hand clamped on her wrist.

Clint again, or had someone else come in?

She screamed once more but couldn't move now, not even her head to watch the doctor. Nell had shifted so that one of her hands held Mariah's chin.

"Mariah!" Nell looked her in the eyes. "Please, look at me. Let the doctor work. Pray with me."

Mariah forced herself to lock her gaze on Nell while the doctor's painful treatment went on with her arm.

Rattlesnakes killed people. Venomous bites.

"I-I'm going to die."

"No, Mariah, you're going to make it. We got to the

bite in time." The doctor tried to sound reassuring, but Mariah didn't believe him. At the very least, she would lose her arm.

Nell prayed. Mariah knew that was all she could do right now. She tried to pay attention to Nell. She heard, "'Yea, though I walk through the valley of the shadow of death . . .'"

There was more, but Mariah grabbed hold of that one phrase. This was the valley of the shadow of death. This moment. And the moment when she'd been shot and buried alive under a stagecoach. And the explosion.

"This isn't the valley of the shadow of death," she snapped.

"No, of course it isn't." Nell clung tightly to Mariah's hand. "You're going to be all right."

Mariah didn't listen to the reassurance. "Valleys are low places you go down, then come up, supposing you survived."

"Yes. That's what a valley is, and—"

Mariah cut Nell off. "This is more like the endless *prairie* of the shadow of death. I came west on a wagon train with my family. A long, level prairie—Iowa, Nebraska, Wyoming." Staring at Nell, she saw her friend's lips moving. Heard a few more words. Healing. Strength. Wisdom. Safety. Nell was praying Mariah through the prairie, the entire Great Plains of the shadow of death.

"God needs a new psalm."

"There are plenty, Mariah. We'll just pray them all."

Mariah kept looking at Nell, kept feeling Clint's weight on her. Kept feeling terrible pain from whatever the doctor was doing. Kept praying. Kept rolling along that vast, endless prairie of the shadow of death. As she prayed, Nell's pretty blue eyes faded from Mariah's vision.

"D-do, uh, do sn-snakebites make you blind?"

"Doc, do you need any help?" someone called. She thought it might be the sheriff.

"We're fine back here. We don't need a crowd." The doctor talked as he worked. Since her vision was vague, framed in black as if she were looking down a train tunnel, she didn't bother to try to see or understand what Doc Preston was doing.

She was sure she didn't want to know.

Mariah heard talking coming from the doctor's outer office. Other folks had come to help her.

"What did you say about snakebites?" Nell leaned so close, Mariah must've whispered or slurred her words. Or maybe she only imagined she'd spoken out loud.

"Do they make you bl-blind?"

"I don't think so." Nell glanced at the very busy doctor. "Should her vision be bothered by this?" Those blue eyes, wide with worry and prayers, faded, along with any sound in the room. It wasn't the snakebite, Mariah decided. It was the panic. The pain.

As she realized she was losing consciousness, Mariah considered fighting it, then decided being awake was more trouble than it was worth.

Clint felt the struggle go out of Mariah. He wrenched his head around from where he watched the doctor practice his rough frontier medicine to see Mariah's eyes roll back in her head, then fall shut.

"What happened?" For a moment of pure heartbroken terror, he thought she'd died. He lifted his weight off to look at her. Despair rolled through him like black fog.

"She fainted." The doctor, fiercely focused on drawing the poison out of Mariah's arm, didn't even look up. "It was all just too much for her. It's best she sleep through this anyway. Being calm was beyond her, and a pounding heart and rapid breathing, tense muscles, struggling—it all spreads the poison faster. I have every hope we got all . . . well, most all of the poison out in time. What did get into her blood isn't a lethal dose. I hope."

Clint swallowed hard, his throat bone-dry. His eyes burned with unshed tears. He glanced at Nell. Her fear was a living thing in her eyes. Clint was sure his were the same.

"She's going to hurt for a while. Not just from the bite or my doctoring, and heaven knows *that* will hurt plenty. But despite how fast you got her here and that I put a tourniquet on her arm right away, some of the venom will have gotten into her bloodstream. And now I have no choice but to take the tourniquet off. While it keeps the poison from spreading, the lack of blood circulation will cause its own harm. She's going to be very sick for a while, but it's the kind of sickness a person survives. You got her here in time, Clint."

"The . . . um, breakfast crowd had cleared out. I was on my way over to see . . . see . . ." Clint felt his throat swell nearly shut. If he didn't stop talking, the doctor was going to have to find some treatment so Clint could breathe. "She was screaming, falling, and the snake kept striking out at her."

"I checked for other bites. This is the only one." The doctor reached across Mariah and patted Clint on the shoulder. "You saved her. And it sounds like she saved herself by fighting the snake and calling for help."

Clint thought with dark dread that screaming like Mariah had done wasn't exactly the same as calling for help. He suspected he'd hear her screams of terror at odd moments and in his nightmares for the rest of his life.

He remembered his mother's screams and how he hadn't been able to get there in time to save her or his family. Of course, he hadn't actually heard her scream. She'd died silently in the fire. But her imagined screams were very real inside his head.

"Nell, thank you for coming."

A ruckus in the doctor's outer office told them more had come. People ready to help. Or maybe just nosy people, yet those types could be put to work, too.

"Nell, I need warm water. There's a hot well on my stove."

Nell went to work.

"I'll need someone to sit with her." The doctor looked Clint in the eye. "If it's going to be you and Nell, you'd better go lock up the diner before you settle in here." The doctor began bathing Mariah's arm with the steaming water.

Clint realized she still wore the leather apron she always had on when she worked over the forge. The leather scarf she tied over her head had fallen off somewhere, and her dark blond hair had come out of the no-nonsense bun she always pinned back at the base of her neck.

Clint had barely cleaned up after the last of his breakfast customers and had been heading out to help at the smithy. "I already locked up. I put a soup on, shoved to the back of the stove to simmer. I planned to close the restaurant and work with Mariah until it was time to start preparing for the noon meal. So I won't open today. I can stay here with her."

The doctor used a clean cloth to dry Mariah's upper arm before wrapping a bandage around it. "Can you hold this end of the bandage just so, Clint?"

Clint could barely order his hands to do the assigned task.

"I'm taking the tourniquet off her arm now." The doctor went about his work, describing each of the steps. Clint wondered if he spoke just to provide some comfort.

And he was right. It did help. It gave Clint time to get himself under control.

At his side, Nell said, "The men who want chaps are willing to wait for them. What choice do they have? But when I ran out after hearing screaming and gunfire, I think I left my front door wide open. I should check, and I could use some fresh air." She looked hard at Clint as if judging whether he was a worthy guard for her friend. "I won't be gone long."

"When you get home, Nell, you may want to take a moment to wash the blood off."

Nell gave a grim frown. "You need that, too."

He watched her leave as the doctor carried the basin of pink-tinged water away. When the doctor turned his back, Clint was there, somewhat alone, to see Mariah's eyes flicker open.

"Rattlesnake." Her voice was faint and laced with fear.

She fumbled with Clint's hand as she reached for him with her right. Her left she didn't move. "Will I die?"

"Doc Preston says no. He got the tourniquet on your arm right away—within a minute or so of your being bit. He said a little of the poison will get into your blood but not a fatal dose." Clint didn't add what the doctor had, that he *hoped*.

The doctor was back as quickly as he could move when he heard Mariah speak. "It's a nasty wound, and your arm is going to be swollen and not work like it should for a week. I cut your arm to make it bleed, and almost all of the venom flowed out with the blood. That was my aim. You'll heal, but I'm afraid there'll be no blacksmithing until I say so. Good news is, it's your left arm. Your right is fine, which means you can get to work faster." The doctor shook his head. "A woman blacksmith. What will they think of next?"

"You might complain louder, Doc, if you didn't need me to keep your horse shod and your buggy rolling."

Doc Preston smiled. "That does keep me from fussing at you overly." He nudged Mariah's chin with his fist. "I want you to rest here for a time. Then if you're able, you can go home. Once you're there, I'll stop in every day. I'm hopeful that after a few days of bruising and swelling, maybe a bit of fever to sweat out the last traces of poison in your blood, your arm will begin to heal quickly. We may have you back at the forge in a week."

The doctor looked at Clint. "Did you get the snake? It's not loose here in town, I hope."

"It's dead, Doc." A shudder Clint couldn't control shook his body when he thought of the rage and fear that had caused his gun to roar to life. Clint knew he was a crack shot, though he didn't use his gun often. "If no one's seen to it yet, I'll bury it as soon as Nell gets back. Then we'll get Mariah home."

"I hope everyone who gets near it is careful." The doctor scowled as he began packing his leather bag. "I once treated a snakebite on a man who went to pick up the head, the severed head, of a rattler. The snake, dead, or so it seemed for over an hour, still bit him. It got some venom into him, too. The man lived, but it never occurred to him that the snake could still be dangerous after so long."

Frowning, Clint said, "I'll be careful."

"I've got to go look in on Latta Blodgett now. She's expecting her seventh child any day, and I have to nag that woman constantly to keep her from working at chores, even with Parson Blodgett and five sons and Joy, her fifteen-year-old daughter, trying to block her."

Mariah lifted her left hand and rested it on Doc Preston's forearm. "Thank you, Doc. You saved my life today. Please understand how much I appreciate it. How grateful I am for your speed and skill."

"Thank Clint, he got you here in time."

"I'll thank him, too, have no doubt. Both of you were ready and able in my time of need. I appreciate it."

Doc Preston, looking at her through his wire-framed glasses, patted her hand, then lifted it gently away from his arm and rested it on the examining table. "Now, I want you to stay here the rest of the day so I can see how you're reacting to the poison. Then we'll walk over to your house with you. I want two men at hand to escort you, especially when you go up the stairs."

"I've no objection to resting quietly while you look in on Mrs. Blodgett." The words, faint, faded away as the doctor picked up his bag, adjusted his glasses, and headed out.

Clint watched the man go. "Maybe I should have been a doctor. I like serving people and I grew up in a restaurant run by my parents. But the doctor is a man who does a lot of good. The parson, too. There are many ways to serve my fellow man." His eyes came back to Mariah. "Blacksmithing is a way to serve, as well."

"I think, if you live right, you'll find yourself serving others just as others serve you. The world works well when we all serve each other." Mariah lifted her left hand again and stared at her bandaged upper arm. "I once knew a man with one arm missing. Lost it on account of a snakebite." Looking at Clint, she said, "Have you told me the whole truth? Am I still in danger of dying? Or losing this arm?"

Clint took her right hand in his right. He slid his hand deep into hers with their palms touching, their fingers entwined. "It's the whole truth, Mariah."

She had such doubt in her expression, she might as well have accused him straight-out of lying.

"It's the truth," he said again. "When the doctor comes back, you can ask him. I'm not saying I might not try to shade the truth if I thought it was a harsh and fearsome truth. But this time I don't have to make such a decision. The doctor had your arm tied tight almost instantly to keep the poison from circulating. He cut open your arm and that let the poison flow out instead of spreading inside you. I do truly believe you're going to be all right. Sore from the cuts from the doctor's scalpel, and swollen from the little bit of poison that slipped free into your body, but you'll heal."

Seeing it was time to change the subject from all the worries that plagued her, he asked, "Can you tell me what happened? You'd been gone from the restaurant for quite some time, and you were outside. So, you must not have come upon the snake right away."

Mariah felt her brow furrow as she tried to remember what had happened. And that made her mad. She'd be switched if she was going to let her head get away with forgetting yet another episode in her life.

"No, the snake was . . . under a basin." Her spirits lifted as she remembered. "That's it. There was a basin and some pails stacked outside the shop this morning. Not unusual for folks to drop things off."

"Who left them?"

Mariah shrugged, then flinched. She had to be mindful of her left arm, as every inch of it hurt. "I had some work inside to finish and then I went out to get what had been left. I picked up everything. The pails, the metal basin. It was upside-down, flat on the ground, or it seemed to be. But how did the snake get under there if it was flat?" She didn't shrug this time.

"They can easily slip into tiny holes," Clint replied. "I suppose the basin had a hole if it was brought in to be repaired. The snake found a dark, sheltered spot to sleep for the night."

"I lifted the basin and heard the rattles. I've heard that

sound a few times in my life and knew exactly what it was. I backed away fast."

She told Clint what she could remember. Falling, the snake hitting one of the pails. She thought she'd felt it hit the heel of her boot.

Clint hurried to look at her shoe. "There's no sign it got you in the ankle. The doctor examined you already. I trust him. But it's hard not to worry."

"For me too." Mariah felt itchy, as if every spot on her body might've been bitten. "My mind's a little jumbled still."

"I was outside right after you screamed the first time. I'd locked the front door and come out the back like always." He came to her side, caught her hand and squeezed tight. "I saw you fall backward, get up, swing the pail at the snake, and slap it aside. I had my gun out by the time I rounded the corner of the diner. The second you knocked the snake aside, I fired. I was terrified I'd hit you because you fell. I must've missed the snake the first time because it struck again, or not killed it at least. I think that's when it got you."

His grip on her hand was growing painful. "If I'd just hit it the first time. If I'd stopped running and taken one second to aim. If I'd—"

"You're hurting me."

He gasped and released her hand.

Then she took back hold of him. "If, if. If you'd taken one more split second to aim, the snake might've used that second to bite me in the chest or my neck. It might've gotten its fangs through my dress and bit my back. Somewhere no tourniquet could help me. Hush now."

"Hush?" Some of his upset faded and he managed a smile.

"You're not allowed to be so upset when I'm the one bitten by a snake. It's me who's upset and I'm not sharing. You just settle down."

The smile widened. "Yes, Miss Stover."

She gave his hand a squeeze. Nell came into the back room then, and Mariah let go of his hand. After they talked Nell through the whole thing, Clint went out to bury the snake.

"The doctor said I can go home after a little while." Mariah frowned at her friend. "Do you know of any territories that don't have poisonous snakes or stagecoach robberies?"

"I don't think there are any of those anywhere. And for certain not any that give women the right to vote."

Mariah was sure Nell and Clint were doing their best to talk about anything but snakebites. Their distractions helped, and the pain in her arm, though still nasty, wasn't as overwhelming as time passed. They had a particularly good time talking to Clint about Mrs. Mussel's visit and Esther Morris and women's suffrage and how fragile the law was right now.

Mariah breathed more deeply than she had for a while. "I think I'll use my vote to outlaw rattlesnakes."

"Good luck getting them to obey," Nell said with a wry smile. "They're notoriously lawless."

Doc Preston came in to catch them laughing. "This is good. Anytime I have a patient who can laugh, it's a good sign. I'm sorry I was gone so long. I caught Mrs. Blodgett on a ladder, dragging a chicken down off the barn rafters.

She has plans for it for supper. Her husband swears he only looked away from her for two minutes. Her sons were out tending the cattle. Her daughter told her to rest while she cleaned up after the lunch dishes." He shook his head. "She got a notion to corner a rooster for supper instead. She's not that far along with this baby. A fall from a ladder could bring on the labor, and it wouldn't survive. Her little ones are a sturdy bunch, strapping boys mostly, and her daughter is no one to mess with, either. But this one needs to stay inside the womb and grow for a few more months. I advised her husband to chain a heavy iron ball to his wife's ankle. He may be over to see you to get one made once you're feeling able to go back to work, Mariah."

Clint came back in. "The snake was already buried. Deputy Willie took care of it. I found a nice long, stout stick and left it in the smithy. From now on, you can poke around the pile of work left for you before you pick anything up."

"I wish I'd thought of that before today. When I think of all the buckets and pots I've picked up without giving it a moment's worry." She shook her head. "Thank you."

"Let's see if you're able to stand, Mariah." The doctor hadn't removed his coat or hat. And the afternoon was halfway gone. Clint had left the diner closed so that anyone wanting to eat at noon—and he usually had a crowd—had been forced to feed themselves.

The doctor came to her snakebit side and, an inch at a time, eased her legs off the table and helped her pivot. The examining table was a high one. "Clint, go over to her right side. We'll stay with you, Mariah, and get you to your own room."

Mariah's arm hurt so badly that she had to glance at it to make sure the snake wasn't still there with its fangs embedded.

Or maybe a wolf had stopped by to chew on her.

Nope, it was only the doctor, and he wasn't touching her arm.

The doctor studied her face. "You just turned pale as milk. Sit there for a minute or two."

"I can stay here with her, Doctor," Nell said, "if we decide she can't walk or climb stairs."

The doctor nodded. "She'll sleep better in her own bed. But if we can't manage it, she can stay here."

Mariah gathered herself. She didn't want to make Nell sit up overnight. The examining table was no comfortable bed, either. "I'll make it," she said.

Clint took her hand, then rested his other on her shoulder.

The doctor slid an arm across her back. "Let's take it slow."

With the doctor urging her forward, and Clint mostly holding her up, she stood.

Mariah took a deep breath, then released it. "The worst of the dizziness has passed. Let's go."

14

They went around to Mariah's house, and once inside, the stairs looked formidable. But she was determined to make it up there.

One step at a time, with Clint beside her, Nell ahead of her handling doors, and the doctor behind her in case she fell, they made it upstairs.

As she stepped slowly into her room, Mariah saw Nell heading straight for the bed to turn down the covers. "I think I'll sit up for a while. I've been lying down long enough."

She saw Clint look across her to the doctor, who'd come back to her side. The two men deciding what to do with her, regardless of how she felt.

What was the point of living in a modern, equality-respecting territory like Wyoming if the men still insisted on directing your life? Mariah moved to a chair beside a little table near the fireplace. She sat down, then turned to glare at Clint with narrow eyes.

"I put on a pot of *soupe de poulet* this morning for the

noon meal. I set it to the back of the stove to keep warm and not overcook. Let me get you something to eat."

"Looks as though you'll be fine here, Mariah." The doctor doffed his hat. "I'm going to head home. My wife will be looking for me. But don't hesitate to call for me if you get to feeling puny."

"Thank you for everything, Doc. I'll keep every scrap of metal you own in good condition by way of payment, but I'll expect you to send me a bill, too."

He nodded. "You're welcome. You're a much better snakebite story than a doctor usually gets."

Once Doc left and the steady drumbeat of his steps on the stairs faded, Mariah looked at Clint. "I know you've got a lot of chores to do out at your place. You go on now and do them. I'd appreciate the chicken soup." She'd been eating at his diner long enough to know what his strange words meant. "But if it's warm and ready, Nell can fetch it for me." Her eyes shifted to her friend. "You've got work to do, too. I'll sit here and eat soup while you go get your work to bring up here. And thank you both for giving up most of your day for me."

This time, Clint and Nell shared a look, like *they* might insist on directing her life. The pang of irritation when the men had done it now made her feel a little guilty. Since Nell was certainly not a man, Mariah decided maybe it had nothing to do with Wyoming and equality and voting and men. It might just be the way you got treated if bitten by a rattlesnake.

Clint nodded. His eyes focused on Mariah, and he studied her for too long before finally heading out.

Nell came to Mariah's side, her good side, and gave her

a firm but cautious hug. "I'm so glad you're on the mend now." Her eyes brimmed with tears. "I should run and get some supplies. I have quite a bit here"—Nell gestured at a table that was set up for her work—"but I need a few things. Do you think you'll be all right here alone?"

"Yes, and it won't be for that long. I know you can get all that leather hauled up here in a few minutes' time. But I would appreciate that soup and a glass of water, too. My throat is parched and scratchy. Probably from screaming at that snake."

Nell nodded, swiped her wrist across her eyes, turned and nearly ran down the stairs.

Mariah sat for a time, listening to Nell leave. Just minutes later, she heard Nell return and rattle around in the kitchen. Mariah said a thanksgiving prayer for good friends, a good doctor close by, and the pure miraculous hand of God preventing this from turning very ugly.

Soon Nell was back in the room. She placed a nice meal in front of Mariah, with a tray that included bread and butter, warm soup, and a glass of water. "I'll be back quick to join you in that meal. I haven't eaten since breakfast, and my throat might be a little scratchy from worrying, if that's a possible cause. You go ahead and eat, though. If you wait for me, your soup will turn cold."

Nell ran one hand over Mariah's hair. Mariah noticed the hand trembling. "You're a mess. If you're feeling up to it, once you're done eating, I'll help you clean up when I get back."

"Um . . . Nell?"

Since Nell was just one foot away from Mariah and paying rapt attention to her pallor, her wound, her hair, and her tone of voice, Nell immediately said, "Yes? What is it?"

Mariah must've sounded strange because Nell looked worried.

"The thing is, I-I . . ." She gestured at the dark blue shirtwaist with the cutoff sleeve. "I was wondering if you'd . . . make me a new work top."

She smiled. "Of course I will."

"And . . . well, I think I need a pretty dress, too. Maybe a lighter color. A few ruffles."

Nell squeaked and clasped her hands under her chin. "A dress? I get to make a pretty dress?"

"Well, my only good dress has a bullet hole in it and was soaked in blood. And besides, it was a dreadful dark dress best suited for funerals."

"I know the dress. You wore it every Sunday to church, winter and summer." Nell gave her a smacking kiss on the top of her head. "I haven't sold a pair of chaps to a single man in weeks who isn't willing to wait for however long it takes for them to be done."

"I guess, unlike broken wheels and leaking basins, there aren't any real huge chaps emergencies."

"I had a man in today wondering if I knew how to make a saddle." Nell squeezed her eyes closed tight. "I told him no, but I'm scared to death I can learn. Because he'd pay really well." She groaned, her voice rising to a near howl. "I don't want to make saddles."

"I could use a new bonnet, too," Mariah said. She didn't really need a bonnet. She just said it to keep Nell from bursting into tears. Mariah might let her friend sew her a second dress just to keep her spirits up.

Did Becky need a dress? They might need to team up with dress orders to keep Nell happy.

"I'm so excited." Nell flashed a broad smile at Mariah. "I've got a beautiful lavender with dark purple flowers sprinkled all over it. It'll be perfect with your hair and eyes."

Mariah had never chosen a dress based on something so shallow in her life. "Pa always told me to pick a color that wouldn't show the dirt."

Laughing, Nell said, "I have to go. If you can't hear my footsteps on the stairs, don't worry. I might be floating." Then she ran out and practically thundered down the stairs. Happy or not, the woman definitely had her feet planted firmly on the ground. She had to support herself and she made very good money creating her boring, sturdy chaps. And who knows what a man might pay for a saddle?

Though Nell was a practical woman who needed to make a living, there was no denying she had a tender love for ruffles.

Mariah tasted the chicken soup. *Soupe de poulet*, for heaven's sake. She was torn between trying to save him from his strange names for food and just supporting him, for although it was indeed chicken soup, it was the most delicious chicken soup she'd ever eaten.

So maybe it deserved a special name. She should suggest *Special Chicken Soup*. Or maybe *Clint Soup*. Yet she didn't think he'd be open to her suggestions.

Sitting in her room in silence, eating the soup that made her realize how hungry she was, she felt the pain and tried to endure it, tried to ignore it. One, well, she had no choice

126

but to endure. Two, she didn't seem able to ignore such pain.

So instead she just ate, and felt, and thanked God that something that could have turned out so badly was instead going to lay her up for a few days or a week. Then she'd get right back to work.

The forge, the smithy—it weighed on her heart at this moment. She understood Nell's love for her pretty dresses and her practical cooperation with the men asking for new chaps.

A woman needed to keep a roof over her head, pay the bill at the general store, and pay for her meals at the diner.

It was nice being independent. She took pleasure in thinking of being able to vote at the next election. She couldn't wait for Mrs. Mussel to come to town to speak.

And through it all, she thought of the pretty iron petals she'd used to adorn the fireplace poker she'd made for the saloon.

She thought of the decorative engraving she'd done once on a row of pots for Doc Preston's wife to plant an indoor medicinal herb garden.

Most people wanted nails, hinges, wheels, horseshoes, pails. But Mariah knew in a very quiet corner of her heart that she liked just a bit of delicate filigree with her work.

Decorative metalwork and ruffled dresses.

She and Nell were a pathetic team, because instead of realizing their dreams, they were stuck making horseshoes and chaps.

Though she knew Nell wasn't happy, did Nell know the same about Mariah? Had she ever spoken of it? She'd felt such pressure to be good enough that Pa would allow her to work beside him. But she'd never really asked herself if she *wanted* to do it. Now, with Pa gone and all the work on her shoulders, for the first time in a long time, probably because the weight was so heavy, Mariah had to wonder if this was what she wanted to do with the rest of her life.

The town needed a blacksmith, but she could train Willie and hand off the job.

Still, she needed to feed herself and she had no other skills that came directly to mind.

Pa would be upset with her. No, even worse and despite how much he'd raised her to be independent, Pa would *expect* her to quit. He'd let her work with him, but he and Theo had always taken the hardest jobs and sheltered her from the worst of it. He'd assumed in a kindly, manly way that she was too much of a woman to do the job.

And knowing that was enough to keep her working on iron for the rest of her life. She had something to prove to Pa, and when it came down to it, she had something to prove to herself.

She shoved aside any misgivings she had about the life laid out before her. Or maybe she shoved them deep inside? Nevertheless, she'd stay with blacksmithing as a tribute to Pa and Theo.

15

"Can I at least help pour coffee?" Mariah was going crazy with boredom, but her arm wasn't strong enough yet for her to do blacksmith work. It'd been badly swollen, flaming red, and so sore that it hurt to think about moving it or touching it all week.

She'd spent a good part of last week in bed with a fever, with Nell sewing chaps in the room with her. Nell told Mariah that while she rested and healed, iron was stacking up at the smithy. New things outside the door most mornings that Willie dragged inside and repaired if he could. Mariah hoped he was watching out for snakes.

Willie was doing basic work, but he didn't know enough to tackle anything complicated. And he certainly didn't know how to shoe a horse or make a wooden bucket.

She'd been depending on the kindness of others to keep her business running.

Her fever had gone down and stayed down about two days ago. She'd been steadily drinking the doctor's fever tea, and it would work for a while before the fever returned. Finally, two days ago, she'd awakened feeling clearheaded for the first time in a while, and the fever was gone for good.

Her arm still hurt like mad when she bent it, yet it was no longer swollen. The doctor said the wounds he'd inflicted to drain the poison had closed and were healing well.

Then she'd spent two days sitting around her house, watching Nell cut leather.

Now she was feeling better. She'd come to the diner to eat but couldn't stand to just sit around for another whole day. She took that to mean she was well or close enough to it.

Maybe she wasn't up to swinging a sledgehammer—she had to use both arms for that—but still, she was so much better. And she was slowly going stir-crazy and saw no reason not to pester Clint to pass the time.

"It's a two-handed job, Mariah. And the pot is heavy." Clint was working over the stove, doing something weird to eggs. He called it *eggs Benedict*, though he seemed to have no idea who Benedict was.

She'd seen poached eggs before, but Pa and Theo had shown no interest in them. Honestly, neither had she. Pa had said Ma used to make them along with milk toast. She'd called it *sickroom food*.

It'd sounded awful to Mariah, though she didn't remember eating any poached eggs or milk toast herself. Her recent tussle with the snake aside, she'd never been disposed to sickness.

And now here Clint was, serving it to a bunch of hardened westerners—not the milk toast, but the poached eggs for sure. He was adding ham under the egg on a piece of odd, round toast. She'd had it herself for breakfast and it had been fantastic.

But it was different from anything she'd ever eaten before. Clint had learned to cook somewhere really fancy. He'd said he was a lowly cook in a fine restaurant in New York City, but he'd learned enough to go out on his own. And he'd certainly gone way out. He'd mentioned his family dying and afterward his leaving the city and its memories behind. Beyond that, when they'd talked about the past, Clint was annoyingly tight-lipped. He liked talking about food, though.

When he'd served her breakfast, he said something about *Holland days sauce* or something like that. Holland was a foreign country. She was almost sure of it.

And the toast was odd. He called it an English muffin, but the only muffins she'd ever had looked far different from the flat circles of bread he was toasting. He even called the ham *Canadian bacon*.

So . . . England, Holland, Canada, and wherever Benedict was from. And yet he said he made it all himself, so there was really no foreign country involved anywhere.

"I could just scramble some eggs. I'm sure you'd get takers."

"I'm trying to develop the palate of the fine citizens of Pine Valley."

She remembered Pa making up a pallet of blankets on the floor in their house for her, and another for Theo. Ma and Pa got the single bedroom. That was a long time ago when they'd first moved to Wyoming. Pa had since added on, including bedrooms upstairs for Mariah and

Theo. Maybe *pallet* wasn't the same thing Clint was talking about, but whatever it was, it had nothing to do with breakfast.

"And besides, if I offer them scrambled eggs, they'll all take it. I won't be able to serve my delicious eggs Benedict. I think I know better what they want and need than they do."

"That is incredibly arrogant." Mariah plopped both fists on her hips, and it startled her so that she forgot what they were talking about. She looked down at her fists. "Clint, look, my arm is working. I left the sling off this morning, but I'm so used to keeping it still that I hadn't noticed how much better it was. It bent and it doesn't hurt." At least it didn't hurt badly enough to stop her from the motion.

Clint finished pouring the strange and yet, she had to admit, luscious creamy sauce from Holland over the eggs, ham, and toast, then straightened to stare at her. A smile broke out on his face.

"Mariah, you're getting better." He set his saucepan aside with a hard *clank*. He took two long steps toward her, wrapped his arms around her waist, and swooped her in a circle.

She squeaked and grabbed at his shoulders. That didn't hurt much, either.

He plunked her down and jabbed a finger right at her nose. "You're going to be fine." He laughed, went back to the two plates he had ready to serve, and snatched them up. "I'll be right back." Just before he stepped through the swinging door from the kitchen to the dining room, he said, "Maybe I can find a job for you in here after all."

He rushed out and was back so fast that she couldn't think what to do, and that was if she knew what in the world he was doing. Clint somehow made cooking very mysterious.

"I know." He pointed at the strange round tube of ham. She had to wonder what part of the pig that came from. "I've got about ten more orders for eggs Benedict and I expect ten more after that. Can you cut twenty slices of Canadian bacon?"

"I can absolutely slice ham." She got to work. Her left arm did little, yet she was fully capable of holding the ham tube in place while she sliced with her right.

Clint rushed around the kitchen doing everything else, but she felt as if she was saving him a step and was glad to be of use. The kitchen was a whirlwind for a time until finally Clint came in with a sigh, carrying a stack of empty plates. "The last of the breakfast crowd is eating. The eggs were a big hit."

Mariah had already started pouring hot water over a basinful of dirty dishes. "I think moving my arm like this is helping. It feels more limber. You remember the doctor told me to exercise it some?"

"It looks so much better."

Of course, she had on long sleeves, so he meant the way it moved. Mariah knew it was still quite ugly to look at.

"It's an answer to prayer. Thank you for your help. I've got to get a few things cooking for the next meal, then I'll take over. I don't want you to exhaust yourself."

"I'm either going to wash these dishes or I'm going to go back to the forge. You decide."

She felt his hands on her waist. She'd just set a clean

plate aside and knew as he whirled her around that he'd chosen his moment carefully.

He might want to scold her, but he definitely didn't want to break any plates.

Instead of a scolding face, though, she saw a wide smile.

"If you think you're up to washing dishes, then do it. But if you get tired, let me know."

She smiled back at him. The steaming water and dish soap were at her back. His delicious eggs and ham made the room smell savory and sweet at the same time. "You're really the best cook I've ever known."

"A compliment instead of your usual sass about my cooking?" He leaned forward and gave her a smacking kiss. Smile to smile.

Then he straightened away, and the smile faded. She was very sure hers did, too. He leaned in again, slower this time, watching her eyes with his gaze occasionally sliding down to her lips. She suspected she copied him in that.

And he kissed her.

Mariah had never been kissed before.

She'd honestly never known she wanted to be.

Well, sure, she wanted to be kissed, but she'd never had a specific man in mind.

And no man had ever shown much interest in being in her mind.

As she mulled all this, her arms rose and circled Clint's neck. He was taller than she was, but not overly so. She needed to hold herself up on her tiptoes somehow.

He turned his head just slightly so their noses didn't touch, but their lips still did.

After far too long, and not nearly long enough, Clint

lifted his head, met her gaze, and said, "It's been a wonder having you so close all day, spending time with you. I've come to think I'd like for us to be even closer, and all the time forever, Mariah."

Her head was a little foggy, but she knew sweet words when she heard them. And she wanted to hear more of them, only slightly less than she wanted to be kissed again.

The door behind Clint, the swinging door to the dining room, swung open. Something . . . that is, someone, said, "Oops."

The door quickly swung shut.

Clint lifted his head again. Smiling, his nut-brown eyes flashing with humor, he said, "I think your friend Nell just caught us. The proper thing to do would be to just walk right into that dining room and tell them all that we're getting married."

"I-I can't get married." She wrenched her arms away from his neck.

His arms were wrapped around her waist and he tightened his hold. "Oh yes, you most certainly can get married. In fact, you're *going* to get married. To me. Just as soon as we can arrange it."

"No, at least not yet. Not for a long time. I have to run the smithy."

"No, you don't. You can leave that hot, harsh job behind. Let Willie take over the smithy. You can be a married woman instead."

They both knew married women didn't work. It was just not done. To take the blacksmith job when there was no one else to do it and she needed to support herself was one thing. But to hang on to the job when there might be a man needing it to support his own family was just too selfish to endure.

"Let go of me, Clint."

Her tone sounded grim as could be, and he must've let it in—past the romantic notions blooming in his head—because he let go.

"It's impossible for me to marry. My pa built something in this town, a business, needed and well-run. And I'm capable of managing it on my own."

"You've missed a whole week because of the stagecoach robbery."

"That wasn't my fault."

"Of course it wasn't. But then you nearly died in that explosion."

"A fluke accident. It will never happen again."

"You can't say that. It's a dangerous job. And now you've missed a week because of a snakebite."

"That could have happened to anyone."

"But it happened to you. I want to take you away from the danger. Let me take care of you, Mariah." Clint's hands closed on her arm. She flinched, and he jumped back.

"It didn't hurt. I just did that to make you get your hands off me."

Clint's brow furrowed. "You acted as though you liked my hands on you just a few seconds ago."

Mariah realized her heart, which she'd felt filling with warmth and hope, had just turned ice-cold.

She tried to undo the wrong she'd done by encouraging him. "Clint, I have appreciated so much all that you've done to help me and protect me. But I don't want you to take care of me."

"But—"

"At least no more than I would take care of you. What I hear you saying is insulting."

"No, it's not."

"Yes, it is. I . . ." She struggled to find the right words and appreciated that he didn't jump in and talk over her. He seemed to understand that this was important.

Or maybe he just decided to let her talk because he had their future planned, and nothing she said would make any difference.

"You know what it's like when a woman gets married. She can work alongside her husband—no one would notice if I cooked in the diner."

"You can't cook." His eyes widened with alarm. "I'm the cook."

She was tempted to punch those alarmed eyes. "Well, then no one would notice if I carried food to the tables and washed dishes."

He relaxed and nodded. "That sounds fine. You can do that."

Clenching both fists, she struggled to keep her temper firmly rooted in mental punishment and not really give him a black eye.

"You're making my point, Clint. Marriage would change everything. People would expect me to be someone else. Your wife. I'd need to close the smithy."

Clint shook his head as if her words made no sense. "Of course you would. You can't be the town blacksmith if you're a married woman."

"I know you believe that. I know everyone in this town would agree with you. In fact, the pressure to do that is so great, I even find myself believing it. And that's why I can't marry you. I've got something to prove to Pine Valley, to Pa, and to myself. And it seems to you, too. I'm going to be the town blacksmith. I plan to do it for my whole life. And I suppose that means I'll never marry, never have children." The weight of that surprised her. She hadn't really known she wanted a husband and children.

"The job is a hard one and demanding," she went on. "It took Pa, Theo, and me working long hours to meet the blacksmith needs of this area. That's what I've chosen now, and marriage would end that. And if I can't get married, then to kiss you is not honorable. I apologize. I hadn't really thought it all through until you started talking about giving up my dangerous job so you could take care of me."

"Mariah, I—"

"Are you going to say you'd be proud to have a blacksmith for a wife? You'll support me and encourage me and be proud of me if we marry and I continue to fire up the forge every morning?"

Clint fell silent. Very quietly, he said, "I'm falling in love with you. I want to marry you."

"You want that, if I change. If I give up my livelihood."

"It's not that I want you to change. I just want you to be exactly what a married woman is. She stays at home. She works around the house and the farm and at my business."

"That's wanting me to change."

Mariah watched him, the ache in her heart real. No married woman worked unless she worked at her husband's side. It just was not done. And to give up the smithy felt like she was living up to all Pa's worst ideas about her.

She had something to prove.

A quiet thought whispered through her mind that she might be able to find a way. Maybe in a territory that prized equality as highly as Wyoming did.

But the look on Clint's face, the absolutely baffled look . . .

He couldn't stretch his mind to include a wife who was a smithy. In fact, Mariah couldn't stretch her mind that wide, either.

And because of that, she dropped her gaze from his and said, "No one's tried to kill me and it's been a month. I appreciate your protection through this time, but now I need to go take care of myself. And that includes returning to work tomorrow."

With a hard jerk of her chin, she left the kitchen, dodging around him. He didn't try to stop her, which was the only answer she needed.

16

Key Larson was breathing hard when he met the boss outside of town. He'd slipped to their usual meeting place as silent as a ghost, but the boss wasn't an easy man to surprise.

"The Stover woman is back to work at the smithy."

"She is?" The boss scowled. "She's well enough for that?"

While the boss made all final decisions, he was a man who'd listen. "I can't see where she's said a word about me."

Key knew his worth. Yes, he was the newest member of the gang, but he'd been there a while and had brought with him a good connection. A man who, for a cut of the money, told them when the payrolls moved. And this last job, with bad information, hadn't been his doing.

The boss crossed his arms and drummed his fingers in a nervous beat. "She's even seen you right up close since the holdup and she didn't react. Killing her is gonna be touchy. One of the main tricks is not to give even a hint where we're from. It's why we travel far and wide for our robberies. It's why we leave no witnesses."

Nodding, Key said, "If we outright kill her, we'll bring the fire straight down on Pine Valley. They might call in the U.S. Marshals, maybe even the cavalry. They'll for certain bring in outriders on the stages like they did a year ago. Which is why we broke off our robberies. We started up again when the outriders left. Now if we kill the Stover woman, the law will rain down fire until we're caught and hanged. And we didn't have good money from the last robbery. We need to go out again faster than usual. Do we dare just let her live?"

"If we do, we'll break two rules. We leave a witness, and we stage two holdups close together. I don't like none of it." The boss scrubbed the bristles on his chin and spent time thinking, which was never a good thing. The boss nearly always thought of something that was going to make their lives hard.

Key pushed his luck by saying more. "You can't meet your payments and you can't make payroll. Not with the money you've got." He figured he'd said about all he dared.

"She knows too much."

"Nope, not now she doesn't. She don't know nothing." Key ran a finger down the scar on his face. It was a bad habit, but he liked to remind himself of the lousy lawmen who were aiming to cut off his head. Every lawman in the territory needed killing.

"She does if she ever remembers. You said she looked you right in the eye, even got a bullet into you."

That still burned. Key quit trying to control the fury. He wanted her dead and he was done being the reasonable one.

"But you're right about raining fire. We can't just shoot

her. The coach line hasn't started up with the outriders again, so we should be able to get in one more robbery before we have to lay low for a while, and I need the money. When folks get to thinking about the close call with the explosion and the snakebite, they'll know those were murder attempts and that we had to be riding right into town. And that might get someone to thinking we're from around here." He slammed a fist hard on the oak tree beside him. "I don't like any of this." His eyes narrowed. "I'm running out of ways to make her death look like an accident. Blast it, that snake should've ended her. I almost got myself killed trapping it. I've got to do something, and do it soon. That woman can ruin me."

"Ruin us all," Key said.

The boss's cold, dark eyes, like the dark of an approaching storm, locked on his. "I've got the most to lose. But it has to look like an accident. If we can't manage that, then we can't do it. It'd give too much away."

Key didn't respond. But he thought about a noose around his neck and knew the boss was wrong. They all had plenty to lose.

Mariah sank into bed, no pain in her arm.

She couldn't believe the comfort. She'd spent far too much of the last month hurting. But here she was, safe and sound. And it'd been a month since the robbery. No one was after her.

She eased off the fretting about killers stalking her from the shadows, only to have it replaced with something else.

Clint.

She'd hurt him.

And he'd hurt her.

The difference was, she'd known she was hurting him. She'd known there was decency in his talk of a future together after they shared that kiss. She'd seen the goodness in him and the interest he had in her. He'd said he'd fallen in love with her.

And she'd gone right ahead and kissed him, then turned around and hurt him.

Because he'd hurt her more.

And the shame of it was that, although she knew she'd hurt him, the baffled look on his face told her he didn't understand what her objection was to a marriage proposal.

What should she have said? And how could she explain it to him in a way that wouldn't hurt? How could she explain the limitations put on a woman?

Pa had done it when he'd trained her in a mighty manly career, but in a way that made it clear she wasn't quite good enough to handle it.

Clint had done it when he suggested she help him in the diner and turn the blacksmith shop over to Willie, who didn't have a fraction of her skill. It wouldn't be right for the town.

The whole world did it when everyone expected a woman to just quietly go home when she got married. Or work at her husband's side. Even on the frontier, a married woman wasn't even allowed to teach school, an acceptable womanly job—or rather an acceptable single woman's job.

Nell might be allowed to keep sewing if she married,

but she'd do it from home. Not from a shop. Not unless her husband took up shopkeeping with her.

Maybe Clint could cook over her forge, but she sure as certain couldn't shoe a horse in his diner.

More than Clint's attitude, Mariah knew she put limits on herself. She couldn't quite imagine working as a blacksmith if she was someone's wife, unless of course she married a blacksmith and helped him.

It was just considered simple decency. A man supported his family. For her to work as a blacksmith was to announce to the world that she didn't trust Clint to take care of her. It would be offensive and insulting to him.

Add to that, for her to keep working was to steal a job from a man who had a family to support. It made no sense, not in a town without a blacksmith. But there was always the minimally skilled Willie.

Then her swirling thoughts swirled around to kissing Clint again. It was a fine feeling. She'd enjoyed kissing him. Enjoyed being held in his arms. She could see how a woman might just give up everything in exchange for a man's strong embrace.

The rioting thoughts went on, and since she couldn't get to sleep, she tried to think about the day of the robbery. That was how she usually spent sleepless nights.

She had a few fleeting memories of leaving Laramie.

At least she thought they were memories of leaving. Yes, she was sure of it because she'd worn a riding skirt and shirtwaist for the ride over, but her drab Sunday-best dress for the ride back, and her memories included that dress.

She had a sense of riding along on the stage, which only

came in small flashes, so how could she be sure she was remembering riding home? She might be remembering riding to Laramie. No, the dress was the thing to anchor her in that day's memories.

She pushed hard to expand the memory, pick out details, hoping to recall more. She had a sudden vision of Theo and Pa on one side of the stage seats, the ones facing forward. Theo was between her and Pa, a tight fit. Two men sat across from them, facing backward.

Her head started to mildly throb as she pushed.

She saw the two men, two strangers, riddled with bullets. She lurched up in bed. That was new, the first memory that included the holdup. An awful thing that was now stuck in her head.

She was remembering the holdup. Hang on to that. Focus on it.

The headache got worse as she pushed harder.

She was punishing herself, she knew, for not being able to get Clint out of her head. The kissing and how hurt she was.

Her mind swooped around like a Wyoming windstorm.

Yet no more memories would come, and her head was wretchedly painful.

At last, disgusted with her muddled head, she threw back the blanket she slept under on these cool summer nights. Rising, she went to the kitchen to find the concoction Doc Preston had given her. It helped with the pain and helped her fall sleep. She didn't take it often because she worked hard all day and sleeping usually came easily.

But tonight, her mind wouldn't shut off, and after that one horrifying glimpse, it wouldn't let her further into her memories. Her aching head was battering her. Her fretful thoughts weren't going to shut off.

Pa had shipped in a nice little stove. Not cooking in a fireplace was a luxury for Mariah.

Part of her routine was keeping a teakettle on at night. She kept it pushed away from the hot center of the pot-bellied stove, and the water stayed just a bit below a simmer. Hot enough to brew tea. She dished a generous spoonful of the medicine into the pretty white glass teapot and poured the water over. She let the pot steam as it brewed the tea.

Her eyes rested on the teapot. It had been her mother's. One of the few pretty, feminine things in the house. How Mariah missed her. Making tea in Ma's pot, white with painted-on blue flowers with green leaves, always reminded Mariah of her ma.

Ma had loved keeping a home. She'd never gone out to the smithy, neither back in Iowa nor here. So Mariah had stayed indoors with Ma . . . until she died. Then, partially so she wouldn't be alone, when she wasn't in school, Mariah had tagged after Pa.

Sitting at the kitchen table, with the pretty teacup that matched the pot, Mariah judged that she'd waited long enough. She inhaled the aroma from the tea that, probably just out of habit now, started to relax her. Maybe there was some property to the steam that actually had an effect, or maybe she just knew relief was coming.

She used the tea strainer Ma had to pour tea from the pot to the cup, then sipped the brew. Doc Preston's own concoction. It wasn't a pleasant drink, bitter and sharp tasting, but she found it soothing.

Letting her mind settle, she finished the medicinal tea slowly and replaced her rabbiting thoughts with prayer.

Not big, sprawling prayers for her future or what to do about the smithy or Clint. Quieter and deeper, more important prayers for her faith to sustain her. For God's protection. Yes, these were big prayers, too. But she trusted in her own faith. She trusted in God. These big ideas, to let God guide her, were soothing.

The tea gone, she went back to bed. Glad to be feeling well. Glad to be a woman of faith.

Her eyelids grew heavy as she snuggled into her bed.

An odd click pulled her out of her drowsing, but there wasn't a second one and she was heavy-lidded enough her eyes fell shut. What a strange, momentous day, the pain mostly gone from her arm, working in the diner kitchen, hurting Clint. Her first kiss.

She let the day end.

Key was a nickname he'd picked up and for a good reason. He was good at getting through locks.

Now he stood in Mariah Stover's kitchen, feeling the quiet, deep thrill he always got from wandering through other people's homes, touching their things. Back in Denver, he'd made a good living at it. But then an old lady had caught him and ended up dead. Though he hadn't killed her, he hadn't minded when she'd fallen down a flight of stairs running away from him.

Back then he'd gotten good at lifting valuable little bits of gold and silver, a necklace now and then, to support himself. His crimes barely drew any notice from the police—until that old lady fell. After that, there'd been a manhunt. Word got around that a lot of things were missing in a rich neighborhood that no one had bothered reporting to the police. The night watch had increased. Vigilance and better locks had spread.

No one had seen him so he didn't really worry, but folks, the rich ones, the only ones worth stealing from, started being wary. Started hiring private watchmen to wander their homes, inside and out. They started locking their valuables in more secure places. He could get to them, but finding hidden safes and cracking fancy combination locks was a slow business. His easy life had gotten hard, and he didn't like it.

He'd left Denver and wandered a while. Then he'd stumbled into a job as a cowhand, not a top one but good enough.

Before long he'd learned how easy it was to rustle a cow or two and sell them to immigrant farmers who weren't wise to the laws of their new land, or to butchers who didn't ask too many questions.

Then he'd fallen in with the Deadeye Gang and found a life he enjoyed. The money was good, the risk small.

He found out he liked killing.

Yep, he liked his new life. But he sure enough missed wandering in other people's houses.

And knowing there was someone asleep upstairs, knowing he risked getting caught, made it all the more thrilling. His heart pounded until he felt it in his ears. Joy he rarely felt any other time almost lifted his soul, if a man had such a thing.

Of course, he was silent through it all. The thrill of

discovery wasn't so great that he actually *wanted* to wake her up. He'd have to kill her if that happened, and it would be best to not do that just yet. When it happened, it was supposed to look like an accident, and he didn't know how to handle that if he was confronted with a woman getting ready to scream and run.

The waiting to finish her was its own kind of fun.

So instead of tempting fate by making noise, he stood there for a long time before the night breeze caught the back door and made it snap shut just a bit too loud.

She didn't come down, though.

For a few seconds more, he stood looking around. What to do to pretty Mariah? What accident? She'd dodged the explosion. She'd survived the snake. Push her down the stairs? Poison?

He shook his head as he considered the options, seeing nothing worth stealing in this place. That was the trouble with robbing poor people. They didn't have nothing worth stealing. Add to that, they knew every little thing they owned.

He could steal a pair of valuable earbobs from a rich old woman and she might not ever notice, or if she did, she'd likely think she lost them. If anyone got blamed, it was the maid.

If you took a few silver spoons, no one counted to check.

Crystal candleholders were always easy to sell, and rich folks owned so many pairs, they rarely took notice.

But you stole the one and only valuable bauble a poor person owned, and they were looking for it the minute they noticed it was gone—which was right away.

And a valuable bauble from a poor person, whose valuables were dismal things as a rule, was usually worthless
and wouldn't get a man very far.

His eyes rested on the single teacup, upside-down, drain-
ing by the metal basin where she no doubt washed dishes.

A teacup. He touched the cup and found it was still
damp. So he'd almost walked in on her in the dark. He
smiled as he imagined it.

His eyes slid to the teapot sitting on a shelf above the
stove, and then he sniffed the air. Something different. Not
tea like he remembered it.

She'd definitely come down at night in the dark because
he'd been watching and there'd been no lantern light. Yet
the moonlight was strong tonight, and the woman must
feel comfortable that she knew her way around her own
home.

She'd made herself a cup of strange tea.

He picked up a small sack by the teapot, opened it, and
sniffed. This was it.

Something she favored late at night. Maybe it helped
her sleep.

Key remembered what the boss had said and pondered
it all. Then, being very sparing, he took out a handkerchief and poured just a bit of the tea mixture into his
kerchief.

He'd take it with him. Talk to the boss about it. If she
drank tea late at night, maybe there would be a way to
very quietly add just the right thing to her tea and kill
her that way. And maybe, with her just recently snakebit,
rather than take their time about killing her, they should
move fast.

The doctor might blame it on a relapse caused by snake venom.

He didn't have anything with him right now or he'd've just taken it on himself to toss something poisonous into her bag of tea.

He'd been around awhile. Not around the boss, not that long, but he'd been around the darker side of life plenty long. And he knew a bit about poison. Including some plants round these parts that were toxic and had a mild flavor if they were prepared just right. He'd even seen a few plants in the area that he could gather and turn into powder.

Poison wasn't his strength, not like locks and keys. Still, he knew a bit. He'd talk to the boss first because that was just good sense when a man had a temper as short as the boss had.

But this needed to be done, and done fast.

Folding the handkerchief carefully around the tea, he twisted the kerchief into a little pouch and tucked it into his pocket. His eyes moved from the kitchen to the corner of a staircase. She was right up there, right now. Fast asleep.

Secure in her locked house, which had a lock a child could get past.

He could go up there right now and finish this. He could toss her down the stairs, and folks would believe she fell. Even if they were suspicious, who could prove anything?

Key rubbed his hand absently over the tea in his pocket and considered it all. He believed himself to be a careful man. Dangerous, but he didn't take risks. Part of why he liked this gang. Leaving no witnesses suited him, and he'd discovered a taste for killing.

No, he'd leave for now and talk to the boss about poison.

But he liked the idea of just finishing her now. He imagined her fighting him. Fighting hard. It fed a hunger in him to kill that was one of his great talents.

Not tonight, though. Tonight he'd leave her be and instead spend some time imagining the kill. Which was its own kind of pleasure.

Key let himself out and used the same skills he'd used to get inside, leaving the door locked behind him.

17

When Mariah was in a bad mood, she liked to make angle iron.

Flat strips of iron about three inches wide and six feet long, turned raging hot about six inches at a time, banged and banged and banged until every ounce of her mood was poured into a defenseless strip of iron . . . and she'd made something useful.

Angle iron made great support legs for tanks and windmills, buildings and wagons. Its uses were endless.

And making it was very satisfying.

There was plenty of call for angle iron, so she was wise to make it ahead of orders coming in, though Pa had a fair amount on hand already. But today she needed to do some banging.

Pump the bellows.

Make the fire roar.

Turn the iron from red-hot to white-hot.

Vise it hard on the anvil with half its width sticking over the edge.

Swing the sledgehammer until six inches of the iron was bent at a perfect ninety-degree angle.

Then do it all over again on the next six inches.

Halfway through the first strip of iron, her muscles were singing with the pleasure of the work.

She was good at this. As she banged along, she quit being angry at Clint and switched to being angry at her pa. He'd never fully respected her work.

It was ridiculous to think that somehow Pa, in heaven now, was looking down, nodding and thinking his girl was a fine blacksmith and he'd apologize to her when someday he saw her come through the pearly gates.

Mariah was pretty sure there were more serious things to do in heaven, like worship the Lord.

Even so, she needed to prove it to herself, if not Pa. And as she banged with the hammer, she decided she didn't need a stupid dress with stupid ruffles. A thought that intruded now and again and made her bang all the harder.

Then, because she loved her pa and wasn't happy focusing her anger at him, she thought of those men who'd killed her family and might even now be considering whether they should kill her. She almost hoped some criminal would try because she was in the mood to make them pay for their effort.

Every outlaw and every rattlesnake in the territory that knew what was good for him would stay well back today from Mariah Stover.

The fourth six-foot length of angle iron was done. Unhooking the vise, she held it with tongs and plunged it into a trough of water to cool it, then tossed the fashioned iron onto a growing pile. She clenched her hand on her sledgehammer, contemplating how she'd make someone pay for threatening her.

She heard the smithy door creak open.

She spun around, already hurling her sledge.

"Ack!" Becky jumped back and slammed the door just as the hammer crashed into it right where her face had been.

Mariah ran for the door. "Becky, are you all right?" She tore the door open.

Becky stood outside, her face in a deep scowl, her hand resting flat on her heart as if she were trying to hold it inside her chest.

"I'm so sorry." Mariah took a few steps toward Becky, and when her friend didn't run or swing a fist at her, Mariah hoped it meant Becky would forgive her. "I'm so glad you weren't hurt. I'm, well . . ." Mariah had an excuse, but truthfully there was no excuse for what she'd just done. "I guess I'm on edge today."

"Really?" Becky's voice nearly dripped with angry sarcasm. She wasn't a sweetheart like Nell. Much tougher. Any yelling her friend wanted to do, Mariah deserved.

"I was just thinking about someone maybe wanting to kill me and sort of daydreaming about how I'd love to fight back, and then the door opened." Mariah gave her shoulders a sheepish shrug and repeated, "I'm sorry."

"You're on edge, huh? Well, you'd better get off that edge and get yourself under control or you're going to have trouble attracting customers."

Mariah looked behind her through the open door at the stack of angle iron. She saw a pile of hinges, three wooden casks of nails, the newly made wooden pails sitting full of water. The horse stalls stood empty now, but soon there'd be horses needing shoes.

"I doubt it. Not much stops the steady stream of emergency need for a blacksmith. Like Nell and her chaps, there seems to be endless demand for my services, although usually her orders aren't quite so frantic. The broken iron just keeps coming."

"I'm over here to see if you'd have lunch with me. You're not safe, Mariah." Becky wasn't one to sugarcoat her opinions. It was a little trying at times, but honestly it was a trait Mariah admired and, to some extent, envied.

And Mariah didn't want to eat with Becky over at Clint's stupid restaurant, either. Yet if they didn't do so, she'd be burdening Becky with having to cook after she'd almost killed her. Too much to ask, even of a very good friend.

A deep, low growl turned Mariah around fast.

Maybe they would eat at her place. "You brought Brutus to town with you?"

The dog stretched to lie on his belly, its front legs out in front of it. Not a dog that would be welcome inside the diner. Its eyes locked on a man crossing the street a dozen yards away.

Brutus was a mottled-furred dog, gray and black mainly, with no known breed. He was gentle with Mariah and anyone Becky was friendly with. But he was a top guard dog and one to attack strangers first and see if his mistress was all right with it later. Mariah noticed him staring at Sheriff Mast as the man walked from the jailhouse to Clint's. Nope, the dog had no place in Clint's diner.

"Yes, I brought him for you. He'd've smelled that rattlesnake and warned you."

"But you can't separate him from Lobo."

"Honestly, that's what gave me the idea." Becky jabbed a finger at Brutus, then at the smithy, then at Mariah's house that was just a bit to the east. "Stay. Guard."

Apparently, Brutus was now on duty. He turned to stare in the smithy, through the open doors. Then he began sniffing along the foundation of the building.

"Lobo just had pups."

Mariah tore her eyes away from the busily sniffing dog. "How many? I want to see them."

Shaking her head, walking toward the diner, Becky said, "Six puppies, and you can see them anytime you want. But don't distract me from the point of this. Right now, as she always does after she has a litter, she wants to kill Brutus."

Lobo was more wolf than dog, though Becky had found her, guided by Brutus, half-strangled with a collar around her neck. The collar was strapped on too tight, as though she'd had it on for years and had run off wearing it. Lobo had let Becky rescue her, with Brutus whining, going between Lobo and Becky as if vouching for the human. Since Becky had removed that collar, Lobo had been Becky's shadow.

She'd been with Becky since before she'd left her pa's ranch to set up on her own. And she and Brutus had puppies every year.

So this might be her fifth litter. And usually six puppies. Most of the dogs in the area were Lobo and Brutus's babies, and they were highly prized because dogs were scarce.

"Lobo won't let Brutus near the pups. He makes her furious, and poor Brutus stays well away."

"They're inseparable usually."

"Yep. She'll get over it when the puppies are weaned. But for the next three months or so, Brutus is like a leper. No, that's not right, she'd avoid a leper. But she seems to hate him, fear him. Thinks he's dangerous to her babies. That's just how she always is. We've been through this every year since I got her."

"So you brought him to me?"

Becky shrugged. "It came to me that he could protect you and save himself a few months of being growled at. I think he'll be all right with a temporary new home."

Mariah looked behind her to stare at the sniffing dog as it rounded the corner of the smithy. "It's honestly a good idea—he *would* have sniffed out that rattler."

"And he can sleep in your house at night, so no intruders will get in. You'll be safe."

A door slammed across the street and drew Mariah's head around. Nell came out of her shop, waving.

"I stopped and asked her if she wanted in on lunch. She said yes real fast, but she acted a little funny about it. What's going on?"

Mariah remembered someone, almost certainly Nell, catching her in Clint's arms. Nell had tried to talk to Mariah, but Mariah was in no mood to talk.

"I'll bet she said yes fast."

Becky, still walking, turned to Mariah and arched a brow, saying nothing. Letting silence apply its own pressure.

"We can't talk about it in a busy diner." Mariah caught Becky's arm. "Nell walked in on Clint and me. We were, uh . . . well, I'm not sure at what point she walked in."

Becky turned to fully face Mariah, waiting.

Nell came up beside Becky. "Are you trying to get out of her what happened between her and Clint yesterday?"

Becky crossed her arms. "Talk. Do it fast. I'm hungry."

Mariah felt her face heating up. She scratched the back of her head and realized she had her black leather head-scarf on still. The apron too. She pulled both off while she worked up the courage to talk fast . . . which wasn't fast at all. Becky kept waiting.

Mariah looked left and right to make sure no one was approaching. She spoke just above a whisper. "Clint . . . he kissed me yesterday."

Nell grinned. Becky gasped. Mariah wondered how Brutus had taken the news.

18

"We're eating scrambled eggs at Mariah's house." Becky caught her by the arm.

Not the one that'd been snakebit. That was nice, or lucky, Mariah wasn't sure.

"No, come to my place. I'm not sure how much food Mariah has at her place." Nell gestured toward her dress shop. She had an upstairs living space similar to Clint's, but she also had a stove tucked in there, a dry sink, and an icebox. Things Clint left down in his diner kitchen.

They changed course for Nell's.

"Start talking." Becky was easily the most strong-willed woman of the three of them. A blacksmith oughta have a stronger will.

"To make a long story short," Mariah said, "he kissed me. He proposed."

"He proposed *marriage*?" Becky nearly shrieked.

Mariah backhanded her arm. "What else?"

Becky rubbed a hand hard over her mouth as if trying to stop more words. Mariah appreciated that.

"He said he'd care for me and protect me all my life. And he was glad I'd quit being the town blacksmith because it was dangerous."

"There's no need to make a long story short." Nell, walking on her snakebit side, slid an arm across the back of her waist. "We don't mind hearing every single, little, teeny-tiny detail."

"I told him the town needs me, and anyway, I like what I do and don't want to quit." Which wasn't strictly true, but it was the principle of the thing. "I asked him if he would be willing to marry me if I kept being a blacksmith, and he couldn't quite get those words to come out of his mouth."

Nell flinched, then glared at the diner as they walked up the steps to the boardwalk that ran the length of that side of Pine Valley's main street. The diner on the south end, Nell's dress shop on the north.

Becky got the door, and they all filed in.

"It would take a strong, independent-minded man to let his wife be the town blacksmith. But Clint, with his love for cooking strange food in a town that mainly eats stew and fried chicken, seems like an independent-minded man. He wouldn't even talk to you about it?"

Nell led the way upstairs. Mariah followed, with Becky bringing up the rear. Nell had a small kitchen table and three chairs for the very reason that the three of them often gathered at her place.

Mariah got coffee started. Becky stoked the embers of the fire to life. Nell got a skillet on the stovetop, then added butter to it to melt. She got out a bowl of eggs from the icebox and started cracking.

The three of them worked quietly together for a time. They'd shared many a meal and many a coffee visit. They knew just how to get everything done with ease and speed.

The stirred-up eggs hit the skillet with a warm crackle while Becky sliced bread and Mariah got out a stack of plates, cups, and utensils.

Nell had three of all of those, too.

"So, are you in love with him?" Nell used a spatula to scramble the eggs. She looked worried but in a kind-hearted kind of way.

"Did you punch him in the nose?" Becky came and sat at the table, wearing a buckskin coat with long leather fringe. She shrugged it off and tossed it on the floor by the door to the stairs.

"You two are the best friends a woman ever had. The fact that you're very different from each other only makes you more wonderful."

Nell sighed as she tended the eggs. "I guess that means you're not in love with him. Or at least you're not going to admit it to us."

The coffee started hissing. They hadn't made a full pot. No sense in wasting coffee grounds.

"It also means you didn't punch him, which he deserved." Becky started buttering her bread thoughtfully.

"The thing is, do any women work?"

Becky chomped into her bread and raised her hand like an obedient student to indicate she did. Her mouth was full, but Mariah got the message. Becky most definitely worked.

"Me too." Nell lifted the cast-iron skillet, brought it to

the table, and scraped out the perfectly done eggs, dividing them evenly.

"No, of course I know you work. We all do. I should have said *married* women. Can you think of a single married woman, not counting a woman who works alongside her husband?"

Becky dug into her eggs. Nell buttered her bread. Mariah knew they both, like her, were racking their brains.

Becky slammed the side of her fist on the table hard enough that the utensils bounced. "How about Esther Morris? She was the justice of the peace in South Pass City.

"That's right." Nell's face lit up with excitement. "And Mrs. Mussel coming here to give a speech—that counts."

Mariah nodded. "And both are married women. I don't know what Esther Morris's husband does, but even if Mrs. Mussel travels with her husband, she still gives the speeches. I don't think having him along as company counts as them working together."

"Then that means Clint needs to climb down off his high horse and accept that his wife is going to be a blacksmith." Becky nodded, then went back to her eggs as if it were all settled.

Mariah got up to pour coffee for them all. "But do I want a fight like that to go on in a marriage? Do I want a husband who I have to nag to let me work? Even if I convince him, can there be any harmony between us? He'll be annoyed and consider himself disrespected and embarrassed. He won't be any good at hiding his feelings, and I'll resent him for it."

"Yep, even if he agrees at first, he might change his mind." Becky let out a huff of a breath. "I suspect the only way to hope you'd be allowed to work is if you found a husband who wants to be a blacksmith. Too bad Willie is married."

Willie, thirty years old, mostly content with the minimal job of being town deputy. Four inches shorter than Mariah and skinny as a rail. Black teeth due to an overly enthusiastic fondness for chewing tobacco. A man with no interest in bathing or changing into clean clothes. Nice enough if you could stay well away from him.

And yet he had a wife who seemed very fond of him.

The three of them started to laugh, and when they finally got themselves under control, nothing was really settled. But they all felt better for their having the noon meal together.

19

Mariah didn't put in a long day. She was whipped. She'd probably needed more time to heal before going back to work. But she was still mad at Clint and bored to death.

Brutus mostly slept through the long afternoon. He showed a fine wisdom in that he kept well away from the fire and the hot iron.

About once an hour, the dog would get up and start sniffing around, then go outside and be gone for ten or fifteen minutes—running a patrol route most likely. Or maybe he was just interested in stretching his legs.

Mariah stepped away from the last piece of angle iron she intended to make for a while. She hadn't gotten much done with the stack of bent and broken iron that had piled up during her week in bed. But today had been a day to get back into the swing of hammering. Not to do detailed, complicated work, but simply to bang on iron.

It wasn't close to suppertime and yet her arms were

already aching, along with her head. It seemed she'd done all she was going to do for one day.

"Let's go home, Brutus." Mariah was putting everything back in its place when Joshua Pruitt shoved the doors of the blacksmith shop wide open.

There was something in his eyes she didn't like. She heard a low growl from Brutus, and considering Brutus had lived at the Pruitt ranch for years, that struck Mariah as bad.

"Shut up, dog." Joshua did a little growling of his own.

Brutus subsided, but the hair on his neck stood on end, and his ears were laid back.

Joshua turned toward Mariah, and she was glad Brutus was with her. Joshua held several things in his arms.

"I've brought you a load of work. Three buckets here, and I've got a small water trough and a bunk that needs work. I don't have those with me. I'll have to bring them in the wagon. I didn't have time for the slow ride to town. Sorry I let things pile up, but I never thought the town would lose its blacksmiths. Now the work is all gonna be for you to do. Sure hope a little woman is up to the task." Pruitt's tone clearly said he didn't think she was up to it.

"Set the buckets down over there, Joshua," Mariah said, pointing. She saw Pruitt's eyes darken, as if her using his first name was an insult.

"I expected the work done now—right away. I'll wait."

It was well known that Becky had left her pa's ranch because she didn't like her father's hard-bitten hired hands. They were a salty lot and known for their bad tempers and short fuses.

"I'm done for today. It's my first day back from being

bitten by a rattlesnake, but I'll get to the buckets tomorrow." Shaking her head, she added, "I've already let the forge die down for the night."

Joshua looked like he was prepared to launch into complaints about being made to wait. Mariah decided to direct the man's attention elsewhere. "What brings you into town so late? Your crew usually comes in midday to eat a meal."

"Just had a hard day and couldn't find time to get away until now, and I need the buckets mended." Joshua gave Mariah a mean look that was unsettling.

At that moment, Clint came in at a near run. He saw Mariah standing there talking to Joshua and almost skidded to a stop. He was behind Joshua, so by the time Becky's pa heard him and glanced back, Clint was the very picture of a calm man acting like he just happened by. Yet Mariah had seen his expression. He'd seen Joshua walk into the smithy. And he knew the man well enough, with his harsh ways and short temper, to not like Mariah being alone with him.

Brutus started growling again.

"Brutus, settle down now. Uh . . . stay." Mariah really hadn't tried giving Brutus orders up until now. She looked at that betrayer with his wonderful kisses and did the right thing to order Brutus to stay back . . . but maybe not the most satisfying thing.

"I've got supper ready for us, Mariah. I finished my work out at the homestead and hurried back to town. The beef bourguignon left over from lunch is warming. Thought I'd come and see if you need help closing up."

"Nope, all ready to go. Thanks anyway, Clint." Mariah didn't especially like being alone in the shop with Joshua, either. Oh, he'd never hurt her, but she might end up getting a tongue-lashing, and coming from Joshua Pruitt, that could sting.

"Joshua, I'll get to what you brought in first thing in the morning, but I'm still not at full strength. I don't dare push harder than I already did." She pointed at the wall where several buckets hung, though they were made of wood, not iron like the ones Joshua wanted repaired. "Buy a new bucket if you need one to get through the next day."

Joshua set his buckets down with a hard thud. "I'm not buying a new one when a solid repair will do just fine for these. I'll come back tomorrow or send someone in for 'em. They'd better be ready when I get here."

He stomped out of the smithy, not unlike an angry guard dog. She mentally apologized to Brutus, who was quite well-behaved.

The door slammed hard, then bounced back open. Mariah waited for Joshua to think of a few choice words she needed to hear, but he didn't come back.

Hooves pounded away, and Mariah felt sorry for the poor horse.

"Um . . . so, did you get a dog?"

"Everyone knows Brutus."

"They do indeed. Did you get the dog from Becky?"

"She came in with him today. Lobo had pups, and she doesn't like Brutus around them when they're real young. Becky thought he might be tired of being snarled at and I might like having a guard dog around the smithy during the day and at my house during the night."

"Good idea." Clint sounded sincerely impressed.

"He'd've sniffed out that rattlesnake." He shoved his hands deep in his pockets. "I mainly wanted you to have some company while Pruitt was around. He came galloping into town like he had a headful of steam about something."

"Thank you."

"But I do have leftover beef bourguignon."

"And what in the world is that?"

Clint grinned and shrugged one shoulder. "It's delicious."

Nell's scrambled eggs were long gone from her belly after an afternoon of hard work. "I'll just bet it is. Everything you make is delicious." Sighing deeply, she said, "And we should talk about what happened yesterday."

She left the smithy with Clint and Brutus and locked up.

Clint nodded at Brutus. "Does he behave himself in the kitchen? If he does, he's welcome to come in."

"Brutus?"

The dog stood and watched her with rapt attention. Mariah really liked him. She wondered if Becky could get along with only one dog and let her have Brutus. Becky could keep one of the pups.

Or maybe Mariah should get one of them.

"Brutus, go on now and hunt."

Brutus leapt to his feet and raced away.

She turned to see Clint watching the dog run off. She said, "Becky took him to your place after we ate the noon meal at Nell's. She said you were close enough to town that his hunting range might include your house. When she brought him back, she spent some time telling him not to eat any of your chickens or ducks. As for your baby lambs, she seemed confident he'd leave them alone, and it matters because he hunts his own food."

"I was out there before she was done. She told me and let me watch her walk around, let Brutus sniff the animals. Told him to guard them. I don't know much about dogs, but he seems like a fine one."

"Becky's got six puppies if you're interested."

Clint turned from where he watched after a now-vanished Brutus. "That's not a bad idea. If the dog stayed out at my place, he could guard the livestock. I've lost a few chickens to weasels and such." He reached out a hand and touched her back, urged her forward. "Let's go eat."

She went with him, trying to gather her thoughts. Trying not to let that kiss influence her overly.

They reached the back door, where she always had gone in when she was staying there. He opened the door like a fine gentleman, and she preceded him inside.

He served her a delicious beef stew that he should have just called by its real name. "This is wonderful, Clint. Better than any beef stew I've ever had in my life. What do you do to make things so unusually tasty?"

Shaking his head as he chewed the amazingly tender beef, he swallowed and said, "I don't want to swap recipes, Mariah. I thought for a long time last night about my clumsy proposal. I thought of what a fine, hardworking woman you are, highly skilled, badly needed in this town. I've decided you should stay working at your smithy."

He looked so proud of himself, so generous, she was tempted to bonk him on the head.

"Giving me permission, are you?" She shoved another

forkful of stew into her mouth and chewed thoughtfully. The carrots she could see were really young. He already had a spring crop. He had pearl onions. There were plenty of spices in the thick stew it all sat in. She would have liked to swap recipes.

"Absolutely." He swung his arms wide like the most reasonable man alive. "And maybe we can work out a trade. I know you keep busy all day long. So you can't work here in the morning, but I could run home and do my chores after my lunch crowd is finished, then get back and work at the smithy in the afternoon. You can train me to help a lot more than I do. I've watched you while you work, Mariah. I know there's a lot to it and I know you're about ten times—oh, probably a thousand times—better at it than I'll ever be. You've been trained by the hands of a master for most of your life."

Mariah continued eating. She saw Clint's satisfied smile slip.

She knew they'd shared a kiss or two. She wasn't sure how to count them honestly. And she knew that no matter how agreeable he was right now, later he would be ashamed of having a wife working as a blacksmith. Even though at the moment he believed all would be fine.

With her plate scraped clean, and his only a few bites later, she picked up her dishes and he got his and followed her into the kitchen.

The kitchen's windows faced westward, and looking through one of them by the sink, Mariah could see her house. Brutus lay stretched out on her porch, licking his chops.

"The thing is, Clint, you do an unusual job for a man.

171

Not cook or own a diner, lots of men do that. In fact, I'd say the diners in frontier towns are mostly run by men."

"I ate at a lot of them on my way west."

That made her smile, thinking of Clint chewing on tough beefsteak. Eating lumpy potatoes and lumpier gravy. "I'll bet that was an education."

Clint came up beside her. "Not really. I grew up in my parents' diner in New York. Our food was good, but it was plain food. Roast beef, fried chicken for the noon meal, ham and eggs for breakfast."

"So, how'd you come up with sauce from Holland?"

Clint gave her a confused look. "We had a fair-sized family. Myself and two younger sisters. Pa and Ma, Sissy and Lila. We all worked in the diner. My next younger sister was seventeen and she fell in love with a young man we'd hired as a waiter, who worked hard and showed real interest in my sister and working in the diner. He wanted to learn to cook. With him wanting more work and the distant sound of wedding bells in the air, there were enough hands to run things and so I struck out on my own. I ended up working in a much fancier restaurant. I learned so much working there. I changed jobs when a better job that paid more opened up. I then got hired to be the lowliest cook in Delmonico's, one of the finest restaurants in New York City. Maybe one of the finest restaurants in the country. I quit moving around and focused on learning everything I could. I got longer hours, learned more, and kept getting promoted there.

"My family was proud of me. I was proud of them. We had a happy family. It was the most natural thing in the world that once Sissy and Earl got married, I'd move out, they'd take my room. I'd get a bachelor's apartment. Monday was my day off at Delmonico's, and I spent it with my family. Working back at the family diner. Sissy was expecting her first child. Earl had gotten good enough, he started carrying a lot of the weight. Ma and Pa had it better than ever. We had a nice life."

He sounded like he was describing something wonderful and yet his tone was sad. He'd lost his family in a fire. She almost stopped him. She didn't want to hear the details.

"And then the restaurant caught fire in the middle of the night. A huge fire that burned the whole block down. No one in my family survived." He fell silent for long moments. "Except me."

Mariah rested one hand on his arm as they stood looking out the window. Losing her pa and Theo was too new, and hearing of Clint's loss made her feel raw and terrible.

"I'm sorry, Clint." Simple words, but they were from the heart and she meant them.

"I dream about it. I dream about going home at just the right time. Even though, of course, I was asleep across town. Sometimes I get there and save them. Mostly I see my youngest sister, Lila, screaming out her bedroom window. She liked to watch for me when she knew I was coming over. She'd stand at that window, which faced the direction I always came from, and wave at me when she'd spot me. Call out a happy greeting. In my dreams she's screaming, burning, falling.

"They found her on the ground. She'd jumped out that window. But her nightgown was on fire. The fall killed her before the burns could. She was the only one . . . well, the rest of them were so badly burnt I couldn't recognize them."

Mariah left her hand there, resting on his arm, giving him what little bit of comfort she could.

"I buried them, then spent some time half mad with grief, until my head finally cleared enough that I knew I couldn't stay in New York anymore. I couldn't stop smelling smoke. It's a big city, lots of smoke everywhere, but I kept thinking things were on fire. I had to get out.

"So I turned what I owned into cash. Pa's diner was in ashes, but the lot had value. Pa had some money in the bank. I had some. I gathered it all up, left New York City, and headed west on the train. I joined up with a wagon train at one point as a rider. I had no wagon. I rode along with that group for a while, but it was like . . . like my memories could catch up moving that slow. And the trains were too fast. I kept getting to places that were nowhere I wanted to go."

He shrugged. "While I traveled, I ate at diners. Worked at a few of them on my way, and when I got far enough away from New York that I couldn't smell the smoke anymore, I stopped."

"You saw the Towers standing guard over this town." Mariah took Clint's hand and led him into the dining room to look out his good-sized front window. The towering mountains showed up in the setting sun.

"They're like a row of angels." Clint gazed out at them. "They were snow-covered when I got here, and that's how it struck me. A row of angels guarding the town."

"I think of them as protectors, too." She looked at the beautiful peaks of the Wind River Range. She'd heard there were a whole lot more mountains farther west, but Pa had stopped here, and so had she. "But my ma died since we've been in the shadow of those angels. And now Pa and Theo. I can't give the mountains too much credit. They haven't protected me much at all."

Clint stood shoulder to shoulder with her, looking out the window. It was a peaceful moment when her life had been so crazy for so long.

"Mariah, will you marry me?"

She wanted to. Right now it sounded like the best idea in the world. But she didn't trust him to mean what he said.

She tried to be as honest as she possibly could.

"Before you say no . . ."

He started talking again before she could reply. She almost smiled because he sounded so sure she would refuse him and yet he'd asked, and very politely, too.

". . . I want you to know that I've had, uh . . . well, I've been interested in you for a while now."

She snapped her head around to look at him, the beautiful towering mountains forgotten. "You have?"

He gave her a sad kind of smile. "I was pretty sure you hadn't thought of me that way. But, Mariah, when those stagecoach horses came tearing into town, and we knew . . . that is, I knew you were supposed to be back, I've never been so terrified in all my life. You weren't conscious, so you probably don't know I came out there with the sheriff. I pulled you out from under the stage while they used horses and ropes to lift it off you. I carried you back into town."

He reached out and took her hand, squeezed it tight. "I want to marry you. And it's not because I've just recently

175

noticed you since you were hurt and I was helping hide you. I've been hoping you'd notice for a while."

"Why didn't you say something?"

His smile widened. "I did. Or at least I tried to. I spoke to you special when you'd come in to eat at the diner."

"You speak to everyone, Clint. I never noticed you treating me differently."

"Well, you were always in here with your pa and Theo. That kept me from being overly familiar. I kept hoping you'd show some sign of interest in me before I spoke to your pa. He was a formidable man. And I'd've faced him without a moment's hesitation if I thought you would welcome my attention. Only now, since you were hurt and we've spent real time together, do I think, that is . . . hope, that my, um, my suit might be welcomed."

Mariah studied him. So this wasn't just a whim. Something new caused by her being hurt and vulnerable. It made it harder to say no.

"I believe it's the right thing to do, to keep being the blacksmith in this town. They need me. Eventually a new blacksmith might come along, but for now, to just quit—"

"I don't want you to quit."

She held up her hand, palm flat, most of the way to his face. "Let me finish. I am going to continue working as the town's blacksmith. I believe once we are married—"

He gasped and smiled bright.

"That is, *if* we get married, well, the thing is, I believe if I keep working, the moment is going to come when it bothers you. You'll want me to quit, and I won't. Right now, you're all happy and willing to let me pursue the work I'm good at. You're almost certainly going to change your mind."

"No, I won't."

"Joshua Pruitt, or one of the Wainwright brothers, or who knows who it might be will say something about me working, and you"—she jabbed him in the chest—"will be insulted, as they will surely intend you to be."

"I can't be insulted if I'm proud of you."

Mariah stared at him, straight in the eyes. She tried to look deeper, tried to figure out if marrying him was the right decision or not.

"I am not going to say yes or no right now, Clint. I'm going to think about it. Pray about it."

Very solemnly, he nodded. "That's wise. I'll do the same."

"If I say yes, it will be because it's God's will. I'm . . . that is, *we're* drawn to each other. I know that. But our promises, well, we can say love, honor, and obey for the vows. But I'm going to need promises from you, too. Maybe not in the vows spoken before the parson, but between us. I do know that right now I feel like this town needs me and I've got to have the courage to stand up to everyone when I get pressured to quit. And I'm going to need you standing right beside me, supporting me while I face that pressure."

"I'll make that promise, Mariah. And we'll both pray about a future together. May I kiss you again?"

And that was the whole problem. Because she really wanted him to, and she couldn't go around wanting to kiss Clint, then up and refuse his proposal. That made her a person she didn't respect.

"I'd like that very much, but I think we should not do any more of that until we've made up our minds."

Clint gave her a lopsided smile. "My mind's made up. So how about I kiss you, but you don't kiss me?"

She smirked. Leaned forward and gave him a quick kiss right on the lips. "Thank you for proposing. I'm honored. It's a fine thing to have a good man want to marry me. And you are a good man, Clint. And thank you for supper. It was real tasty. Now I'm going to get Brutus and go home where I'm well away from temptation."

He wiggled his eyebrows. "I'm a temptation?"

She swatted him on the chest but soft enough that it was almost a caress. "Good night, Clint."

She turned away from those towering mountains and went out through the back door. Clint followed and ended up walking her all the way home. Brutus came from around the back of Mariah's house. Clint let the dog sniff his hand.

"We met already today at my place, then at the smithy. We're friends now."

Mariah went up the two steps of her front stoop. She swung the door open and said, "Brutus, go on in."

As the dog ran inside, Mariah glanced back at Clint, who'd stepped up beside her. He drew her into his arms and kissed her thoroughly.

"I'm sleeping in town for now. I spend nights at my homestead as a rule, but for a while longer, I want to be close enough to see if that dog barks at anything in the night." He turned and headed back toward the diner.

When she went inside, her lips were still warm. Her heart too. Then Brutus, the tough old growly dog, came up and nudged her hand with his nose, and she drew her hand along his silky head. Yes, Brutus knew how to protect what he considered his, but he was a big old softie in his heart. She was glad for his company.

She thought about the dog and the man. Clint knew how to protect what was his, too.

It was too early for bed, so she settled in to read her Bible and spend some sincere time in prayer.

God's will?

How could it not be as clear as the Wyoming air? She thought it was, but then she wanted to marry Clint something fierce at the same time she was worried about how they'd handle the pressures of the future.

"Guide me, Lord. Guide me."

Brutus lay across her feet, and the two of them spent long, quiet minutes together as the sun set.

20

A growl that could curl a woman's hair jerked Mariah up in bed.

Brutus was rushing out of her room.

Mariah flung the covers back. Leapt out of bed and fell over in a heap with a loud crash. Her head banged on the floor. She untangled herself from the blanket that had tripped her and ran after Brutus, whose growl had turned to barking.

Mariah was halfway down the stairs when she heard the back door of her house slam shut. By the time she got there, hoofbeats were pounding as a horse galloped away.

She wrenched the back door open and found it unlocked. But then she'd heard it slam already so she knew it had been opened. She always locked both doors. Pa had been a cautious man. Mariah was more so since Pa and Theo had died.

She knew without a doubt she'd locked the back and front doors tonight.

The unlocked door had been firmly closed. Brutus was barking wildly. She caught the fur on the back of his neck, not sure if it was safe for the dog to run off after whoever it was.

Seconds later, Clint was pounding on her front door. "Mariah, are you all right?"

Her two protectors.

"Yes, I'm all right. I'm coming." She tugged on the thick ruff of fur around Brutus's neck, then let him go. Maybe Clint would know what should be done about her intruder.

She struggled for a moment with the lock, then got it open, gasping for air as Clint stepped inside.

With a vicious growl, Brutus dashed past Clint and into the night.

"No, don't let him go."

Clint whirled to grab Brutus, but he was gone. Silent as a ghost.

"He's going after him. Brutus will get shot!"

Clint caught Mariah as she tried to push past him. "He's gone, Mariah. We'll never find him in the dark. We just have to hope he comes back."

"But he could be shot."

"Shot by who? What's going on here? What happened? I heard the dog barking. Did I hear someone riding away?"

Mariah flung herself into his arms. "Yes. Someone came in the back door. Brutus woke me up and ran downstairs barking." She told him everything, including that the back door was unlocked.

Clint caught her by the upper arms. "Someone broke in while you were asleep?"

Nodding, Mariah noticed he had some sort of nightshirt on. He was barefoot. He'd come running without a moment's delay. "They must have wanted something in here."

"They? More than one person?"

"No, I have no idea about that. I heard one horse gallop away." Mariah turned to the door again, and her hands clung to each other, her fingers twisting nervously. "The rider got a good head start. I don't think Brutus will catch up with him."

"I hope you're right."

The two of them looked at each other for a long time, then Clint pulled her tight against him. His nightshirt. Her nightgown. Both of them barefoot. This was completely improper. But she couldn't bear to let go, not just yet.

When she was beyond simple clinging, maybe Clint could breathe again. He said, "The house stood empty for a time. Could someone be, uh, sleeping here maybe? Was there any sign of an intruder when you moved back?"

"Sleeping here? Like someone who lives in town? Someone who already has a house? Or some vagabond who's been in town a while, but no one's noticed a newcomer?"

"No, that can't be. But what else? A husband whose wife kicked him out, who thought the house was empty?"

"And this man knew how to get through a locked door? Because that back door was locked when I went to bed, Clint. And it wasn't *broken* open. Someone got through the lock. I heard the door slam shut, and when I checked just now, it was unlocked."

Clint ran a hand through his hair. It stood up almost straight, and she had to fight the urge to smooth it down.

"Two men who share a cabin that's really crowded? So thinking the house was empty . . ." He paused and shook his head. "No, that makes no sense."

"It has to be someone." Mariah swallowed hard. The

bruise on her forehead, from when she'd jumped out of bed, tripped and hit the floor, began to throb. "Clint, it has to be someone from the Deadeye Gang."

Mariah thought of the last month, or at least the weeks since she'd regained consciousness after the stage robbery. "Do you th-think . . . the exploding forge?"

Clint said, "The rattlesnake?"

"It has to be." Mariah hugged him again, more gently this time, less like a clinging, frightened woman . . . which was exactly what she was. "What am I going to do?"

Clint held her against him. "First, we'll thank God for Becky giving you Brutus."

"I was deeply asleep. If Brutus hadn't been here to wake me up and scare that intruder away . . ." Mariah's voice broke.

"That dog may have saved your life."

"He's my hero." She looked at Clint, disheveled, exhausted, filled with fear and concern. "And you, Clint you're my hero, too."

"Mariah, I spent time thinking and praying tonight. About us. About whether God has laid out a future for the two of us together. Can you tell me how your prayers came out? Because I'm feeling almost frantic to not leave you alone in this house. Brutus is a fine protector, but a husband would be one more. You're a strong woman, Mariah, but if I could, I'd surround you with an army regiment. Or at least I'd surround you with me."

Mariah pulled him close. She knew exactly what her heart wanted to do. And nothing in her prayers had led her in another direction.

"Yes, I'll marry you, Clint."

He smiled and whispered into her ear, "Let's go wake up the preacher."

Key swung the door open and heard a dog growl.

He froze. No dog there. No dog in town.

Then the growl turned into a bark. Key turned and ran. He slammed the door shut behind him, sprinted for his horse.

Key ripped his horse's reins loose from the brush, leapt into the saddle, and kicked his horse. They were in a hard gallop before they'd gone two steps.

A dog. Panting, sickened by the fear, Key knew for a pure fact that the worst possible thing, in the view of any robber, if someone wanted to protect their house, was to get a dog. Any dog. A little yipping dog was as good as a big monster. But this dog sounded like both. Noisy and big. The dog, unlike a human security guard, could head straight to a man. There was no slipping around silently and avoiding notice.

Don't go home. Don't lead anyone to where he spent his days.

He spurred his horse straight east. He'd shut the dog inside, but that fool woman might release it to chase him. A dog could run as fast as a horse but not for as long. Key's horse was a strong one, fast and with good stamina.

Galloping on, Key felt as if he were being pursued. As if a dog's padded feet were closing in.

Bending low over the saddle, Key touched his gun. He didn't draw it, but it was satisfying to know it was there. But the noise of a gunshot . . . if the dog was leading someone else, the sheriff maybe, it'd bring them right to him.

Instead, he pulled the knife out of its scabbard that hung around his neck and inside his shirt. He shifted the reins and the knife so that he held the knife in his left hand. The trail was steep to the right, and the dog wouldn't come from that direction.

Key gripped the saddle horn and reins tight. He didn't want this to come to a fight, but if it did, the dog would lose.

He rode on. His horse was blowing now.

Had it been long enough? Had he left that dog behind? Could he slow down yet?

A bloodcurdling snarl sounded from behind him, and then razor-sharp teeth sank into his arm.

He pulled hard on the reins, and his horse skidded until it was nearly sitting on its haunches.

Key kept tight hold of the knife and slashed at what he could reach of the dog. With its teeth in his arm, he wasn't sure if he could hit anything. Then his horse reared up.

The knife caught hold of something on the dog.

The beast finally dropped away. Key quit worrying about a gunshot giving away his position. He threw himself off the horse before the animal went over backward. He landed solid on his feet, spun around, drew and fired, then fired again.

A yelp from the dog gave him a bitter satisfaction. He fired once more and heard the dog running away. He knew what a gun was.

That was when the throb started in Key's arm. There wasn't time to chase the beast down and finish him. Whirling back to his shaking horse, which hadn't run off during the gunfire, he mounted up and rode more slowly, listening for a posse heading his way.

He came to the steep bank of a creek and suddenly his panic was replaced by relief. He knew exactly where he was.

Guiding his horse down the bank, he left the trail and rode upstream. He'd stay in the water if need be, unless he heard someone coming after him.

His arm felt wet. It was too dark to see very well, but for sure he was bleeding. No doubt about it—his arm was torn up bad.

Yanking his kerchief off his neck, he wrapped it around his arm and knotted it tight. Awkward to do while riding, but it felt like he was losing a lot of blood, so much so he was frightened. He kicked his horse into a trot. Then later, to galloping.

No dog was after him.

No posse.

Only his own ghosts. The feeling of being chased.

He hated the feeling, he hated the dog, and he hated the woman who'd sicced the dog on him.

Killing her had been about no witnesses. Sneaking around an occupied house had been about savage pleasure. No more. Now killing her was going to be simple payback, and he couldn't wait.

Clint wasn't about to leave her alone to dress. He stayed downstairs while she hurried up to her bedroom. He inspected her back door. It was a good, solid lock. Not one to be opened with a skeleton key. The kind of lock a blacksmith might have on his, or her, home.

He did his best not to pay attention to the sounds Mariah made moving around upstairs. Dressing.

All he had to do was think of what might've happened without Brutus for his heart to speed up. His breathing to turn into near gasps.

A litany of prayers rose to God as he waited for Mariah. Prayers of thanksgiving. Prayers for protection. Prayers for them to have a marriage that was within God's will and to make a fine life together.

And he might have lost her without Becky bringing Mariah a dog.

Clint prayed every moment he waited.

Mariah came down at last, though honestly it was probably only minutes. It just seemed like forever to Clint.

"Now we'll go to my house, and you can stay outside my bedroom while I dress. Then we'll wake Parson Blodgett. I don't want to leave you alone for even a minute."

"I agree with you, Clint. I don't want to be alone." She took his hand, and they carefully locked her front door as they left.

They headed for the diner. Upstairs, Mariah waited in his main room while Clint dashed into his bedroom and got dressed in record time.

When he was done, they joined hands again.

"Where do you want to stay tonight?" Clint had a whole list of questions. He doubted they'd get to many of them as they walked swiftly toward the parsonage.

"Oh, um, I thought we'd go back to my home, but if you'd rather—"

"Your home is fine. But I need to stay out at my homestead most of the time. I think tomorrow we can go out there to sleep, if you agree." He was being very careful to not say a word about her work. "We can decide if we want to move out there right away. As a rule, I sleep out there every night. It's close so I usually walk back and forth. I have to sleep there six months out of the year, and I'm close to six months for this year already, so we could stay at your house."

"We always boarded your horse when you had enough supplies to haul into town for the day's cooking."

Clint held her hand tight as they reached the parsonage, which was on the edge of town. The parson had homesteaded and spent his spare hours farming. Two of his children were mostly grown boys, and all of them were old enough to be a big help, and his wife, of course, was indomitable.

"We'll stay at your place tonight. We'll, uh . . . we'll decide about everything else later." He knocked firmly on the door.

He really wanted to decide now. But the time for talking was past as the parson whipped the door open, looking concerned, as anyone would be at this hour.

"What happened now, Mariah?"

"We want to get married." Clint took her hand.

The parson's eyes shifted back and forth between them, fully dressed in the middle of the night.

His brow knit as his wife came to his side.

She spoke over his shoulder. "Get yourselves to the church. We'll be right behind you."

21

All Mariah could think was that she wished they'd woken Nell up.

Not having her friend at her wedding seemed wrong. She wasn't asking for a white dress or a bouquet of roses. She didn't mind that there was no ring, no veil, and no music.

But Nell should be here. And Becky.

Mariah should be paying attention to her soon-to-be husband and Parson Blodgett. His rounded-bellied wife came with him to stand as witness.

Doc Preston had said the woman was tough, and Mariah saw her anew. Of course, Mariah saw her every Sunday morning sitting in the front row with her six extremely well-behaved children, but somehow, right now, in the darkest hours of the night, Latta Blodgett looked like the kind of woman to settle the frontier.

Parson Blodgett had neatly trimmed brown hair that could use a comb, a tidy mustache, and he'd hastily dragged on his clothes. To put it politely, the man was disheveled.

Mrs. Blodgett, however, came to the wedding dressed

for church. She wore a pretty calico dress, extra fabric around her belly. Her red hair looked apt to curl, but she had it under control in a bun at the back of her neck. She had on nicely laced-up black boots.

Parson Blodgett had on boots that didn't match. One brown and scuffed up, one black and highly polished. Yet he had a kind smile and didn't rush right into the vows. Instead, he talked with them for a surprising length of time, given that it was so late.

Clint and Mariah explained the situation with the dog and the intruder.

"I wonder if Brutus is all right?" Mariah glanced over her shoulder at the door, worried for her furry new friend.

It was clear the parson had imagined something far less respectable as their reason for marrying in such haste.

He pulled her attention back to the wedding. She and Clint both spoke of their prayers for guidance and their decision to marry immediately solely because Clint was wanting to keep Mariah safe, but that they would have married soon regardless.

Once things were clear, Parson Blodgett talked quietly with them about the danger and possible ways to reduce the threat. Afterward, he performed very sincerely a nice wedding ceremony.

As he asked for huge, lifelong promises to God and to each other, Mariah stopped thinking of Nell and worrying about Brutus and instead began to want her father. For that matter, she wanted her mother.

Her eyes burned. She had to speak her vows past a lump in her throat. In the dimly lit church, she hoped it didn't show. She did want to get married. It was just that the moment underscored how alone she'd be if not for Clint.

Clint had a firm grip on her hand and seemed to notice her tension. He edged just a bit closer to her and slid an arm across her back. Those little motions seemed to coincide with the vows to love, honor, and obey. The parson, based on the story they'd told, included talk of God protecting them.

"I now pronounce you man and wife." The parson smiled wide at them.

Mrs. Blodgett clapped her hands, then held them clutched right under her chin. She gave a smile as wide as Wyoming.

Mariah felt a smile not quite as generous on her own face. Where was Brutus? They had to find him. If he caught up to that intruder, he could be in danger. The dog had been away for too long.

"You may kiss the bride," the parson said.

Clint's strong hands took possession of her shoulders. Through her dark-colored shirtwaist, she could feel that his hands didn't have enough calluses, not compared to Mariah's father.

But his strength was solid. He'd come running when the stagecoach horses tore into town. He'd come running when her forge exploded. He'd come running when the snake attacked her. And tonight he'd come running when the dog barked. He was a good man, and she was happy to be married to him. Yes, there might be trouble ahead with his dealing with her work. But they'd face that trouble. Handle it like mature adults, and they'd find happiness together.

Add to that, he was the best cook she'd ever known.

She saw Clint's smile and knew at this moment, at least, he was very happy. He turned Mariah to face him, leaned forward, still holding her shoulders, and gave her a warm but brief kiss. A perfect kiss for the moment.

Clint then shook the parson's hand. He reached in his pocket and gave the man a coin. Mariah barely noticed the gesture.

Mrs. Blodgett came and hugged Mariah. "I'll be praying for your happiness and for your safety."

It was an awkward hug, what with Mrs. Blodgett's belly in the way, but it felt nice regardless. Mrs. Blodgett wasn't an old woman by any means, yet she was older than Mariah by quite a bit and it felt good to be held in her motherly arms.

Mrs. Blodgett leaned close to Mariah's ear and asked, "Do you wish for a bit of time with me to speak of the wedding night ahead?"

Considering Mrs. Blodgett was expecting her seventh child, Mariah figured the woman knew what was what.

But what about Brutus? Mariah couldn't think of much else but that for now.

"Thank you, but I'll be fine." Mariah hugged her again and felt her eyes burn with tears that neither her ma nor her pa was there. Nor Theo. And never would be. Nell and Becky, well, maybe she and Clint should have waited a bit. But how would they get through the night with Clint unwilling to leave her and Nell not really being a gunslinger?

Clint's arm came around Mariah's shoulders. "We'll let you folks get to sleep now."

"You should talk to the sheriff." The parson stood beside his wife at the front of the church, facing Mariah and Clint. Now he moved around them, holding Mrs. Blodgett's hand.

"We're going to wait until morning." Clint glanced at Mariah. In the light of a single lantern, which the parson was carrying out, she saw his question. His request for her to speak her mind.

She nodded. "The morning is soon enough. It's possible a good tracker could find that rider's trail. But not in the dark."

The parson looked doubtful but nodded. He and his wife led the way out of the church, while Clint stayed right at Mariah's side.

"Good night," Clint said. "Thank you for your wisdom and being part of our wedding. God bless you." He began walking with Mariah toward her house.

"Good night, youngsters," the parson replied.

At his side, his wife called after them, "We'll be praying for you."

"We appreciate it," Mariah called back. She was sorely afraid they'd need every breath of their prayers.

Clint made his way back to her house, his arm around Mariah. He felt her tension. She was utterly silent. This was a ramshackle business to rush into a marriage like this and not give his bride any of the fine details of a proper wedding ceremony.

She even had her usual dark shirtwaist dress and black skirt on. Nell was making her a new dress, and if he'd heard the story right, it was almost done.

"We shouldn't have gotten married."

Mariah gasped and whipped her head around. "You're sorry you married me already?"

"No!" Clint jumped back, facing her. They were still outside. It was like two gunslingers meeting at . . . well, at high midnight. Or whatever time it was. "I wanted to marry you. I've wanted that for a long time. I'm just sorry the wedding was so slapdash. You could have had your friends there. We could have invited the whole town. We could have found flowers and—"

She put her hand on his mouth. Then jerked her hand back and closed it, rubbing her fingers against each other, as if touching him bothered her. Being touched by her bothered him, too. But probably not in the same way it bothered her.

"Listen, Mariah. I'm so happy to be married to you. As we walk toward your house to sp-spend the night together, well, it's all really sudden. My heart has just barely stopped pounding with fear for you and now it's started pounding with fear of the night ahead."

Mariah's eyes went wide. "I can't believe you admitted that. I was going to die before I admitted such a thing." A small smile escaped. She glanced at his . . . smile, then he leaned forward and kissed her.

"I want to be married to you, Mariah. Tonight, let's just get some sleep and leave . . . married things for another time. I'll even sleep on the floor downstairs in front of the fire."

Mariah looked at him. She was beautiful. Washed in moonlight. Fear and humor in her eyes. Her dark blond hair reflected the blue of a bright night.

"You're the most beautiful woman I've ever seen. I'll thank God every day of my life that you married me."

"I sincerely hope that's true. I'm bound to test your patience on occasion."

"As I will yours," he said.

"Let's go to your place and get your nightshirt."

He shook his head. "I'll take my boots off but sleep in my clothes. I think the floor by the fireplace will suit me. We need to do some serious talking before we share a bed. I want you to know you won't test my patience. I'm determined to know you well enough that you can abandon those worries."

Mariah nodded, reached her hand out for his, and they turned to walk on to her house. She didn't tell him, but the words he'd spoken were deeply true—she did worry about those things. She did expect him to regret marrying her and grow impatient with her.

It didn't matter because she'd made her vows and she intended to keep them. But she didn't expect everything to go as smooth as hammered iron.

Just as she reached the steps leading up to her front door, a sudden blur of motion and noise stopped her.

"Brutus is back. Oh, thank heavens." Then she heard him whine and she smelled blood.

"Get inside, Mariah. Turn the lamps up. He's hurt." Clint swept the big dog up in his arms. Mariah barely stayed ahead of them.

She turned up every lantern in the kitchen. Clint knelt beside her kitchen table and set Brutus on the floor.

"Oh, Brutus!" His black-and-gray-mottled fur was soaked in blood. Too much blood.

"Go find some bandages, scissors, a basin of water," Clint said. "And needle and thread—he's in need of stitches."

Mariah was running before he finished his list.

The next hour was spent in a hard, fast fight for Brutus's life.

"This crease here is a bullet wound. And these two are knife wounds." Clint had a steady hand.

"I've tended a few animals at the stables if you need help."

Clint looked up from the needle he was threading. He smiled, and the intelligence and determination shone in his eyes. "You're helping so much, I hardly have to think of what I need and you have it at hand for me."

Mariah ran her hand gently over the dog's head. He'd lain calmly while Clint snipped away fur, cleaned the wounds, then stitched them closed. When she got her hands close enough, the dog's pink tongue reached out to lick her hand.

"So many dogs wouldn't have put up with this. Did Becky teach him?" Clint went back to stitching. "This one is the deepest. I don't think the muscle is cut, but maybe the doctor should come take a look."

"We've both stitched up hurt animals before. I don't think the doctor would do anything different from what you're doing. But we can take Brutus to see Doc in the morning, that is, if we change our minds about needing his help."

Clint nodded and worked on. When he was done, Mariah took away the basin and tossed the blood-tinged water out her back door. The door that currently stood unlocked, which worried her. But she'd tossed out multiple basins of water and she wasn't going to relock the door every time.

She came back to Brutus's side and gathered up the cloths Clint had used to bathe the wounds. Clint was wrapping Brutus's shoulder with a white bandage. The dog had a cut on his cheek, shallow and short. Another on one of his legs.

"I wonder what went on out there?" Clint muttered as he fastened the one bandage.

Mariah wasn't sure how best to bandage a dog's face, and his leg probably wasn't serious enough to need a bandage.

"Who's the best tracker in town?" Mariah asked.

Clint was silent as he finished bandaging and leaned back, sitting on his haunches. "I've heard Becky's got a good tracker at her place. Her new foreman."

"Nate Paxton. I've met him. Becky thinks he's doing good work. I need to let Becky know about Brutus anyway. I can ride out there to tell her and ask Nate if he'll help."

"Not you, Mariah. Maybe the sheriff can ride out for him. You're not wandering around in the countryside alone."

Mariah nodded. It occurred to her to object to his orders, but she completely agreed so it would be a waste of time for them both. And Mariah was suddenly so exhausted, she wasn't sure if she could climb the stairs to bed.

"It's time for bed." Clint stood, worrying about the dog and those bandages and the wounds and Mariah . . . oh, and he needed to pray for forgiveness for not letting the Lord carry his burdens.

"You don't have to sleep on the floor, Clint." Mariah's kind voice sent his spirits soaring.

"Well, if you're sure, that would be—"

"You can sleep in Pa's bedroom. It's down here, I'm upstairs. He's got the biggest room in the house. You don't need to sleep on the floor in a house with three bedrooms."

Taking all his courage in both hands, he said, "Will that be our room then?"

One minute she was holding his hand, the next she was crushing his hand. The woman was strong.

He wrenched his hand free before he lost the ability to stir batter and break eggs.

"I'm sorry. I didn't mean to hurt you. I guess I don't know my own strength." She covered her mouth with both hands and looked . . . well, wide-eyed, almost frightened. Like she was scared she'd really hurt him.

Now *he* was a weakling. Not the impression he wanted to make on his new wife.

"I just wasn't expecting us to talk right now of . . . of future sleeping arrangements."

Oh. That would probably make a woman's hand clench tight. "We'll decide all of that tomorrow," he assured her. "Tonight we get some rest."

She nodded and took one step to probably run upstairs and shut her door firmly.

He caught her upper arm very gently, and she turned back.

"I think between a husband and wife, even a husband and wife who aren't quite ready for all the intimacies of marriage . . ." In the lantern light he saw her blush. He wondered if he wasn't blushing himself. He cleared his throat and went on. "A kiss might be the proper way to say good-night."

A sweet smile bloomed on her face. "That would be nice."

Words to warm a husband's heart. He leaned close. She came to meet him. He was about four inches taller than she was, and she wasn't a small woman. Their lips met with absolute perfection.

The kiss caught fire. He tilted his head and pulled her fully into his arms. He felt the warmth of her arms as she wrapped them around his neck.

"Mariah," he said during tiny breaks from the kiss, "I'm so glad we're married."

He wanted her to say the same back to him, but instead she clung tighter to him and let the kiss go on. By the time they finally broke off the kiss, it took all his willpower not to try to lure her into the bed he'd been assigned.

But he didn't want their wedding night to follow the fear of the intruder and the suddenness of their decision to marry—and Brutus's wounds, and her exhaustion. Privately he admitted he was tired, too. And he'd like them to spend their first truly married night when none of those things might interfere with their being fully united.

"Good night, beautiful Mariah. Thank you for marrying me."

She rested one pretty, callused hand on his cheek, and smiled up at him. "You are very welcome." She kissed him one more time, quickly, which was wise of her. Then she headed for the stairs.

He looked down at Brutus. The dog had stopped lying flat and had gotten into a more normal position, legs folded under him.

"We're quite a pair, aren't we, boy?" Clint crouched low, hoisted the dog, and carried him into his bedroom.

Then, with a barely functioning brain, he went to the kitchen. Mariah had locked the back door. He checked the front and found it locked, too. He turned down three of the four lanterns Mariah had brought into the kitchen. He took the other with him to his bedroom. He was determined it would not forever be known as *Pa's room*.

The room was clean. He smelled the fresh air and sunshine. He knew Becky and Nell had spent time in here when Mariah was recovering at Doc's, packing up but not discarding Pa's and Theo's things. They'd stripped and washed all the bedding. They'd kept the dust down. They didn't want Mariah to be faced with the task when she got home. She also would be allowed to decide what she wanted to keep.

Clint shucked his boots. Removed his gun belt and set it on the table beside him. Emptied his pockets, which didn't contain much, then lay down on the tidy bed in his clothes on top of the blankets. Sleeping in Joe Stover's bed felt wrong.

He tried to shake off the strangeness of it, and it helped when he heard Mariah moving around upstairs, most likely getting her nightgown back on and going to bed.

It was good that he was downstairs, close to any doors that someone might slip through uninvited.

Joe's room was fairly large. Clint wondered what Mariah's

room was like and how long it would take him to talk her into sleeping down here with him.

Brutus rose painfully to his feet, then sniffed around the room, probably looking for rattlesnakes and would-be killers. Or maybe crumbs on the floor. The dog limped out into the hallway that separated Joe's room from the kitchen and lay back down at the base of the stairs, midway between the front and back doors. Protecting everything at once. He rested his chin on his forelegs. Poor, battered, heroic dog. Soon he was snoring quietly. If Brutus thought it was safe enough to sleep, that was good enough for Clint. Of course, the dog might be well beyond exhaustion.

The snoring was soothing, though. Clint took a moment to marvel at the fact that he was now a married man.

He fell asleep with a smile on his face, and with thanks to God in his heart.

22

A fist hammering on the front door jerked Mariah out of a sound sleep. She sat up in bed.

She heard footsteps downstairs, inside, and almost screamed. The intruder was back. She sat there, terrified.

Only there were two intruders. The door knocker, which was an odd kind of intruder, and whoever was in her house being noisy as all get-out.

"Mariah, you get down here and open this door."

Nell. Mariah flopped back flat on the bed.

The sun was barely lightening the eastern sky. Still, it was time to get up and it appeared she had company.

"Hi, Nell."

Clint! The morning fog, laced with terror, cleared. Mariah leapt out of bed and began yanking on her clothes.

"So it's true? You two got married last night?"

Nell was inside the house with Clint. Mariah quick pulled her skirt on and then the shirtwaist—her wedding dress, for Pete's sake. She rushed downstairs barefoot.

Nell's mouth gaped at the sight of her.

Mariah knew that appearing so clearly just out of bed, in front of Clint, had shocked Nell to the marrow of her bones.

"Yes, it's true," she said. "Clint proposed earlier yesterday. I went home to pray about it. Later, Brutus woke me up barking at an intruder in the kitchen in the middle of the night."

Nell's eyes darted to Clint.

"No, no, not him. Good grief, Nell. Clint heard the dog barking and came running. The trespasser's horse was galloping away from the back of the house while Clint was banging on the front door. Not unlike you did this morning."

Mariah glanced at Brutus, who was panting at Clint's side. She rushed to him and dropped to her knees. "Brutus went after the man who broke in and he was hurt. We think he was both shot and stabbed." Mariah began inspecting the bandages and the stitches Clint sewed. "Poor Brutus had three cuts that needed stitching up."

Nell's mouth closed finally, but then her jaw dropped and she had to drag her mouth shut again. The woman was looking for all the world like a landed trout.

"Mariah, I think with Brutus here, and Nell," Clint said, sounding somewhat skeptical about them both, "I can go home, do the milking, and get back here in time to start breakfast at the diner. Finish dressing while you tell her about last night, then come on over and eat something."

He rushed back to his bedroom and came out with his boots on a couple of minutes later. He dodged around Nell, who hadn't managed to say a word the whole time.

Brutus limped after Clint. Clint noticed, then jabbed one finger at Mariah and said, "Stay."

Mariah was pretty sure he was talking to the dog. That was what kept her from wringing her brand-new husband's neck. "Come upstairs, Nell. Brutus, stay." She didn't want the injured dog to attempt climbing the stairs.

Nell was still gaining control of her mouth, not gaping anymore at least. Hopefully she wouldn't get control of herself for a while, so Mariah could get her story told.

Sure enough, Mariah told Nell everything while she pulled on stockings and shoes. Then she apologized for not waking Nell the night before. "I would've loved to have had you with me at the wedding."

"I'd have loved to have been there." Nell then brushed that aside with an impatient sweep of her hand. "You think it was someone from the Deadeye Gang who broke in here to try to kill you last night?"

Mariah straightened from tying her bootlaces and stared straight at Nell. "Maybe I panicked. Maybe I jumped to conclusions. But we talked over the possibilities last night, Clint and me. Neither of us could come up with anyone who'd go and break into my house. And there's no damage to the lock. I checked last night. Clint did too. My key for that door, the front door, and the smithy are both accounted for. Pa kept them hanging on a nail inside the kitchen cupboard behind a stack of plates. They weren't out where someone could have found them easily, and no copies exist."

By the time Mariah had finished recounting all that, she had her hair braided and coiled into a tight bun low on her head. She anchored it with pins that were sturdy enough to keep a woman's hair from dangling over a forge and catching fire.

Nell looked nervously around the room. "Let's go to the diner. I don't like being here."

Mariah thought Clint would be a while getting back from his homestead. And his diner was definitely locked.

"Let's make coffee here and give Clint a chance to get back." She led the way downstairs and went straight to Brutus. He was lying down again.

Nell came up and knelt beside the dog.

Mariah looked Brutus in the eye. He sat up, panting, watching her. The white bandages were in stark contrast to his dark fur.

"You think someone shot him?" Nell asked.

Mariah nodded. "Clint sewed him up." There were a dozen stitches on Brutus's jaw, six under the bandage on his leg. "The wound on his shoulder is likely from a bullet. I'm not sure how Clint decided that, but he thought it looked like it was from a gunshot. We need to find the sheriff and tell him what happened." She looked up at Nell. "Becky said her foreman is a skilled tracker. I'm going to ask him to pick up the trail of the low-down dog shooter."

Mariah was gentle as she stroked Brutus's fur. "And I need to tell Becky that Brutus got hurt. She loves this dog, and I've been wrangling in my head about trying to steal him for myself."

"She won't like that. But, considering everything, she might work with you on it."

Brutus whined and nudged Mariah's hand, and she realized she'd quit stroking. The dog was enjoying it and wanted more. He was the very picture of a big old softie.

A softie who could rip out your throat.

"Poor Lobo was probably tired of having a litter of puppies every year." Nell scratched Brutus behind his ears. "Though she seemed to like the puppies, and she likes Brutus when she isn't trying to kill him." Nell smiled at Brutus. "You're the finest dog who ever lived. You deserve steak for every meal from now on."

"He hunts his own food. It'd cost a fortune to feed him steak, and the only steak handy is at the diner—from Clint's cows. Don't give Brutus any ideas about them being food."

Nell rose from Brutus's side. "I want to see the back door." She started heading for the door.

"You're a lawman now?"

Nell stopped and looked over her shoulder. "Well, my husband was a lawman. I listened when he talked about solving crimes."

"That's right. Sorry, that was rude of me."

Nell's husband had been a lawman in a little border town between Missouri and Kansas. He'd been shot trying to stop a bank robbery. It had prompted a grieving Nell to pack up and move west with her brother.

"Don't worry about it. It was a long time ago. I like that it's something you don't think about very often anymore."

Mariah wondered if that meant Nell *did* think about it often.

"Honestly, you're holding up really well." Nell then leaned close and whispered, though it was more of a hiss, "But I can't believe you married Clint."

Mariah shrugged. "I can hardly believe it myself."

They got to the back door, locked. "The key please."

Nell studied the door while Mariah got the key and gave it to her.

Unlocking it, Nell opened the door and swung it wide. She crouched by the outside doorknob and looked. "See these scratches by the lock?"

"I do, but I'd have never noticed them if you hadn't pointed them out."

"When someone picks a lock—"

"*Picks* a lock?" Mariah interrupted. "You mean like when they go to a store and pick which one they want? Because Pa made these at the smithy."

Nodding silently, Nell stayed hunkered down and leaned ever closer as she continued her inspection. "No, I didn't mean that. Pick is, well, I guess it's a lawman word for opening a locked door without a key. It's not that easy. Few people even attempt it."

She fell silent and ran her hand over the keyhole. "This lock wasn't on the door when you moved here? It couldn't have been if your pa made it."

"No, Pa added the whole back of the house on. It was just the front room with the fireplace for cooking and a single bedroom about half the size it is now. Ma and Pa slept there. Theo and I slept on cots Pa built by the fire. He and Theo, with some help from Ma and me, added the kitchen, enlarged the bedroom down here, put in the stairs, and added the second floor and two more bedrooms."

"There are quite a few scratches here. And the fact that your pa made this lock, that means it's well-made because your pa didn't do anything poorly. So, picking the lock, opening it without the key, wouldn't have been easy. But,

Mariah, I think . . ." Nell looked up and over her shoulder, her brow furrowed with worry.

"You think what?"

"I-I . . . Mariah, whoever broke in here last night, I don't think this is the first time. There are too many scratches. This lock has been opened several times."

"So, whoever it was—let's call him 'the louse'—was in here while I was gone? Wandering around?"

"Is anything missing?"

Mariah thought of Pa's money, stashed in a hidden compartment under his mattress. She whirled away and ran for his bedroom.

She took one second to note that the bed needed to be made as she rushed around it to the side away from the door.

Pa didn't just slide money under the mattress, though. He was a little more careful than that. He fixed the wooden bed frame so it had a little hidden box that slid open, which looked like a normal part of the bed.

Mariah opened the box by pressing in a certain way Pa had rigged. It was a tricky hiding place. She reached into the box, pulled out a small bag, weighed it quickly in her hand, then tucked the bag away.

It felt like the usual amount of twenty-dollar gold pieces was in there. She knew how much he'd saved because they'd all worked hard to set money aside in case of trouble. Pa knew that being a blacksmith wasn't a job for a man past his prime. The farrier part of the business was especially hard on a man—and a woman. Mariah could attest to that fact.

Pa wanted to be able to provide for himself and have money enough if anyone couldn't work through injury.

Mariah suddenly had to fight tears. Pa was a wise man. And he was gone forever.

Brutus was standing in the bedroom doorway, watchful as ever. He must have sensed her mood. He came around the bed to where she knelt and whined quietly, then licked her cheek.

She swiped at the wet spot and then found one on the other side of her cheek, too.

She hadn't held all the tears inside.

Standing, she squared her shoulders, gave Brutus's back a gentle rub, and left the room. Nell hadn't followed her in.

Instead, Nell was still studying the lock. Finally, she rose and said, "We need to talk to the sheriff, and you need to add another lock or two to your doors. There are some simple hooks you can latch when you're inside. You can make them yourself. Web used to lock our house extra thoroughly because there'd been threats against him. It'll make you safer overnight."

Mariah impulsively hugged Nell. "Becky bringing me the dog. You with ideas for locks. Clint marrying me to protect me. I've got the best people in the world in my life." Her voice broke, the grief and tears over her pa pouring out.

Nell held on tight.

A few moments later, the crying eased and Mariah loosened her grip. Nell pulled back to look her in the eyes. "All these tears aren't because you've just realized you got married, I hope."

The last of Mariah's tears vanished and she erupted into laughter. "I really am too close to being hysterical,

I'm afraid. I don't regret marrying Clint. Maybe the haste of it, but—"

"He's a good man, Mariah. I'm happy for you."

It'd been a few years since Nell's husband, Web the sheriff, had died. For the first time, Mariah wondered why a fine, sweet-natured woman like Nell hadn't remarried. The town was full of available men, and a pretty single woman like Nell was a rare find.

But Nell rarely talked about her husband, rarely talked about her backstabbing brother, who'd abandoned her. She showed no interest in or longing for a husband.

Mariah had always liked having Nell as a friend, and the two of them, along with Becky being single, had suited Mariah. Now she had to wonder. Becky, she somewhat understood. Becky was tough and self-sufficient and sour on men because of her pa.

But Nell?

Mariah made coffee while Nell had a look at Brutus's bandages and wounds. "He's leaving them on nicely. I'm surprised."

"He was feeling poorly last night. I don't think he had the energy to do much but sleep."

Nell said, "He's not going hunting today." She went to the icebox and found a few things a dog could eat while Mariah got the coffee boiling.

By the time the dog was fed and watered, the coffee was ready. "I'll go see the sheriff and see if he'll go out and talk with Becky. I don't plan to ride anywhere alone until this trouble is settled."

"Trouble. Hmmm. Not quite the word I'd have used."

They discussed more of what had happened last night.

Nell proved to be a skilled questioner, and Mariah remembered seemingly small details that Nell said might not be important, but it was good to know everything.

Enough time finally passed that Clint would be back now. Together they walked over to the diner.

Mariah pondered the complications of her life as they entered the diner to the hiss of boiling coffee and the smell of something wonderful. Mariah wouldn't venture to guess what Clint was cooking, but she was sure it would be delicious.

Her husband's food would be delicious.

Her husband.

The idea startled her.

But it did nothing to lessen her appetite.

Quite the contrary.

23

The sheriff asked almost as many questions as Nell did. Then he rode out to Becky's place to bring her and Nate Paxton in.

Nell accompanied Mariah to the doctor with Brutus.

Because Brutus was limping badly, Mariah didn't expect a whole lot of protection from him. Instead of firing up the forge, she walked back to the diner and led Brutus to the kitchen, where he collapsed in a corner.

"How is he? What did the sheriff have to say?"

Mariah began washing dishes while Clint hurried to keep up with the rush of hungry Pine Valley residents. She talked while he cooked, and by the time she'd finished her story, Becky came barging into the kitchen.

"You two got married?"

"Yep."

Becky seemed about to say more when her eyes slid to Brutus, who'd lifted his head and whined, but hadn't gotten up.

"Poor boy." Becky rushed to his side.

"We took him to the doctor this morning. But Clint did the work on him last night, and the doctor thought it was done well."

The kitchen door swung open again, and Nate walked in. A tall guy—"rangy," Mariah would say. Skinny might describe him better. His hair seemed to be fighting to curl up tight, and he kept it very short. His eyes were as blue as the lake west of town, where it reflected the sky above the towering mountains.

He looked at Brutus and his brow furrowed. "Is it all right for me to be in here, Clint?"

Clint was busy concocting something. He filled two plates as he answered, "Sure, stay out of my way is all. These are the last, then I'll make up plates for us and we can talk." Clint rushed out.

Nate frowned. "What is that he's making?"

Mariah plucked a towel off a nail by the washbasin. "He said a word I couldn't quite understand, so he told me to call it 'French toast.' No matter 'cuz he can't cook a bad meal."

"I've had plenty of meals in here. You speak the plain truth." Then he went to fuss over Brutus until Clint came back with a stack of empty plates.

Mariah kept washing and drying while Clint went to pour more coffee. Brutus, meanwhile, reveled in all the attention.

When Clint returned with more dirty plates, he said, "This is the end of it except for a few coffee cups. Nate, I'll show you the direction I heard that horse take off last night, but I won't ride with you. The sheriff wants to go along. I don't want to leave Mariah completely alone.

213

Becky stood from where she'd crouched beside Brutus. She turned to the room with fire in her eyes. "I'll ride along with you, Nate."

"Mr. Pruitt, I'm going to have to be gone a few days. I just got word my ma is ailing, not expected to make it. She lives down in Denver." Key had wrapped his arm tight. Made sure the bandage didn't show below the end of his sleeve, and then he was getting out of here for a while. He hadn't seen his ma in fifteen years, and she wasn't a likable woman on her best day. Liked to wander, following one man or another. If she were still alive, Key would have no idea where to find her. And he wasn't going to Denver, neither. Things might still be a little tense down there.

"It's only a couple of weeks until roundup and the cattle drive. I need every hand for the job."

Key knew how to barter, especially when he didn't really care how it came out. But he liked it here with Pruitt. He had a good setup.

"I understand. I'd like to come back after I've seen Ma. If there's no work for me, I'll drift."

"I didn't say you could go." Pruitt had a mean temper, and he lurched to his feet. His face an unhealthy shade of red. Idly, Key wondered if he could say just the right word to make Pruitt so furious, it'd give him a heart attack.

Might be fun to find out, but Key didn't waste time on it now.

"I'm sorry for the misunderstanding, sir." Key was keeping it real polite. He really would like to come back. Just not enough to not leave to begin with. "I wasn't ask-

214

ing permission. I have to go. I've no choice. I expect you'll replace me if someone comes along. But I'll stop through here when I get done burying my ma. If you've a need and can see your way clear, I'd be obliged to continue working for you." Key turned on his heel and walked out before Pruitt could say something that'd make it impossible to come back.

Pruitt shouted after him, but Key made a point of not listening. He strode out the door and mounted up, favoring his left arm. He had to ride out of here before someone started asking questions. There'd be talk of the dog, no doubt found dead. And they might be able to pick up a trail, though probably not once he went into the water. Still, some men were good enough that his horse's hooves might be recognizable. And the sore arm would be a big clue.

He kicked his horse into an easy lope and headed down the trail toward Denver. His arm hurt like that dog was still dangling from it. It was swollen and so stiff, his skin had a shine to it.

It wasn't just bites, neither. His arm was torn up bad. There might be a chunk of skin missing, he wasn't sure. The bleeding had slowed and didn't drip if he kept it bandaged, yet he needed the arm sewed up if he wanted it to heal decently. Denver was too far. Even if the furor had died down about him there, he wasn't going to ride that far. He'd pass the next town south and maybe the next. He had ridden through some little cow town every twenty miles or so on his journey up here. But he'd meandered some and didn't rightly know where all he'd been.

He'd ride until he found help, though not too close.

Blame his injury on a wolf, then heal up and get back here. The Deadeye Gang had hoped for a good haul on that last holdup. They needed to strike again and soon, before the stage lines added outriders again. And the boss knew it.

And when they did strike, Key wanted his cut. And that was when Key knew right where to go. He had a friend who fed him information about gold shipments. He'd ride to see him, spend time healing, then get back in time to be such a hero that he'd have a place in the gang for life.

By the time Becky had heard the whole story and checked Brutus and consulted with Nate, they'd also eaten lunch. Clint made his coq au vin again. It was a town favorite, and he'd learned to make a really big batch. Good thing his chickens kept hatching chicks or his flock would have gotten thin.

Nate spent such a long time studying tracks around Mariah's cabin that Clint had time to finish up the noon meal and go along. So did Becky. The sheriff knew how good Nate was at tracking and offered to guard Mariah instead of following. Turned out he also knew how to do farrier work and could help shoe horses and even make the horseshoes.

Clint was no hand at following a trail left by man or beast, but even he could see what Nate was doing.

They'd ridden out a while. Becky following along behind Nate. Gesturing toward the tracks, she asked, "Have you seen this horse before, Nate?"

"Nope. And I'd recognize it if I had. A good-sized horse, tall. And a light rider. Figuring it to be a man, and

I'm only guessing about that, he's a small man riding a big, fast horse."

"The kind of horse an outlaw would ride." Becky kept her head down and her words quiet.

They'd been on the trail a while when Nate said, "Right here. Blood." He swung down from the saddle, Becky a second behind him.

Clint dismounted, but he wasn't sure what to do so he stayed back.

"Here, look." Nate pointed at the ground. "The tracks—this is Brutus running. Bleeding." His voice was tight, grim.

Becky's jaw flexed, but she didn't say a word, just followed Nate as he walked along. Clint decided to continue staying back. He held the horses and wondered if even that was any help. Then he looked down at the tracks of that good dog. The tracks running away. Smart, good dog.

Clint had a thought. "If it was just a bullet wound, that outlaw might've been a ways off. But those were knife wounds."

Becky looked up from where she'd hunkered down to study the trail. "You're sure?"

"Yes, I am sure. I know knives and bullets. Brutus had to get close to get cut."

Nate had gone on ahead while Clint talked, but Nate nodded as he walked. "Right here. The dog is right on top of the horse. Blood, a lot of it." With cool satisfaction shining in his eyes, Nate looked back. "And the dog runs off that way, for home. The vermin who tried to sneak into Mariah's house took off that way, and there's a blood trail with him, too."

"Brutus got a chunk out of him." Becky was still tense, but there was pride in it. Her dog had bought into a fight, and he hadn't left his opponent unscathed.

"Our outlaw," Nate said, "has a dog bite or two somewhere this morning. He oughta stand out in a crowd."

"We've been thinking," Clint said, "the reason these outlaws leave no witnesses—even to the extent of trying to kill a woman who can't identify them—is because they might be folks who live right beside us."

Becky's eyes narrowed. "Folks from right here in Pine Valley?"

"Well, at first I just thought they might be known men in the area. The robberies are spread out, after all. But the longer this goes on, the more I believe they could be right here in town. Someone has been in Mariah's house more than once."

Nate tugged his Stetson off his head and ran a hand through his hair. "You think Nell knows what she's talking about?"

Nell had told her story about the scratched-up keyhole. Now the three of them, standing around the tracks and blood, pondered it.

Becky answered, "Her husband was a lawman. She never talks much about him, just that she's a widow. Which now that I say it out loud, I have to wonder why she doesn't talk about him."

"Grief?" Clint figured it was that simple.

"Maybe." Nate crossed his arms. "Or maybe she's left something behind and doesn't want it brought up here."

Becky glared at him. "Nell isn't running from the law."

Nate jerked one shoulder. "I s'pect that's right. But she

might be running from something else. You're sure her husband is dead? She's not on the run from him?"

Becky froze, staring at Nate. Silence reigned for long moments. Then Becky slowly shook her head and shrugged. "I only know what she's told me. I've found her to be an honest woman, and really, not overly scared that something out there might be a danger to her. But I'll think on this and see if she'll talk about it."

Becky turned back to Clint. "To listen to her this morning, the words she used, it's clear she'd talked about clues and such before, and has some knowledge of how to investigate a crime. Almost certainly she learned these things from her husband."

"She sounded sure to me, and I wouldn't say she's a woman to act that way if she had doubts. She'd say right up front if she was just guessing."

"There are plenty of places to hide out in the Wind River Mountains." Becky had been here longer than any of them. "But if someone is coming into town at night, sneaking around, well, that's a lot of work. But it's possible. Still, if whoever killed Joe Stover and Theo and all the others on that stagecoach was someone we knew, it'd stand to reason they wouldn't want witnesses."

"Yep, and that's mighty mean," Nate said. "Most robbers aren't cold-blooded killers like this. They might fire their guns. They might not care if someone gets killed in their robberies, and that's bad enough. But they don't usually kill every witness, never leaving a single one alive. It's even worse that they'd try their best to kill a woman. Not many men who'd do that. They might just be ruthless, vicious killers, but there might be more to it than that. They don't want a witness for a very good reason."

"This was the first robbery in over a year. The U.S. Marshals were combing the area. The stagecoaches ran with outriders. Everyone thought the gang had moved on or disbanded. We let down our guard."

"And the outlaws are close enough to town to know that."

"Whoever it is has been able to get to town more than once." Becky looked back at the trail toward town. Thinking, trying to add it all up. "To my knowledge, there's no robbers' hideout around here, so whoever got into Mariah's house last night has to be close by."

"I don't like that we've left her behind in town." Clint's wife. His very own God-approved wife. And he'd ridden off and left her with killers after her.

"She's with the sheriff, Clint." Becky rolled her eyes. "He'll protect her."

"Probably better'n you," Nate added with a grin.

"He's a tougher man than I am." Clint turned toward his horse, done with this search. They'd finish it on their own. "Better able to stand watch. Faster with a gun and a fist. All true. But the sheriff won't care as much as I do. And that makes a man stand fast even when there seems to be nothing to fight against."

Becky rested one strong, sun-browned hand on his arm, and he turned back. "You care about her, don't you?"

"Of course I do. I married her."

"No, a man might marry a woman for many reasons. There's no 'of course' about it. I figured you both panicked last night, and you jumped in to save her life by marrying her."

"I've been . . ." Clint stopped and glared at Becky. He shouldn't be telling her this. "I've been interested in Mariah since the first day I saw her walking the streets of Pine Valley. Before I'd even opened my diner."

"That's two years ago. Why didn't you court her until now?"

Clint jerked one shoulder sheepishly. "Because I was penniless. Because I wanted to come to her with something to offer. I needed time to build a house, and when homesteading proved to be a miserable way for a man of my skills to earn a living, I started the diner and poured every minute of my life and every penny I made and every ounce of my strength into getting my homestead and my diner up and running. Things looked good since last fall, but then winter hit, and life was rugged running the farm and the diner. And . . . and, well, um . . . I've been working up the nerve since spring. She never gave me one speck of encouragement, so I was afraid of how she'd respond."

Clint leaned close to Becky, who leaned in close to him. He whispered, "And her pa was kinda scary."

Becky straightened, then started laughing. Nate chuckled, then laughed loud. Clint felt his cheeks heat up, but he couldn't help but smile. Soon he was laughing along with them.

"I knew Joe Stover just a little," Nate said. "He was a tough man."

"He'd've probably put you to the test." Becky giggled and then clapped her hands over her mouth.

Nate turned to look at her, his eyes wide with surprise.

Clint said, "I've never heard that noise come out of you before."

Becky got her giggles under control. "It's the bane of my existence. Makes me sound like a ten-year-old girl."

"I'm going back to town." Clint turned and headed for his horse.

"We'll follow this trail wherever it leads."

Clint swung up on horseback and saw Becky look at Nate.

Nate said, "Yep. We'll see what we can find. You go look after your woman."

Clint left them to it. He wondered if Mariah had ever heard Becky giggle. But he wouldn't tell. He didn't want Becky mad at him.

24

Mariah banged on a thin sheet of iron with a precision she rarely used. A lot of blacksmithing was raging fire and brute force, but it could be so much more.

She'd watched Pa do the fine work when he'd made the locks on their house. Small pieces, carefully and finely made. Making the key took the same delicate work. And getting the key to fit the lock, two different keys front and back, had been the work of a master artisan, though Pa refused to admit as much when Ma had made a fuss over the detailing.

Mariah had watched him work on that lock and on other things. And she'd tried her hand with it to the point Pa, feeling like the delicate work was more suited to Mariah than the heavy forging of iron, had let her learn it.

She hadn't done it much. Pa admired a well-made lock and occasionally needed other such fine work, but he had little use for decorative work. She'd once spent far too long making iron leaves to adorn a fireplace poker as a gift for Ma.

She'd crafted steel toes for boots, then etched that metalwork with a chisel to adorn a pair of boots for herself.

Pa had scoffed at the waste of time, but later admitted she'd done a fine job of it.

She'd spent time earlier today collaborating with Nell to fashion latch locks that would be hard to break through. She made a pair for each door, and she'd install the hook of one with an end that curved up, and the hook of another with an end that curved down. Then install them so close together that no one could reach through with a knife or any other tool to lift or lower the latches.

Nell had some excellent ideas to thwart a break-in, and Mariah wondered again about Nell's husband and how much danger he'd lived with and brought home to Nell. And why she rarely talked about her days before Pine Valley.

She'd spend the evening installing the locks, but right now she was making fancy spurs. She'd also suggested to Nell a way to make elaborate metal eyelets for chaps. Nell agreed to let her work on one pair of chaps, then see if Nell could coax more money out of her cowboy customers if that detail would be added.

Mariah could create elaborate belt buckles, too. She needed to make notes and figure out all the ways she could have more fun with her blacksmithing.

Business wasn't always hectic, and when she had time, she loved turning her attention to beautiful metalwork. Now, without Pa to scold her, she could work on details. So she was indulging in making these beautiful spurs. She'd hang them up on her wall alongside the wheels and buckets and see if they'd sell.

She especially loved using her etching tools to carve lines and curves into iron. It was beautiful when it was well done, and Mariah believed hers were well done.

When there was no work, Pa had always pushed ahead with practical items. Hinges. Nails. Buckets. Wheels. Horseshoes. Angle iron. They all sold well and sometimes quickly enough that they were glad to be ahead.

She had killers after her. Probably.

She had poor Brutus to care for. She straightened from her work and saw him snoring quietly by the front door.

She had the sheriff watching over her. He was a decent hand at basic blacksmith work. He'd shod two horses and patched three metal items, two pails and a basin that looked like a horse had stepped on it.

He'd also done the heavy work of making the iron ring that wrapped around a wheel. She'd had two done up, finished but for adding the iron rim, but wrapping the wheel in iron took all her strength. It and farrier work were by far the jobs where she most missed Pa and Theo. She hadn't given them enough credit for the backbreaking labor of those heavier jobs.

And she was married.

Killers, dog, sheriff, husband.

Honestly, she worked a little faster to forget the madness all around her.

Not that she counted marrying Clint as madness. She really was sure it had been the right decision. But the suddenness of it qualified as madness. So she decided madness described her life pretty well and turned back to chiseling a curlicue into a finely wrought pair of spurs.

Pa would have nagged her to make more nails.

She missed him like she'd've missed an arm. And Theo. A quiet man. Hardworking. He had an easy partnership with Pa. Mariah had teased him about taking a wife. She'd even hinted that he should try courting Nell or Becky.

Theo refused to even discuss it.

She loved them both fiercely and fought tears, which still seemed to spring out at her instantly when some little thing would remind her of them.

She wondered if what she felt for Clint would ever grow into something that strong. It would be different, of course. But love had its own power, and she welcomed it into her life . . . if it would just come.

"Miss Mariah, I think it's time we finished up today. You said you wanted to work on putting those locks in." The sheriff set a finished basin aside. Its hole, punctured by a misplaced hoof, was neatly patched and back to its original shape.

She'd just finished the second spur and was willing to straighten away from her work. "You've done fine work here today, Sheriff Mast. I sincerely thank you for the help. You'll get the money I'm paid for those pails and the shod horses. And that wheel you finished, well, I'd've been hard-pressed to do it as well as you did. I've been paying Willie when he's here working, and the same will go for you."

The sheriff waved her offer aside. "I've enjoyed it." He looked at the ironclad wheel with some satisfaction. "I'm protecting you and earning a sheriff's salary while I do it. I won't take a cent. It wouldn't be right. Willie's different. He's only part-time."

"I'll at least pay you for the shod horses, Sheriff. That was all your work."

"They were your horseshoes. So, if you take out their value, I'll take what you're paid for them. That is, if you're sure it won't hurt you for money. Your pa would be mighty upset with me if you went without while I earned pay from two jobs at once."

"Pa would sincerely thank you. And I thank you, too."

"I'll walk you over to your house and get you and Brutus inside. I'll make sure no one is in there, but I won't stay in with you. I'll sit out on the front stoop while I wait for Clint to come back."

Clint had come in and checked on her, reported the findings of the trail, then gone out to do his work at the homestead.

They walked the few yards from the smithy to her house. The sheriff let her unlock the door. He drew his gun, aimed it in the air, and stepped inside. Mariah followed him in. She hadn't been worried much about this until he drew his gun.

Brutus was at her side, but the poor guy had mainly slept all day. She'd fed him well, Clint had brought scraps over and two meaty bones, and she'd given him lots of water. She really didn't know how else to speed his healing.

The sheriff moved to the back of the house. "Back door is locked. I'm going to check the upstairs."

Mariah put some coffee on. Not sure how late Clint would be and wanting to make the sheriff comfortable and to have something to offer Clint when he got here. They'd yet to cook a meal together. She wondered how that went when your husband could cook so much better than you.

Mariah got out her locks and proceeded to the back door to attach them.

She had a second pair for the front door and other pairs for her windows. No one was going to be able to slip quietly into her house. Not ever again. Break a window, of course, but there was nothing quiet about that.

Mariah had just begun working with her wood drill to attach the first hook when she heard hooves pounding into town from the south, the direction the rider had gone last night. The direction Becky and Nate had gone hours ago.

The sheriff came downstairs fast. "I saw them riding in. It's Becky and Nate. I thought they'd never get back."

It crossed Mariah's mind that she hadn't worried about them. But maybe the sheriff had. Maybe she figured her tough friend was unstoppable. But if they were chasing after someone who'd never left a witness, then it was a dangerous man.

Her stomach twisting at the thought, she set her tools aside and hurried to the front door a pace behind the sheriff.

Becky swung down from her beautiful palomino stallion. A sturdy, fast horse that Becky favored over all her others and whose beauty was legendary around Pine Valley.

Nate rode a black thoroughbred stallion. He'd ridden in on it. Though working as Becky's foreman, he switched between all her horses to keep them well exercised.

Still, Nate preferred his own horse, and he could usually be found riding it when he came to town.

Becky said Nate was letting her use the powerful animal to breed her mares—for a modest stud fee. Becky paid it willingly. She took pride in her horse-training skills and sold her horses for a top price. She had the palomino and a couple of other thoroughbred stallions that she crossbred with tough mountain-bred mustangs to get a strong, fast horse. But she often spoke of anticipating the first foals to be born from Nate's stallion.

Now they both tied up their horses to the hitching post in front of Mariah's house and came in, their spurs clinking.

"Come in and sit down. I want to hear what you found." Mariah was talking over the sheriff's shoulder. "You come back in too, Sheriff. I've got coffee on. I'll get you a cup. Becky, Nate, have you eaten since you got to town?" They'd left after the noon meal. Now it was suppertime.

"Have you got eggs and toast?" Becky smiled. Their favorite meal.

"I don't. Honestly, I need to see what I do have. Whatever it is, you're welcome to join me."

"That would be appreciated, Miss Mariah," the sheriff said. "My wife has learned hard lessons about when I'll get home and doesn't worry overly. She knows I've been staying close to you today. And I want to hear what you two found."

"We didn't find much on that trail." Becky jerked her gloves off and tucked them behind the buckle of her belt. She went to Brutus and knelt beside him, frowning.

Mariah could make her a much prettier buckle. "Come into the kitchen and talk while I cook."

She hadn't gotten a single cupboard open when Clint came walking in with a good-sized pot of chicken stew and a plate covered with a checkered cloth. She hoped it was his biscuits.

⁓

"Have you told them what you found? Where did you go after I left? I want to hear everything."

Clint had intended for Mariah to come to his house tonight. He'd left food on the stove in the diner, on very low heat after the noon meal. When he saw Becky and Nate's horses over here, he'd grabbed the stew and come running.

"We haven't talked yet. We just got here." Mariah opened a cupboard and pulled out plates. Becky got utensils. Nate drew up chairs. Five of them.

Clint had been told Mariah had five because her family of three often invited Nell and Becky over for a meal.

That was perfect for this rather grim gathering of people talking about home-invading murderers.

They were seated and eating within minutes.

Becky repeated what Clint, Mariah, and probably the sheriff already knew, then started with what happened after Clint left.

"We followed the trail to the stream that runs to the north of my property." She glanced at Nate to see what he had to add.

Nodding, he said, "We could tell he went into the water because he was still bleeding, and there was enough of a trail, I know he went toward the east."

"That stream is one my cattle water out of, but it's a long stretch from my house. He could easily have walked that stream in the night without anyone noticing."

Nate went on. "We rode upstream for miles. I was sure hoping I could tell where he got out of the water, but there are too many stretches of pure rock. It's why we're so late. I scouted both sides of the stream, followed stone until it turned into a trail with enough dirt to leave a hoofprint. I just rode all over it. Becky too. And she's as good a tracker as I am."

"I'm not. But I'm mighty good." Becky scooped up some chicken. "This is tasty, Clint. You're a fine cook."

Clint didn't respond to that. "You couldn't find him and track him?"

Nate chewed with glum disappointment. "Nope. And I like to think I'm real good at it. So, this man knew what he was doing. He picked his spot to leave the water with a lot of skill."

"Just like he broke into my house with a lot of skill." Mariah hadn't said much, just listened and ate. Frowning over all she'd heard.

The sheriff said, "But you know he went upstream. Not much up there."

Nate added, "I think he went in the wrong direction on purpose so as not to lead us to wherever he'd hiding out or living. If you're thinking that Deadeye Gang never leaves witnesses because it's someone we know, then he might've ridden a long way before circling back and just coming right on into town. He could be right next door to you, Mariah. Right here in our midst."

Clint had a fight on his hands not to go door to door, shaking people until they confessed.

Yet that'd be useless and bad for business. Both his and Mariah's.

"It's worth remembering our housebreaker had teeth sunk into his body somewhere." Becky looked down at Brutus, who noticed and came over to whine a little. She reached down and stroked the dog's black-and-gray fur.

Becky acted mighty tough, but she had a soft side

too, and Brutus was bringing it out of her. "How is he? I was afraid he'd chew the bandage off and bother at the stitches."

"He's been quiet all day, resting. I was glad he wasn't called on to do anything too exciting."

"I had a nice collection of scraps from the diner for him." Clint smiled at the dog. "He didn't have to hunt his food today."

Clint sat at Mariah's rectangular table right beside his wife. So close their shoulders touched. Becky was next to Mariah at what might be called the head of the table. Nate around the corner from her, straight across from Mariah and Clint. He was on the side of the table with the wall at his back. The table had been pushed up against the wall when they'd decided to have five people for supper.

The sheriff sat at the other head of the table. Clint figured they had two heads here and no feet.

Brutus was sitting on his haunches between Mariah and Becky, being fussed over. "You might've picked up those tracks today, Nate. But Brutus catching the varmint and biting him is the reason we can be sure you have the right man."

"More than that," Nate added. "Because Brutus helped us be sure we followed the right tracks, I'll know the horse's marks if I ever see them again."

Nate looked at Becky. "You too?"

"I might not be as confident as you, but I think so. The horse had a long stride, and the rider had him stretched out galloping for a long time. Like a man might who was running from a pack of wolves." Becky stroked Brutus's head again gently.

"Yep, had to be a tall horse but not all that heavy. I'd say a skinny rider on its back. You'd recognize the tracks." Nate sounded real proud of his boss and real sure of himself.

"I had a look at the tracks, but I'm not good enough to identify the rider from them."

"Clint had me look at the trail, too." The sheriff finished eating with a contented sigh. "I might not know the horse, but I'll know what sort of horse and rider to watch for. Enough to eliminate a lot of men. And we can all be on the lookout for a man who's wounded. Any sign of someone who is nursing a dog bite."

Brutus yawned as he sat between his women, as if tired after a good day's work.

They talked over what to do to keep Mariah safe as they finished their meal.

"Mariah, do you want to go out to my place? We've still got the light, and I think it'd be safer out there than in town. Brutus would warn us if anyone tried to get in, but it'll be a while before he's at full strength."

"Is there any reason I need to stay here, to guard it in case whoever broke in last night comes back?"

"I-I think . . . that is, I'm afraid the only goal last night might've been t-to harm you." It turned Clint's stomach to admit that. "If you've got valuables here, fetch them and bring them along."

"Pa's, uh, coin purse is here."

He wondered why she'd hesitated over the words *coin purse* but didn't ask.

"Bring anything you think best."

It was still full light outside. They could walk to his

place, which was only about a hundred yards out of town, and get settled in, even walk along slowly enough to let Brutus set a slow pace for himself.

Mariah looked around the kitchen, then turned to Clint. "I think getting out of here is a good idea. Living in here, without Pa and Theo, hurts my heart. Add in someone tried to sneak in here, maybe with the intent of murder."

Clint nodded. "Both good reasons to get away."

"Let's go out to your place. I'll take a change of clothes, just enough to spend the night there. And I guess I'd better take Pa's money—my money now, I reckon. We don't have to load everything up tonight."

"I need to get back to the Idee." Becky rose from the table and picked up two plates. "Mariah, you gather what you need. I'll wash the dishes. Nate and I are on horseback, so we can pack along anything heavy you want to take. We'll help get a few things moved."

"Thank you."

The sheriff stood. "I'll wait outside, keep an eye out. Then I'll walk with you out to Clint's. I can saddle up my horse, even my wagon, and carry a load of things if need be."

"Not tonight." Mariah sounded exhausted. "We can leave what's here till later."

The sheriff looked at the dog. "Brutus, come on out and keep me company."

Brutus went along, limping a little but calm enough. He acted as if he and the sheriff were old friends.

Clint picked up plates and headed for the sink, along with Becky.

Becky shooed him off with a flick of her fingers. "Go

help Mariah pack a few things. Nate, you too. I've got the dishes."

Clint liked to run a kitchen himself, but Becky looked fierce, and it was only washing up that needed done. He followed Mariah into her pa's bedroom. Giving himself a mental shake, he thought, *No, my bedroom.* Then he caught himself again. *No, our bedroom.* And then he thought of his one- bedroom cabin. He'd escaped sleeping on the floor last night, but tonight might be a different story.

25

Mariah was reluctant to take Pa's money out in front of Clint and Nate. No, *her money* out in front of Clint and Nate. Both men had followed her in as if she were going to disassemble the bed and ask them to carry it over to Clint's house.

She had to shake off the misgivings she felt. She trusted Clint. She'd better, as he was her new husband. Nate, well, she didn't know him that well, but then Pa's hiding place was a secret that would no longer matter since she was taking the money with her and it would probably never be hidden there again.

She was leaving her home, after all.

"I just realized we own three homes, Clint, if you count the room over the diner." Mariah forced herself to dig out Pa's—her—money. *Hers. Hers. Hers.* It broke her heart to think of it.

Pulling out the small, bulging bag of twenty-dollar gold pieces, she shook her head. "We scrimped and saved for this. Pa had considered the money saved for his old age if the day came he could no longer work. Or if the day came we had to pay someone to work at the smithy. He wanted to be ahead in case of trouble. We have for a fact found trouble, but it's nothing this money can solve. It hurts to claim it and take it away with me."

She thrust the money at Clint. He caught the heavy bag and must have heard the clink of coins. Without comment, he slid the bag into his pocket.

He probably trusted Nate completely too, but he sure as certain wasn't flashing it around. She found that she respected his common sense.

"Anything else in here going with you?" Clint asked.

Mariah shook her head. "Is there anything you want? You were in the kitchen. Do you have enough plates and forks and such out at your place?"

"I could use one more chair. I built only one. Mine is sturdy but not as finely made as yours. Your table is much better than mine, too. In fact, take all you want, Mariah. You should have your things around you. For now, we can take one extra chair for tonight and get more tomorrow."

She nodded and said, "We probably won't even sit out at your place. You come into town to cook and eat at the diner yourself, don't you?"

"I'll often bring something for supper and sit at the table. Besides that, I use the table to work on. But I haven't slept out there since you were hurt in the robbery. We wouldn't really need another chair until tomorrow night. I'll bring my wagon to town tomorrow, and we can haul whatever we want home."

"I've still got a few things upstairs I need to take now. I'll go get them. You don't need to come with me." Mariah grabbed her satchel and headed for the stairway.

In truth, she had three satchels—she'd gotten Pa's and Theo's back. The robbers had apparently dug through them but there were no valuables to steal. They'd taken the few coins Pa and Theo had in their pockets, and the rest of the satchels' contents were left behind and strewn about the place. All of it had been returned to Mariah's house while she was still unconscious.

After packing a nightgown, a clean riding skirt and shirtwaist, a few underpinnings, extra hairpins, a comb, and a few other things she'd need overnight, she was done. She hesitated to leave. She looked around the room, her home for a long time. She barely remembered their home back in Iowa. Her throat felt full of unwept sobs. Her eyes burned with unshed tears. This was no longer her home now, even though she owned it. It was almost certain that she'd never live here again.

All the memories of Ma that had become like old friends were in this house. Now she'd walk away from that, along with leaving behind the still-raw memories of Pa and Theo.

Swallowing hard, she swiped her wrist across her eyes in case a few tears had escaped, then squared her shoulders, lifted her chin and her satchel, and headed back downstairs.

Clint was holding a cloth bag. From the scratchy clanking and the shape of the bulges, she thought he'd taken a few kitchen utensils. "I'll leave my pan and the plate I brought. We can stop here in the morning. They belong in the diner."

Mariah went into the kitchen and opened the cupboard where the house keys were hidden—one for the front door, another for the back. Then she picked up the bag of hook-and-eye locks she'd made for the house but not yet installed. She might use them out at Clint's place in case a would-be murderer decided she still needed killing.

She returned to Clint's side. "I can't think of anything else."

"We'll get more tomorrow." Clint held the large bag, with the small cash bag of Pa's money—no, *her* money . . . honestly now, *their* money—in his pocket. "This is hard for you, Mariah, leaving this house. How about we hang on to it, and you can use the house however you wish?"

Which gave her another thought. "Or I could sell it. I wonder what a house would be worth?"

They left the house as she said those words.

The sheriff, who'd been sitting on the front steps with Brutus, rose when they came out. Brutus lumbered over to greet her, panting.

The sheriff said, "I know the Wainwright brothers are crowded upstairs of the general store. They've got the money to build, and they've talked about hiring someone to put up a house for them, but they've never found the time. Maybe the two of them would like to buy your house."

Nodding, Mariah said, "Maybe. Let me think about it."

She walked away from the house. In pain from missing Pa and Theo. Hurting because she was leaving her home. Slightly sickened to think of someone breaking in. She was heartbroken to be going at the same time she was glad to be leaving it all behind. A mixed-up woman for a fact.

She had a sudden fierce desire to sell it. She couldn't imagine ever spending another night in that house. But now wasn't the time to make that decision. She wanted to let some of the pain ebb before she turned the house over to someone else. And she needed to talk it all over with Clint.

She noticed that Becky had Brutus draped over her saddle. She petted the wounded critter as though he were a long-lost friend. Mariah was never going to be able to talk Becky out of that dog.

Nate had a single chair on his lap. A little awkward but he seemed to be managing just fine.

They rounded a wooded stretch until soon they were mostly there. Clint's house was small. A bit nicer than the usual homestead but not by much. He had a log barn that was much bigger than most. It was new enough that the logs weren't fully weathered yet. There were several smaller sheds with well-built pens around those sheds.

She heard a cow mooing from the barn, and chickens clucking from the coop. Other animal sounds created a ruckus, and a woolly sheep came charging to the fence with others hard behind her.

Clint was beside Mariah on her left. He had the bag in his right hand, but he shifted it to his left, then hooked his arm through hers. They walked on, arm in arm, toward Clint's house.

"They know you're home," she said.

"Yep, I usually get a fine welcome. The cow, though, she's just fussing because she needs to be milked."

"You come out here every day?"

"Twice a day when I sleep in town. Gotta milk morning and night."

Becky and Nate had ridden ahead. They dismounted,

and Becky gently lowered Brutus to the ground. Nate set the chair by Clint's front door.

"It's unlocked," Clint called out. "Go on in. Get Brutus settled." He waved them on. They'd shown good manners not to barge into someone else's home, but Clint didn't mind them going in.

Nate opened the door and went inside, carrying the chair. Becky followed more slowly, with Brutus limping beside her.

"You tend all these animals and your garden, too. You do all of this while living in town to watch over me." She squeezed his arm. "Thank you, Clint."

Mariah had seen Clint's house from afar plenty of times. From Nell's upstairs room she could see it because it was just outside of town. From her own place there was a cluster of trees that blocked the view.

"Your animals live nicer than you." She heard those words come out of her mouth and almost bit her tongue. Glancing at him nervously, she said, "I don't mean to criticize your house. It's a fine house."

He smiled at her. "I've got a lot of animals. Chickens and ducks, geese and turkeys. The turkeys were hard to find but raising them is a lot faster than hunting them. I've got sheep, cows, pigs. I've been gathering animals anywhere I can find them from the moment I got here. My chicken flock is doing well, and it had better keep growing. I get enough eggs to run the diner from them. And I hatch out chicks as often as I can. I make a lot of chicken dishes."

She could agree with that, and they were all delicious.

"And the big garden behind the house is at its peak right now. I've planted fruit trees but they're a few years from yielding yet. But the Wainwrights provide apples for me and canned fruit, lots of other things as well. The house hasn't been a priority, but now, as a married man . . ." He slid his hand off her arm to take her hand. "I need to get busy adding on. We'll get it all done, Mariah. I promise you."

"I can't believe how much you've gotten done in just two years. But that's the West. Always building. We added a lot on our house since coming here. I know a little about building and I can help with the chores and tend the garden. We had a garden, though I haven't given it a thought since the stagecoach robbery. There are probably some vegetables out there. I'll have a look tomorrow."

Becky had left the door open.

Clint and Mariah approached the house, still holding hands, Clint lagging enough behind to let her go in first. The sheriff bought up the rear.

They met Becky and Nate coming out.

Becky glanced at their connected hands but didn't mention that. Instead, she said, "I left a lot undone out at the ranch. I've got good hands and I'm sure they've kept up, but there is work for two more, Nate and me. We need to get going."

Mariah let go of Clint and hugged Becky tight. Her friend hugged her back. "Thank you, Becky. Thank you for Brutus and for tracking whoever that was last night." Mariah pulled back and said to Nate, "And thank you, too. I appreciate both of you giving up a day in the busy season—and I know they're all busy seasons on a ranch— and studying that trail. Whatever we know about that man, I owe to your skill. And I owe my safety to Brutus." She tipped her head to look at Clint. "And you too."

Looking back at Becky, she said, "Would you consider letting me have Brutus?"

"No."

"Don't give him to me to own. Just let him come and visit me forever."

"No."

Becky turned to Clint. "As you know, I had a talk with Brutus yesterday. He won't be bothering your livestock. I've got chickens out at my place too, but he might've gotten overly excited at the sight of ducks and such. Sheep? Who knows? But he understands they're his to protect, not hunt. I'll let you keep him until we've cleared up the danger you're in, Mariah. I can save a puppy for you. But a puppy isn't going to be as well-behaved as Brutus around flapping critters that look to him like dinner. So you'll have to think that over."

Becky patted Mariah on the arm. "Good night."

Nate followed her out, the spurs on their boots making a happy kind of sound as they left.

"Great supper, Clint." Nate nodded as he mounted up. He looked at Mariah. "Have a care, Mrs. Roberts." He tugged his Stetson as he reined his horse toward home, following Becky for a few paces, then catching up so they could ride two abreast.

As the sheriff watched them go, he said, "Well, I know you've got chores, so I'll get on." He bade them farewell, then started walking back toward town.

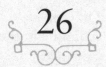

26

"Come and settle into the house. I'm going to get some coffee on, then go check the animals while you explore." Clint realized how nervous he was when he thought about taking her hand again and dragging her along with him. Inside and out.

And it wasn't because she had killers after her. It was because he had no idea how he ought to behave as a married man alone with his very own wife.

Disgusted with himself, he realized he should be worried about killers, for heaven's sake.

"There's one bedroom. It's got a back door out of it and a small lean-to that slows the wind when the door gets opened. Other than that, this is the whole house. Won't take you long to explore."

He went to his table, in the same room they were in, adjusted the chair Nate had set at a perfectly correct angle to the table. Two chairs. Two people living in this house.

He had a wife!

He quickly got the stove stoked and coffee brewing.

He was so aware of Mariah moving around the small space, it felt like she was knocking into him when of course they didn't so much as brush elbows. She left the room to look at the bedroom, and he was reminded that he hadn't yet offered to sleep on the floor out here. He kept stopping himself from saying it because he was hoping they'd soon start to feel like they could share a room. He gulped . . . and a bed.

The coffee was on, a quiet hiss coming from its base, where a drop of water had rolled down its side and sizzled on the stovetop.

Brutus had settled himself beside the stove. Clint had a bigger stove than most homesteads. In fact, many homesteads cooked over a fire. But once he decided to open the diner, he'd ordered this from Wainwright's store. He justified the expense because he did a lot of cooking out here for the diner. Especially canning his vegetables. So he needed a good stove.

And he had the money. He was by no means a rich man, but he'd left New York City with some money in his pockets. Plus he'd worked his way across the country until the Cirque of the Towers and the pretty little town of Pine Valley, Wyoming, caught his attention.

He set down roots to homestead and ended up with a piece of land that supported his diner.

Mariah emerged from the bedroom. "What's the plant in here?" she asked.

"It's a peppercorn. I've just started using the corns."

"Peppercorn?"

"An ingredient I use in a lot of my dishes."

"It's a pretty plant."

"Well, it's a lot more than just pretty. It's got spicy little round seeds that I grind up and add to recipes."

She nodded. "Exploring's all done. I'd like to watch you tend the animals. I know how to milk a cow. We haven't had one out here, but we had one in Iowa and I learned how to milk it. I can gather eggs and tend a garden, and I'd like to help."

Clint felt a smile break out on his face. She wanted to stay close to him.

He pushed the coffeepot back a bit, away from the hottest spot on the stove, to keep it from boiling over. "I'd appreciate that."

He reached out his hand. She smiled and took it. They left through the front door.

Brutus raised his head as they left but seemed content to snooze by the fire.

Clint hoped the poor guy returned to his full health soon.

"I've always enjoyed tending animals. Pa wouldn't let me shoe horses, but he let me feed them and brush them down if we had time." She grinned at Clint. "I like being a farmer's wife, even if the farmer is a cook."

She was honestly impressed with Clint's setup. The house was humble, but once you stepped outside, it was a vibrant, well-run homestead.

"It's probably a little late for hoeing the garden tonight." Clint had stayed close as she worked until he was sure she was capable. But he didn't criticize. Just the opposite. He thanked her repeatedly for her help. Then he'd feed the critters while she milked and did whatever else needed doing.

"I don't mind fighting the weeds, either." The animal chores were done, the eggs and milk inside now. She'd followed Clint to his huge garden. "It's a battle to tame a wild land, and one I'd like to help win."

Clint smiled. "No weeding tonight, but I need to pick tomatoes and onions and garlic. I also need to gather potatoes, carrots, herbs, and a few other things. A lot of vegetables are ripe. I often plan what to serve at the diner based on what's available in the garden."

Mariah threw in to work with him. He showed her the ripe tomatoes, which she'd never grown. There were crisp green beans that also needed picking. She'd grown them before so she knew how to judge the ripe ones. They stayed busy in the garden until nightfall. It occurred to her then that this was possibly the longest day of her life. She'd gotten very little sleep last night and now she'd worked until dark. Well, she wasn't one to sit around. And considering the Wyoming winters, there'd be plenty of long nights, so she enjoyed the work.

With bushel baskets full of vegetables, she followed Clint to the wagon beside the barn. "I'm taking the wagon tomorrow. I don't usually haul quite this much to town, but these vegetables will provide enough food at the diner for a week."

They set the baskets in the wagon, and with a clink of metal on metal, Clint raised the drop-down back of the wagon and latched it.

"It's late, but before we go inside, I'd like to show you one more thing."

"What is it?" Mariah asked.

"Follow me." He led her to the root cellar. She'd noticed the low, sloped door slanting up out of the ground. He opened it, and she wasn't expecting the smell. It wasn't unpleasant, just different somehow.

They went down into the space farther than she expected until soon the walls opened up. Clint lit a lantern, and she blinked at the strange shelves and crates. Then he guided her to a door built into the cellar wall and opened it to reveal stacks of white circles and dangling ropes of something. *Onions?* she wondered.

"This is where I make cheese."

"Are those onions?"

"No, garlic. I cook with it."

"I've heard of garlic, but you make cheese underground?"

He approached the nearest stack of round circles. About a foot across, flat on the top and bottom, wrapped in paper. She now saw the white was some kind of paper or cloth.

"This is a wheel of parmesan cheese. I have mozzarella." He swept a hand to indicate a few more wheels. "That over there is cheddar."

"I've heard of making cheese but not different kinds."

"I learned it as a child. My father didn't like what he could find for sale in the markets, so he and Ma learned to make their own. Ma was an especially skilled hand at it, and she trained me. My chicken parmesan has two kinds of cheese. I use them for several of my recipes. The cheese is a big part of why my food tastes a little different from what you're used to. The garlic is a vegetable with its own unusual flavor that I really love."

They spent a long time in that cellar. Mariah had a lot of questions. "How do you make cheese? Can I help?"

"I would love your help."

She fought a yawn, and he smiled wider. "Let's go back to the house."

They walked together toward the house. He didn't take her hand again, which she noticed. Holding hands seemed overly familiar for two people who'd married so hurriedly.

Still, she wouldn't have protested if he had.

Inside, the coffee had simmered for a long time. Clint poured them each a cup. Mariah washed her hands and face, then sank into a chair. Ready for a quiet stretch, then bed.

In a cabin with one bedroom.

Sipping the coffee, she wondered what she should say about that.

Clint blew on his hot coffee, then took a cautious drink. He pulled deeper, apparently finding the brew at an acceptable temperature.

"Mariah, are you ready . . . uh, that is, are you *comfortable* allowing me to share that room with you? I'd prefer that. We can . . . I mean, I can just sleep. M-maybe we could share a good-night kiss. But further . . . um, familiarity can wait until you're . . ." His voice, tortured and stammering, fell silent as if he had exhausted himself.

She hadn't thought he'd stay in there with her. Clearing her throat, she said, "Yes, we can sleep in there . . . t-together." She felt a blush deepen the color on her cheeks.

His worry seemed to ease as he nodded and smiled, then took another sip of his coffee. She'd rather that he just keep drinking. Talking about sleeping arrangements was awkward. And sharing that room was going to make talking about it feel like the good old days.

What could they talk about while they finished their coffee? Sipping it required talk between the sips. Gulping it down seemed to imply she was eager for bedtime.

Her eyes landed on their sleeping guard dog.

"Becky isn't going to let me have Brutus, is she?"

"She did save your life by lending him to you."

"But I love him."

"It would be very ungrateful of you to take her dog, considering Becky's idea to loan you Brutus might well have saved your life."

"True."

"It doesn't sound like she'll give him up."

"She said we could have a puppy, though."

"I like the idea of having a dog around. One who could keep wolves and coyotes, even snakes and weasels, away from my poultry pens. But a puppy's going to take some time to train."

"I wonder if she'd let us keep Brutus for a while after the puppy comes to live here. A puppy can be an unruly little guy. Maybe if we had calm Brutus on hand, the puppy would learn from his sire's example."

"Maybe. Well, time for bed. It's been a long day." Clint set his cup down with an unusually loud click.

She jumped and only then realized she was wound up tight and talking about the dog had just been her stalling.

"Go on in and get ready for bed. I'll wash up the cups and pot."

"I can wash up."

"Nope. Go ahead." Clint stood too fast and knocked

his chair over. He turned and took too long picking it up. Almost like he didn't want to look at her. A glance at his averted face told her his cheeks were as red as hers probably were.

She got up and bolted for the bedroom.

Talking, as well as thinking, had just gotten too hard.

Clint knocked softly on the bedroom door. Or maybe his hands were just shaking. Clint had never involved himself with women. He'd never objected to the idea; he'd just been ambitious and had poured everything into his work. Any spare hours he had he spent with his family.

But there had been a beautiful young lady he'd met while working at Delmonico's. A daughter of a wealthy man. She'd been far out of reach for him. But she had stolen a few moments to speak to him and encouraged him to meet her in the park. They'd gone on walks together, and for the first time he'd wondered about a future with a wife and children.

Long before anything could truly develop, his family died in the fire and all he'd been able to think of was to get away. Escape the memories. Escape the city.

And now here he was, entering his wife's bedroom. His bedroom.

"Come in," she said.

He swung the door slowly open and saw that she was in bed, on the side nearest the window. He had a feeling that was because it was the side farthest from the door and him. She watched him move into the room. She had the blankets pulled up over her mouth and nose, but her eyes were visible and wide.

Then she snapped them shut.

The sun was just now set and it was still dusk. No lantern was necessary.

The blankets crept higher until she'd covered her eyes, then her whole head. Her nerves touched a tender spot in his heart. She was as unsure of herself as he was.

Determined to behave sensibly, he got changed for bed. Finally, he slipped beside her in the bed. This alone was so sweet, so pleasant, he'd never ask for more.

"I'd l-like to give you a good-night kiss if that's all right." He wouldn't ask for more.

The coverlet crept down. He watched her hair emerge, then her eyes, then her nose. At last her lips.

He smiled at her, and she managed a weak smile back.

He rolled to his side, bent down, and kissed her. He felt it all the way to his heart.

He didn't push for more. He didn't deepen the kiss, or at least not much.

"Good night, Mariah." Rolling back, he reached under the covers, found her hand, and took it in his. "I'm happy to be married to you."

He felt her move and looked to see her rolling onto her side. She bent down and kissed him back. He could barely see her expression in the deepening shadows, but he thought he saw happiness there.

"Good night, husband. Marrying you so quickly was unexpected, but all in all I think it was a fine decision. I'm happy to be married to you, too."

Brutus came to their bedroom door. Clint thought he'd latched it, but apparently not. The dog looked in as if he were walking a guard route, then turned back into the main room, sniffing around the far corners of the house. That wouldn't take him long.

Feeling unexpectedly safe considering what had gone on with Mariah lately, Clint squeezed her hand and felt his body relax into sleep.

27

Mariah's eyes drifted open.

The room was wrong, but confusion vanished quickly. She'd been moved around a lot lately, so she was in the habit of not being disoriented for long.

Clint's house.

She heard quiet footfalls outside the bedroom. Probably Clint, or Brutus would be barking. But she'd also learned caution. She flung off the blankets, rushed to the closed door, and peeked out to see Clint working over the basin he used to wash dishes.

He was working on . . . she felt a little confused by what she was seeing and finally decided it was potatoes.

"Good morning," she said.

Clint was close by. Everything was close by in this small house.

He turned his head, still bent over the basin. The day was just now breaking. Light came through the window beside the table, as the shutters had been thrown wide.

"Good morning, wife." His eyes crinkled as they did when he was smiling inside.

How strange that she knew that. It helped her realize she'd really known him for a while now, even though the marriage had been sudden.

"How long have you been up working?"

"A couple of hours. My day usually starts around four."

"You should have nudged me awake and told me to get busy and help."

A smile fully bloomed. "You've had a few hard days. I'll nudge you tomorrow."

"Four o'clock every morning, Clint? You sure do start your days early."

"I open the diner at six. I've got morning chores, and there are some vegetables I don't like to pick until the last possible minute. Then I clean up before I haul them to town. And today is roast chicken, so I had to gather up a few of my older roosters to butcher."

"I'll get dressed and help." She had a lot more to say, but not in her nightgown.

By the time she was ready to go, and she'd been quick about it, Clint was gone. The front door stood open. She went to see him hefting a basket into his already-loaded wagon. She saw other things in there but couldn't say what. Brutus stood by Clint, who picked the dog up and settled him in the wagon box.

For some reason, seeing a strong man handle a wounded dog so gently made her want to weep. A foolish thought. Swallowing the lump in her throat, she said, "Are we ready to go?"

He latched the back end. "I am if you are."

She darted inside to fasten the shutters, then came out and closed the door. Clint was there to lock it. She wasn't satisfied with the lock, but she could fix that later.

"Clint, I'm going to the smithy now. The sheriff is walking me over, and Brutus is coming with me."

Clint straightened from whipping up the eggs for omelets. He'd been making them as fast as he could all morning. There was an unusually large rush for breakfast because the freight wagon came in on the second Wednesday of each month. Today's mid-September arrival meant a lot of people were in town for supplies, including more women than usual. Clint could see he hadn't been the only homesteader in the last few years. And these women tended to cook for themselves and their families, and they almost always came here with a husband and children.

This September freight wagon was particularly critical because winter arrived real early in Wyoming. People were stocking up, afraid the trails would close before the next freight, which was scheduled for mid-October.

While the freight wagon usually made it through without incident, there were stories of bad spells as well, so it was wise to stock up for the whole winter if possible. That brought folks to town, and that meant business for Clint.

He couldn't go with his wife, not now.

"Be careful, Mariah." He was ready to pour the omelet into his perfectly heated and buttered pan, but he had to step away from his cooking to give her a kiss goodbye.

"I will be. Once the sheriff is satisfied there's no danger, he'll stay until Nell comes over. It turns out she's a crack shot."

"Nell? Sweet, delicate little seamstress Nell?" Clint had his doubts, but the sheriff would be there, so swallowing his worries, he went back to cooking. He poured the whipped eggs onto the hot pan and enjoyed the sizzle. Next, he sprinkled fried onions and diced ham over the eggs. He had two pans going, and the second one was ready to flip.

Which he did by shaking the pan to make sure the eggs were loosened all around. Tossing the eggs up, he watched them turn in the air and then caught them without the slightest spill.

"I love watching you do that," Mariah said.

"It looks fancy, I suppose, but after you've done something a few thousand times, you get pretty good at it. You yourself prove that every day at the smithy."

She smiled. "I've taught you to make nails and a horseshoe. The winter gets slow around here for both of us. Maybe you can teach me to flip eggs?"

"Maybe I can."

Mariah ducked out of the kitchen, and Clint forced himself to concentrate on the meals he was turning out as fast as he could.

Finally, things tapered off and then quieted completely. With a sigh and a rub of his sore back from bending over all morning, he prepared the chickens he'd brought and set them to baking. It'd be easier than fried chicken or coq au vin on a day he wanted to be able to abandon his post if necessary.

It was an all-morning chore to get ready for the noon

meal. Mariah came in to say hello, and since she was right there with him, he could stop fretting for a while.

He cleaned up after lunch, shed his apron, and headed for the front door of the diner. He met Mariah coming in and wearing . . . He blinked. "Is that . . . where did you get that?"

Nell was a pace behind her, so of course he quickly figured it out. Even so . . . "Mariah, you look beautiful."

"Do you like it?" Mariah's cheeks turned a pretty pink with some embarrassment but also, he thought, with some pleasure.

The pink cheeks were a nice complement to the light purple dress sprinkled with dark purple flowers. He'd never seen her dressed in such a feminine way.

She had on a pretty straw-colored bonnet with purple ribbons adorning it. Her hair was peeking out with a few ringlets around her temples and covering her ears.

And she had no soot on her face.

"Mariah, you are so beautiful. I've always known that, but the dress only makes it more obvious." Clint had seen it right away, soot or no soot, but dressed up like this, with her hair in curls . . . she looked stunning.

"I asked Nell if she'd make me a dress. She had this fabric and, well, she came to the smithy and set up to make chaps in there while I worked. I finished up most of what I needed to do before lunch, so she told me my dress was done, then dragged me to her shop to see if it fit."

Brutus came in without even a glimpse at the dress. Clint, meanwhile, couldn't tear his gaze away. "It's perfect," he said.

"Thank you. I wanted you to see it. I suppose getting

such a fussy dress was foolishness." Mariah ran her hands over the skirt as if worrying over any wrinkles. "I'll change out of it to work this afternoon, of course. It would never hold up to the dirty work of blacksmithing."

"That dress is not foolishness," Nell interjected, poking Mariah in the back, which got her to move forward a step. Nell slipped past her, not unlike Brutus had, and took a seat at the table, watching them.

Clint wondered what she saw.

"You needed a new dress, Mariah," Nell said. "Your Sunday best was ruined during the robbery. I mended it as best I could, but a pretty new dress was called for, and you don't always have to pick your clothing based on how it holds up to a forge."

Mariah nodded.

"So, are you done with your work or has more come in?" Clint asked.

Mariah replied, "I'm caught up for now."

"Since we brought the wagon to town today, why don't we see what all you want from your house and load up?"

Nell, the sheriff, Willie, Doc Preston, and even the Wainwrights came over to lend a hand. There wasn't a lot of room in Clint's house, so they didn't take much, though a few of her things, well-built by her father, were an improvement over Clint's. In the process, Mariah sold her house to the Wainwright brothers for an amount that made her wonder if she was cheating them . . . though she didn't wonder enough to protest.

Sheriff Mast, who lingered until everyone else had left, said, "I need to talk to you both."

Clint and Mariah, standing outside the barn, exchanged a look before giving the sheriff their full attention.

"I sent out a warning about the man who attacked you. I told lawmen from five different towns to be looking for a man with a wound, that he might've been bitten by a dog that was protecting his mistress."

"That's good thinking, Sheriff." Clint was impressed, but then he wasn't a trained lawman.

The sheriff shrugged a little sheepishly. "It was Nell's idea."

Nell the gunslinger. A woman full of surprises.

"I got a telegram back today from South Pass City. A man clutching his arm stopped for bandages and such at the general store there. He ate a meal, then hurried on. No one could describe him—not well, anyway—just that he has yellow hair, is skinny, and favors his arm. The man never gave a name, never spoke except to ask for the bandages and order a meal. But he was seen riding south on a trail that leads straight out of the area. I'm hoping the dog bite might've been enough to get him to quit the country. I wired the next town down the trail, warning them he might be coming and that he's considered dangerous. No promises, Mrs. Roberts, but you have reason to hope the danger might be over. We'll either catch him or he's running far and fast."

"That's good news," Mariah said, sounding relieved.

Clint wasn't completely done with his worrying, but it helped. "Thank you for doing all that, Sheriff. It eases my mind some."

They talked a bit longer, after which the sheriff made his way back to town.

Setting to work on chores, Clint got them done in half the time, thanks to Mariah's help.

"I have leftover chicken from the diner for supper," he told her.

"Sounds wonderful," she said.

They walked along hand in hand toward home. With that outlaw heading for the hills, and his wife in her pretty purple dress at his side, Clint decided he'd gotten himself a fine life.

Key rode into Bear Claw Pass, Wyoming, late at night. His arm still ached like the dickens, but it'd been five days since that nasty dog had bitten him and the wound seemed to be healing. He didn't need the drunk doctor in this town, after all.

But he did need a place to rest up for another week or so. He didn't dare go around Pine Valley favoring his arm.

Instead of stopping in town, he rode out to Oliver Hawkins's place. He and Oliver had known each other just a bit back in Tennessee. They'd met up over the years, and now Key needed a favor—and Hawkins owed him one.

Riding up to the monstrosity of a house Hawkins had built, Key went to the barn and left his horse in a stall. No one was around; it was late enough that everyone had knocked off for the day. And since Hawkins tended to hire sluggards, no one paid any mind to a lone rider coming in.

He knocked on the back door of the house, and soon a pretty little woman answered. She had a pallor that seemed at odds with the long Wyoming summer. Key figured Hawkins had found himself another woman to abuse.

"I'm a friend of Oliver's. Can you fetch him for me?"

"Step inside." The young woman left him in the entryway, where Key hung up his hat and went on into the kitchen, wondering if there was any supper left over.

Oliver was a while coming, and the woman didn't come with him.

"Oliver, howdy. Been a while. I need a place to stay for a few days."

Oliver nodded. No hesitation. He knew exactly what he owed Key. Oliver would've had his neck stretched a whole lotta years ago without Key giving him a phony alibi. They'd met in Tennessee but had known each other in Chicago, too. Oliver had killed his in-laws, and Key was glad to bear witness that Oliver had been with him all night.

"Have you eaten?"

"Nope—a few bites of supper would be welcome."

"Amelia!" Oliver raised his voice. "Can you come and fetch a meal for my guest?"

Key could've rummaged through the kitchen on his own. He didn't need anyone waiting on him. But he knew Oliver, knew he enjoyed lording it over anyone who was under his power. So Key didn't deny the man his fun.

Amelia entered the kitchen and, without looking either man in the eye, set to preparing a decent meal. Better'n Key expected. Oliver was hard on housekeepers, and because of that, he often found himself without one.

Mariah wasn't sure if she was safe, but she put her trust in Brutus, Clint, Nell the gunslinger, and the sheriff and went about her life like normal.

Normal except that her life had completely changed.

The Wainwrights were living in her house.

She was living in Clint's.

She had a pretty dress she put on every night after she walked home with Clint from work.

And she slept beside a husband every night.

"Mariah," Clint said, holding her hand as he lay beside her, "would you be . . . that is, we have feelings for each other, don't we?"

"Yes, I certainly think you're a fine husband, Clint. Being married to you is a wonderful thing."

"Then, uh, do you, I mean, do we . . . should we maybe do m-more than just exchange a good-night kiss? Every night? At bedtime?"

Mariah pulled her hand free of his and heard him sigh. Then she rolled onto her side to face him. He did the same.

"You lost your whole family in a sudden and shocking way, didn't you?"

"I did."

The room was dark, but her eyes had adjusted until she could see him enough to know he was resigned.

"Did it take you a while to feel like, well, like you weren't betraying them by being happy?"

Clint gasped quietly. "Is that why you don't want to be with me in married ways? You feel like the closeness to me is wrong when your family is so newly dead?"

Mariah didn't answer. It sounded strange, foolish even.

"I do remember feeling that way." Clint leaned forward,

kissed her softly, then pulled back. "I remember quitting my job, a job I loved and was eager to improve in and impress my bosses and learn enough to deserve a promotion. I just sat in my humble little room I'd rented. I only came out for funerals and to sell the lot my family's diner had been on. I packed the bare minimum of my things, bought a train ticket, and headed west. Staying at that job, enjoying my work, even liking the room I stayed in felt like a betrayal."

"That's what it feels like to me to be more, um, fully married. Every time I find myself smiling, every time I realize I haven't thought about Pa or Theo for a few hours, it's like I didn't love them that much. I'm forgetting them too easily." She stared into his eyes, slowly leaned forward and returned his kiss, just as gently and perhaps for just a bit longer.

When she ended the kiss, he said quietly, "I wandered for over a year before I found my way out here. I was still roaming when winter hit. I spent a whole winter in a little town in southern Iowa, cooking in the kitchen for an elderly couple who owned a tiny hotel. Then the next spring I moved on, even though they asked me to stay and were really kind to me. I didn't want to make friends. I didn't think I deserved to be happy. Just like you said."

"It feels selfish to not be a wife to you in all ways, Clint. I want us to be truly married. We will be. Just maybe not for a while yet."

"If it wasn't for that man breaking into your house, we'd've taken much longer to get married. But we got ahead of ourselves for reasons of your safety. But now we can slow down a bit. You'll have your time to grieve, Mariah."

He was so kind about it. She wanted him to know how much she appreciated his patience. She leaned forward and kissed him again. Resting her hand on his cheek, she deepened the kiss to thank him and show him how much she respected him.

Then something lit up inside her, a fire she'd never known existed. She pressed closer to him. And he to her.

Before she knew it, she'd pulled him down on top of her. And she didn't think of anything or anyone but him for a long time.

And it was a great relief to realize later that she didn't feel one speck of guilt for not thinking of her family during that time. Only later did she think of them. And she knew without giving it much thought at all that her pa wouldn't mind a bit if she was happy.

And she surely was.

Clint couldn't believe how much his life had changed.

Now that he truly had Mariah as his fully married wife, he couldn't believe he'd waited two years to let her know he was interested in her. Two years of not showing that to anyone. It had only worked because he'd had no idea of the wonder of marriage.

They spent time together, and time apart working.

No one came around who favored his arm, which gave him high hopes that the danger to her was in the past.

She still couldn't remember much about the day of the robbery. But her headaches were gone, and all her other aches and pains had healed up.

No one had tried to kill her for nearly a month.

Brutus was healed up, but Becky wasn't coming around to demand her dog back so she must still have concerns.

Worried or not, still on edge or not, Clint hoped that the gap in Mariah's memory had put everyone's fears to rest. If *fears* was the right word to describe the murderous inclinations of a bunch of killers.

Clint pulled a haunch of venison out of the large oven in the diner kitchen.

Change indeed.

He hadn't made eggs Benedict in weeks, and he'd gotten to thinking of coq au vin as chicken stew.

What's more, he was proud of himself for letting go of what now seemed like arrogance. Or maybe it was better to say he'd turned sneaky. He still made his version of coq au vin, yet his customers chose to call it chicken stew. His customers didn't want beef bourguignon; they wanted beef stew. If he made it with all his skill, made it delicious so his customers ate with gusto and gave him lavish compliments, and even better for his diner's profits, they came back again and again. Clint was educating their palates, only with a lot more stealth.

28

"Mariah, I've got a note from Miss Becky." Henry was jogging when he came through the door. She was done with all the work that'd been brought in and had turned her attention to the fine detailing of another set of spurs. The first pair had sold fast.

She set aside her sledgehammer and came to meet the general store owner, reaching for the note.

Reading it quickly, she looked up. "She wants me to bring her nails and four hinges?"

"One of her hands was riding in a terrible hurry. Something about the horse crashing sideways through a door."

"I know she brought in some mustangs she caught in the wild. Probably trying to break them. Was anyone hurt?"

"The man picking up supplies made me think someone was hurt. Or maybe only the horse was hurt because he didn't go for the doctor. He asked if you could bring out the things ordered. Sounds like they've got men standing sentry to keep the horses and cattle from breaking out. He hurried back to the ranch with the supplies. Looks like there's a storm coming in, and he apologized if it ends up with you getting a soaking. But I think the storm is still off a ways."

"I'd better move fast then. Thanks, Henry."

"Welcome." He tipped his hat and headed back toward the general store.

It suited her to be more formal with men. She remembered how she'd called Joshua Pruitt by his first name, mostly to gouge at his arrogance. She was a businesswoman after all, and Pa had always called customers by their first names. Mariah never had. Except there were two Mr. Wainwrights—no one had time for that—and Henry and Pete had urged everyone to use their first names just to keep things simple.

Mariah quickly untied her apron and got saddlebags down from where they hung from a row of nails. She heard the rumble of thunder as she filled the bags.

Mariah saddled Blue, the faithful roan mustang that had pulled the wagon from Clint's homestead this morning. She slid the saddlebags in place, then led Blue over to tie him to the hitching post in front of the diner.

She knew better than to go haring off into the country without telling Clint.

Clint was elbow-deep in profiteroles for dessert when Mariah rushed into the kitchen waving a piece of paper in the air.

"This just came in from Becky's place," she began. "Someone went to the general store for supplies and asked Henry Wainwright if he'd bring the note to me. Becky had a door broken off by a bucking bronco. The horse snapped the hinges free, collapsed a fence and a section of the barn wall. She asks in the note if I'd bring them nails and hinges."

"Why didn't the hand who picked up supplies get those things?" Clint kept working on his dessert. It was a delicate thing, and he didn't dare look away from it right now.

Mariah shrugged. "In too big of a hurry is my guess—trying to beat the storm and keep the cattle and horses from getting in with each other or spreading out over the countryside. So I'm going to ride out to Becky's with the nails and hinges. I'll take Brutus with me. He'll keep me safe."

"That's true. What about Nell? Take her with you too and tell her to bring her gun. Or wait an hour. Let me get through lunch and I'll come along."

"You know it'll be more like three hours, Clint, and it sounds like they need the supplies right away. If it's the door and fence that keep the cattle and horses apart, she'd have to post men to keep the cattle and horses from mixing with each other. The horses sometimes harass the cattle, trying to herd them. And with the storm coming, I'm sure her critters are stirred up. I'd better hurry. I'll fetch Nell."

Clint nodded, regretting his unusual choice for dessert that took so much attention.

But it had been almost two months now since the stage holdup. And there'd been no sign of trouble since the break-in at Mariah's place. Becky's Idee Ranch wasn't far out of town, and Brutus *would* keep her safe. Not to mention Nell's being with her.

She'd been patient about the restrictions that had been

placed on her. It was time to trust. "Don't let Becky keep Brutus, even if she begs."

Mariah laughed. "I think he loves me now more than her. He wants to stay with me."

"You may have Becky beat, but not Lobo."

"Maybe Lobo's ready to wean her pups. I'll bring her back with me, too."

Clint smiled and waved her off.

A niggling of worry had him pausing at his baking, but then he thought of Brutus, Nell, and, good grief, Mariah herself was tough. He went back to his dessert.

Mariah enjoyed riding horseback for the first time in a long time. And now that she was back at the smithy full-time, Mariah had been able to reopen her small livery and so had a few horses available for rent.

Nell rented one of her horses, for no money, which Nell protested but finally accepted since she hadn't let Mariah pay for her new dress.

"We'd better move fast if we're going to beat that storm. It's too bad Becky picked today to need our help."

"But the storm might be the reason she needs it." Mariah glanced at the dark clouds. Yes, they were distant. Some storms moved fast, while others built and built for a long time before they struck. The fast-moving ones were often more violent and yet shorter in duration. A slow-moving one could be a soaker.

"Was it Nate who rode into town with the note?" Nell asked.

Mariah was finding hidden depths to her sweet-natured

friend. Quick with a gun. Very able on horseback. Maybe making chaps wasn't so far outside her ideas of what she wanted to do. She complained about it, but she was good at it and kept making the chaps, also making good money.

"I didn't see who brought it. Henry Wainwright came to the smithy to hand it to me and said they were in a hurry."

Nell nodded, her expression thoughtful. "I wish you'd carry a gun, Mariah. It's not a safe part of the world we live in."

"I do have that knife in my boot, the one you gave me. And the leather sheath you attached to the inside of my boot is perfectly comfortable."

Nell looked around as they rode. It was about five miles out to Becky's ranch. In the scope of the rugged land to the east of Pine Valley, that wasn't far at all.

But there were rocky outcroppings, boulders jumbled here and there. A meandering stream cut the ground so the trail they rode on went down the banks and up every half mile or so for a good part of the ride.

The wind took on a howling sound and gusted past them, blowing about even the tidy riding skirts they both wore. Blue was a steady critter, but Nell's horse skittered around, spooked by the billowing fabric.

Up ahead was a particularly high and tight jumble of boulders. The trail narrowed until they were forced to ride single file, with Brutus trotting ahead of them around a tight bend. In the wind, Mariah thought she heard a high-pitched sound. Maybe a yelp from Brutus, but not much of one. It did make her think of rattlesnakes. But if he'd seen one, or even if one had bit him, he'd have made a lot more noise than that.

Nell circled the rock and was out of sight, then Mariah came around.

A rope lashed out from behind the nearest rocks.

As the lasso snagged around her, she saw Nell, roped and unconscious on the ground. No sign of Brutus. Then she was falling as a man wearing a mask rushed toward her and slammed a fist into her face.

White sparks flashed in her eyes.

There'd been no sound except for that one yelp from Brutus. A cry of pain? What had they done to him? Something certainly.

Had they killed him? Had they killed Nell?

No gunfire. And near as Mariah could tell, only one man and he'd never spoken a word. She didn't see or hear any other riders.

Something—a gunnysack maybe—was then pulled over her head and tied tight around her neck. She was hoisted up and thrown over a horse. She couldn't see a thing now, and her thoughts were muddled from the blow.

Trying to clear her head, she listened so she'd remember anything that could help later, assuming she survived this.

She still couldn't hear other riders.

The man mounted up behind her, then they took off at a fast gallop with the saddle horn gouging her belly hard enough, and the sack tied over her head tight enough, that she struggled to breathe.

Fighting for each breath, she thought of the knife in her boot.

The lasso was around her arms, but her hands weren't tied. Draped over a saddle, reaching her boot was impossible. But she'd remember. She'd stay alert so that when her chance came, she'd fight.

The Deadeye Gang—it had to be them. Or at least one of them. Was he taking her to the rest of the gang? Would it be her against five men? Ten?

It came to her then that the note from Becky had been a ruse to get her out of town. Someone had been there, waiting to strike. Even ready to handle a dog and a riding companion.

Clint would go to Henry Wainwright and ask who had brought the note to town and then they'd know just who'd done this. Did that make Henry a witness now, too? Was his life in danger?

She was in the clutches of a gang who left no witnesses. Not even a witness who had no idea what she'd seen.

29

"Clint, get out here!"

Clint heard Sheriff Joe Mast shouting. In the middle of serving the usual crowd for lunch, Clint dropped everything and ran.

He got out front of the diner to see Blue trotting into town. Riderless. A second horse came in behind Blue, one Clint recognized as the horse Nell often rented. He tore off running for home before giving it a second thought.

"No, Clint, stop! I've got a horse right here. Ride mine. We'll take these other horses with us."

The sheriff was strapping leather on a horse while Willie mounted up. He and the sheriff had their horses tied out front of the jail. Clint sprinted toward an extra horse and swung up in the saddle. He was going at a flat gallop before he reached the edge of town and took the trail to Becky's ranch.

He heard shouting behind him, but he didn't recognize what was said. He was too scared. A woman could fall off her horse. Anyone could. But both women? That was unlikely. And where was Brutus?

He wasn't a full minute in the saddle when Sheriff Mast came up beside him. The sheriff rode a massive stallion that was the fastest horse around. Mast and his horse flew on ahead, and after another five minutes of wild galloping, Clint saw the sheriff's huge chestnut skid to a stop.

"Whoa! Whoa, boy!" The sheriff was on the ground before the horse stopped sliding.

Clint soon caught up with Mast and reined the horse he rode to a halt. Willie almost ran him down as Clint dismounted and rushed toward the sheriff.

Nell!

A second later, he spotted Brutus. Lying on his side, heaving as if every breath were his last.

Nell was moving. The sheriff at her side. Clint paused to see Nell's eyes open. She sagged with relief as Sheriff Mast tended her. She was gagged. Tied up. Flat on her belly on the ground. Then her eyes met Clint's, and fear gripped him when he saw all that was in her expression.

Willie hurried over to untie Brutus. "He's lassoed around the neck so tight it's choking him near to death."

Clint pulled out his knife and slashed the ropes binding Nell's feet as the sheriff dispatched her gag and went to work on her hands.

"They took Mariah." Nell started talking the instant she was able. "I didn't see anything. I just know we were attacked and she's gone."

"You're bleeding, Mrs. Armstrong. You must've taken a blow to the head." The sheriff took the kerchief used to gag her, folded it, and pressed it to the back of her head. She'd had a bonnet on when she left town. A practical cotton bonnet with strings that tied beneath her chin, made of fabric that matched Nell's pretty blue calico dress.

There was a bloodstain high on the back of her head, soaked through the bonnet. The blood had run down around her neck and onto the front of her dress.

But she hadn't seen anything. Which was very likely why she was still alive.

Nell took the kerchief from the sheriff and pressed it to her head as she sat up, then all but collapsed again. The sheriff caught her before she fell.

Just then Henry Wainwright and Doc Preston rode up. Clint saw Parson Blodgett coming fast, as well as Brandon Nolte, a homesteader who'd just been in the diner for lunch. The parson and Brandon led Nell's and Mariah's horses.

"Doc, could you take Nell to town?"

"I was thinking I'd stay and help search for Mariah." Nell sat up again but had to drop the kerchief to brace her arms on the ground and remain upright.

"We'll let Brutus lead us. Nell, you're too injured to help. Let the doc take care of you."

Nell glanced at Brutus, who was on his feet but looked as unsteady as she was. "Get him water. It'll help ease his throat some. And help me to my feet and onto my horse. Doc Preston, I would appreciate your assistance."

As they talked, a peal of thunder in the distance drew their attention to the clouds.

The sheriff helped her to her feet, then handed her over to the doctor. "Willie, ride to Becky's ranch. Get Nate out here. We need a good tracker. Brutus will help where he can, but he's in bad shape. If the rain starts, we won't find any trail left. And if whoever took Mariah has the simple chore of silencing a witness for good, she may not have a moment to spare. We've got to move fast."

"Willie's better on a trail. I'll go for Nate," Henry said and strode toward his horse. He mounted and started riding for the Idee without waiting for anyone to admit that was a good idea.

Clint's stomach sank until it made his knees weak. He went to Brutus, crouched down, and looked him over. Seeing the dog was on the fragile side, Clint shouted after Henry, "Bring Lobo too."

Wainwright waved to acknowledge he'd heard as he galloped away.

The sheriff had a canteen on his horse. He took off his hat and poured a little water in it. Brutus lapped up the water. His legs seemed to gain strength with each swallow. After no more than a minute at the water, Brutus lifted his head and stared in the direction directly south, away from Becky's ranch. Away from town. Very good chance it was the direction Mariah was taken.

Again Clint knelt beside the dog. "Can you find her, Brutus? Can you lead the way?"

Brutus took off at a trot, not a full loping run like usual. But considering the state the dog was in, it was a valiant effort. Unfortunately, it wasn't fast and they didn't have a moment to spare.

"I see tracks." Sheriff Mast pointed at the ground. Between the dust blowing with the rising wind and the bending, dancing grass, Clint couldn't see a thing. "Same ones we saw a month ago. Same horse as the man who broke into Mariah's place."

"They'll vanish when the rain comes. Brutus may not be able to keep to the trail." Clint clutched his reins so tight, his horse shook its head, fighting the bit. Forcing himself to loosen the reins, they rode on. Much too slow.

Mariah roused from a shove and the terrifying jolt of falling before slamming onto the ground again.

"What are you doing here?" The man who'd thrown her from the horse asked the question in a harsh voice. "No!"

A loud blast of gunfire, together with the impact with the ground, seemed to jerk free memories she'd buried. She saw lead slamming into the stagecoach. Smelled the sulfur of gun smoke. Her father and Theo, firing until their guns were empty. Pa had leaned forward to reload and let her take his place firing her gun.

In that moment, she remembered the man who had come up beside her door and shot the two men who'd sat across from her. She'd fired at him and drawn blood, but it wasn't a killing shot.

She recalled his face then and knew she'd seen that same face since. He worked for Joshua Pruitt. No name came to her, but it would in time.

She abruptly came back to the present. Someone was walking around. Only one person, and it had to be the man who'd shot her kidnapper. She was sightless and could sense nothing else, either. No smell. No identifying sound. If she lived, she wouldn't be able to tell anyone about this killer.

A heavy thud from beside her made no sense. Almost like a punch. A fist punching a body. But it wasn't a fight.

Then there were more footsteps. Was he coming closer to her? Ice sleeted through her veins as she waited for the man to silence the only living witness to murder.

No shot was fired. She no longer sensed the killer coming close.

There was a creaking of leather, then hooves pounded away.

With the horseman gone, the worst of the terror ebbed. It seemed the man who'd fired a gun was gone now. She thrashed around and realized her hands were free. She clawed at the gunnysack over her head but couldn't get it off. The only sound was a horse nearby that had stopped and was cropping grass.

She smelled blood. She thought she smelled death.

Sitting in the shrouded darkness, Mariah reached for her boot, found her knife, then sought out whatever tied the hood on her head—a rope wrapped around her neck. Careful not to cut herself, she sliced the rope. As the gunnysack loosened, she pulled it away.

Scrambling to her hands and knees to look around, she saw a man, dead beside her, with a bullet wound centered right between his eyes. A knife was sticking out of his chest. The knife had been stabbed through a note.

Sickened, she thought of Nell and Brutus—lying unconscious back where she'd been taken—and lurched to her feet. With her thoughts focused solely on saving Nell, she left the dead man where he lay and rushed for the horse.

The horse shied away. A thunderclap and her own frantic need to hurry were scaring the poor critter. Fighting to stay calm, to get her breathing under control, she slowed her movements, spoke kindly to the nervous animal. Soon it went back to chomping grass.

Mariah gathered her wits and approached the horse one slow step at a time. Finally she was able to get her hand on one of the reins. Then, grabbing the second rein, she reached up with her other hand to grasp the pommel. For one long moment, she let the horse take her weight as she leaned close to the big animal and hoisted herself easylike into the saddle.

From her high seat, she examined the ground, not really sure where she was. Hoofprints led in two directions. She studied them and saw one set riding on. She'd have to backtrack the other set, which likely belonged to her horse.

She noticed a PR brand on the horse. Pruitt Ranch. Joshua Pruitt had some explaining to do.

She set out to follow the trail left by this horse. For the first ten, maybe twenty minutes, the ground was good grassland broken up by stones and jagged crags of rocks high as a house. Then the land would smooth out again and she could see for a long ways. The sky was dark to the west, the clouds having grown into thunderheads.

She saw a streak of lightning, then another, both striking over the mountains. There was time to get back to Nell before the worst of the storm hit. Maybe find men who could track the killer who'd spared her.

How long had she been unconscious? How far had she been taken from Nell? How badly was Nell hurt?

Mariah fought down the worry and tried to steady herself with prayer. As she did that, heading into the oncoming storm, she heard horses approaching. All her hard-won calm deserted her then, replaced by terror as sharp as the lightning heading toward her.

Where could she hide?

Then a deep bark shoved all her fear aside and she guided her horse toward that familiar sound. She'd ridden only a hundred feet or so when Brutus rounded a boulder and gave out a happy yelp. He picked up speed.

He was alive. And what about Nell? Right behind Brutus was the sheriff, and next she saw Clint.

Clint was here. He'd come for her. Her hero.

Soon more men appeared: Deputy Willie, Parson Blodgett, and Brandon Nolte.

But no Nell.

30

"M ariah." He whispered her name. So deeply relieved to find her alive and well, it was almost beyond him to speak.

A trembling deep inside almost knocked him off his horse. But he clung on and rode to her side.

"Where's Nell?" she asked.

"She's going to be fine." Sheriff Mast took over the talking.

Clint struggled to think who *she* might be. Mariah was obviously fine.

"Doc Preston rode out with us and took her back to town. But she was conscious and walking. A blow to the back of her head left her shaky. How'd you escape?"

Oh. Nell. Clint chastised himself for forgetting, yet his only concern had been his wife.

"I didn't escape," Mariah said. "Or I guess I did, but it was no doing of mine. The man who took me is dead. I had a gunnysack over my head and was mostly knocked out as we rode. I have no idea how far we've come. I was dazed and only fully regained consciousness when I got dropped to the ground. I heard my captor speak to someone. Someone else was there. The man who took me said—" she stopped and shook her head—"I can't remember what. I think a man from the Pruitt ranch took me. On this horse. I met him once, maybe saw him another time."

She turned back to lead them to her kidnapper. They rode alongside her. Brutus trotted at her horse's heels. Clint came up close on one side—so close she reached out and took his hand. He looked at her. Held her hand almost desperately. Impossibly glad to see her alive and well.

They rode for a fair distance. Mariah had left her captor far behind. Finally, ahead, Clint saw a man flat on his back on the ground.

"Key Larson," the sheriff said. "Joshua Pruitt's new cowpoke."

"That's right," said Mariah. "Mr. Pruitt introduced him to Becky, to Nell, and to me. But I remember more than just his face. When I heard that gunshot, my memory of the stagecoach holdup came rushing back. I remember he rode up to my window on the stage. He was one of the robbers. The only face I saw. I witnessed him kill the two strangers who rode with us. And he was taking aim to kill me when the stagecoach rolled over."

Clint recognized him. A killer who he'd fed at the diner. Clint wanted to hurt the man. Slam a fist into his face. But he was long past punishment.

The day was growing dark early. A distant rumbling drew Clint's eyes to the western sky. Storm clouds moving nearer.

"I'm glad you were able to best him, Miss Mariah." The

sheriff tugged on the front of his hat and gave her an approving nod. "We need to get you back to town before this storm hits."

"I didn't kill him. Larson said something to the man we met at this spot. I suppose that's why we stopped here. Larson said, 'What are you doing here?' The man who'd rode up didn't answer. Then I heard a single gunshot. All while I was in a heap on the ground. I don't think Larson had dismounted because I heard him fall off his horse. I still had that gunnysack over my head," she added, pointing at it.

Clint fought the urge to go into a rage. That wouldn't help the situation. Still, he hated that his wife was made to suffer such a painful ordeal.

"The other rider started walking around, and I thought I was next." Mariah shuddered.

Clint came up to her and pulled her close to his side. She leaned on him, and he felt honored by it. Just because a woman could stand on her own two legs didn't mean it wasn't helpful to lean on another. Nice for her, and nice for the man she leaned on.

"If this was part of the Deadeye Gang, then I knew that whoever killed Larson would shoot me next, the only witness who'd lived. And though the gunman didn't know it, I'd just gotten my memory back."

Mariah gestured to the knife in the man's chest. "The killer, he must've left that note. Pinned it to Larson's chest with the knife and rode away. I never heard anyone but the one horse, the one man walking around. The strange noise I heard was him stabbing the note to Larson's body."

The sheriff crouched beside Larson to read the note.

Clint watched him read it several times, based on how long he studied it. Clint would've liked to read it too, but he was busy holding his precious wife. Mariah had her eyes closed and her head resting on Clint's strong shoulder.

"How'd you know to come looking for me?" she asked.

Clint told his side of the story—her horse coming home, the wild, panicked ride—and he squeezed her tighter with every word until he was close to strangling her. She didn't object, so he held on. She'd survived. He felt a trembling deep inside her that matched his own. She seemed likely to shake apart, so he kept on holding her together in his arms.

Clint turned to the sheriff. "Mariah's about all in. She should maybe see the doctor."

"And I want to see if Nell is all right," Mariah said.

The sheriff nodded. He looked down at Brutus, stretched out on his side and panting. "I'd like to see if Brutus here could follow the man who killed Larson." His eyes darted back to the note.

Mariah pulled away from Clint and went to Brutus. Clint followed her. She knelt beside the dog and petted him, whispering her thanks.

Clint said, "What's the note say?"

The sheriff shrugged. "I believe it's a sort of apology to Mariah. It says, 'You didn't see nuthin'. Larson shoulda left you be.'"

There was an extended silence.

Finally, the sheriff said, "We brought Blue with us." He jerked his thumb toward the horse. Brandon Nolte had led Blue near, but they had stayed back a bit, ready to help if needed.

Though Clint didn't know the man well, he appreciated that he'd come along to help them.

Clint and Mariah rode back toward town mostly in silence, Brandon with them, and only as fast as their exhaustion would allow. Brutus seemed to perk up a little as time went on, as if tired legs were his only problem.

Clint hoped that was true.

Reaching a fork in the trail, Brandon said, "I should be getting back home. I hope to beat the storm. My young'uns are tough, but the lightning and thunder might scare 'em." Brandon tipped his hat and rode off toward his homestead at a fast clip.

Mariah headed into Pine Valley with Clint.

She saw the Cirque of the Towers looming over the town. Standing guard. "I've always thought those mountain peaks were a kind of sanctuary."

"They're one of the reasons I decided to stay in Pine Valley permanently," Clint said. "That and meeting a pretty blacksmith and finding a nice piece of land—and a town in need of a good restaurant."

"Admit it, we were in need of *any* restaurant. The fact that you made it a good one was a bonus."

Clint smiled as they picked up their pace to outrun the oncoming storm. The wind had started whipping up in earnest around them.

As they rode on, she looked up again at the magnificent guardians of their home. "It's all nonsense, isn't it?" She turned away from the mountains.

"What is?" Clint asked.

"It's nonsense that those mountains can provide any kind of safe haven for anyone. Oh, maybe they slow the wind down a little. This is an unusually comfortable town as far as the weather goes. Gets mighty cold in winter and hot in summer. But Iowa was worse."

"New York City was worse. But you're not talking about the wind."

"No, I'm talking about how I look at those mountains and they make me feel safe."

"You've been anything but safe for a long time," Clint said.

"Guess that's true," she replied.

"Now, let's get the horses and Brutus inside the smithy. The animals are in need of shelter."

They led the horses into stalls and made short work of stripping the leather. Brutus settled down and looked comfortable enough, if worn clean out. Finished, they rushed toward the doctor's office in the increasingly heavy sprinkles and ducked inside.

"Those tracks will be washed away in the storm, won't they?" Mariah asked.

"You didn't see anyone but Larson, right?"

She shook her head. "And the man who killed him today almost certainly was one of the men who killed Pa and Theo. Now our chance to follow him and catch him is sure to be lost in the rainstorm."

As if on cue, the sprinkles switched to a hammering rain, coming more sideways than straight down.

Doc Preston chose that moment to step out of the back room. "Nell's fine. She's got a headache, but I didn't need to put in stitches. Come on back."

Nell was sitting up on the examining table.

"You're supposed to be resting, Nell," Doc said.

Nell looked down at her shirtwaist, frowning. She wore a dark riding skirt, which was fine, but there was a large bloodstain on the front of her pretty top.

"If I go home right now, I might be able to get the bloodstains out of this and my bonnet."

The doctor shook his head. "I told you no more work today."

Mariah smiled at Doc. "We'll walk her home, and I'll wash out her things. You can talk me through removing the stains, Nell. Later, you can come home with us to Clint's place. I don't want you alone tonight."

Clint slapped himself on the forehead. "I just ran out of the diner. I abandoned everything."

"Pete Wainwright served the noon meal, Clint," Doc said. "He was just finishing up when I got back to town with Nell. He might not've done it to suit you, but he said everyone ate things right up. He stopped in and gave me your key." Doc pulled it out of his pocket and handed it over. "He said he washed up, too. Several of the men helped. The money's on a table in the kitchen. Mayor Pete also apologized for not riding out to search for Mariah. He said he'd stayed to help here in town as plenty had gone out."

Clint shook his head to clear it from the panic he'd felt. He looked at Mariah. "None of that was important when I knew you were in danger."

Smiling, she patted his arm. "Help me get Nell back to her place. She and I will get her blouse washed up while you make sure the diner is settled for the night." Mariah turned back to Nell. "We'll see how you're feeling. You can ride if you're not feeling up to the walk to our place."

The rain had since changed to hail. The roof bore the brunt of the onslaught, causing the building to shake. But because they built things tough in Wyoming, mostly with shutters instead of glass windows, the hail wouldn't do much harm in the end.

"All of you just settle in for a while. I've got coffee on." Doc moved to the little potbellied stove he had in the examining room.

Only then did Clint realize he'd smelled the coffee, and it was part of what eased his terror over what Mariah had gone through.

His wife, alive and well. Seeing Nell sitting up. The safety of shelter from the storm. A good dog curled up in the stable. Coffee bubbling pleasantly.

"A cup of hot coffee sounds great," Mariah said. Then she asked Nell, "Are you up to walking to the table there?"

"With an arm to lean on, yes." A few moments later, all four of them were sitting around the table and enjoying coffee together.

Before long, the hail ended, though the rain continued to pour while Nell, Mariah, and Clint gathered their strength.

31

The rainstorm had put an end to everything related to Mariah's kidnapping.

The sheriff had met Henry Wainwright with Nate and Lobo and he'd sent them both home.

Larson would be buried as soon as the rainwater stopped dripping. The sheriff had found mostly healed dog bites on his arm that were proof of yet more of the man's crimes.

Clint had found the diner to be in satisfactory shape, and he'd been in good spirits when Mariah and Nell arrived. The three of them walked to his house.

Nell was given, despite her protest, the bed. Mariah slept beside Clint on the floor by the fireplace. Clint had suggested she sleep in the bed with Nell, but Mariah couldn't bear to be separated from him. Just letting him go tend the diner while she helped Nell change into clean clothes, wash out her stained shirtwaist and bonnet, and gather a nightgown had been enough to make her near frantic.

It seemed as if she wasn't quite over her frightening experience.

Now here they lay, side by side. A fire crackling nearby. The smell of woodsmoke and the welcome heat driving away the damp of the rain and the chill of oncoming autumn.

A pallet of blankets on the floor did little to soften it. But it didn't matter as long as they could hold each other tight.

"Those towers of rocks didn't protect me today, Clint. You did."

"Yes, and the sheriff and Willie. Henry and Brandon."

"True, it was the people of this town who kept me safe. Doc Preston and Nell with her holstered six-gun. Becky lending me Brutus. But mostly it was you, Clint. You kept me safe, but more than that, you made me *feel* safe because you made me feel loved."

Clint lay on his back, with Mariah resting her head on his strong shoulder. He shifted and took her upper arms in his gentle hands and lifted her higher so she could see his eyes in the flickering firelight. She lay nearly on top of him now.

"You feel loved because you *are* loved. You know I love you, don't you, Mariah?"

"Yes, I know you do. And it's a wonderful feeling." She bent down and kissed him. "One I share. I didn't quite admit it even to myself at the time. But now I know I'd have never agreed to marry you, no matter how frightened I was, if I didn't already love you."

The wood shifted in the fireplace and sent sparks up the chimney.

The warmth of the fire. The gentle rain falling down outside. Brutus snoring quietly nearby. Nell safe and sleeping in their home.

Clint's arms around her.

She adjusted her position so she could rest on her elbows on either side of him and smiled down.

"I was so terrified, Mariah. I felt like the light would be gone from my life forever if something happened to you. I don't suppose you'd agree to let me pack you in cotton wool and keep you by my side at all times. We could buy the cotton from Nell—she could use the business."

She laughed. "What would the people of Pine Valley do for a blacksmith?"

"I know. I married a woman just like God recommended in Proverbs thirty-one."

Mariah thought of that chapter in the Bible and quoted, "'She worketh willingly with her hands.'"

Clint added, "'She riseth also while it is yet night. She girdeth her loins with strength, and strengtheneth her arms.' You've strengthened your arms, Mariah, swinging that hammer of yours." He slid one hand down her arm, paused to squeeze the muscle in her upper arm, and smiled.

"How about, 'She perceiveth that her merchandise is good'?"

Clint's hand slid on down her arm to take her hand. He kissed her palm. "Calluses. You work very willingly with your hands." Then he kissed the tips of her fingers. "And yet you are all that is woman. Strong muscles and callused fingers, but soft and sweet and very beautiful."

"Thank you, Clint. I didn't realize it until recently, not since Pa and Theo died, but I've spent a lot of time turning away from some of the softer things because I was so eager to prove to Pa that I was strong enough to do the work

292

of a man. But the truth is, I like pretty dresses. I like the bonnet Nell made for me. I'm going to be a more proper sort of female when I'm not working over a forge."

"That sounds just fine. Be more proper if you want, but I love you just the way you are." He smiled and kissed her, then tucked her head under his chin with his arm wrapped tight around her shoulders.

They lay together at the end of a terrible day, and before sleep claimed her, Mariah let herself fully enjoy the marriage she and Clint had forged in love.

Mary Connealy writes romantic comedies about cowboys. She's the author of the BROTHERS IN ARMS, BRIDES OF HOPE MOUNTAIN, HIGH SIERRA SWEETHEARTS, KINCAID BRIDES, TROUBLE IN TEXAS, WILD AT HEART, and CIMARRON LEGACY series, as well as several other acclaimed series. Mary has been nominated for a Christy Award, was a finalist for a RITA Award, and is a two-time winner of the Carol Award. She lives on a ranch in eastern Nebraska with her very own romantic cowboy hero. They have four grown daughters—Joslyn, married to Matt; Wendy; Shelly, married to Aaron; and Katy, married to Max—and seven precious grandchildren. Learn more about Mary and her books at

maryconnealy.com
facebook.com/maryconnealy
seekerville.blogspot.com
petticoatsandpistols.com

Sign Up for Mary's Newsletter

Keep up to date with Mary's latest news on book releases and events by signing up for her email list at maryconnealy.com.

More from Mary Connealy

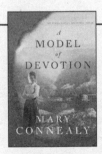

A brilliant engineer, Jilly Stiles sets her focus on fulfilling her dream of building a mountaintop railroad—and remaining independent. But when a cruel and powerful man goes to dangerous lengths to try to make Jilly his own, marrying her friend Nick may be the only way to save herself and her dreams.

A Model of Devotion
THE LUMBER BARON'S DAUGHTERS #3

You May Also Like . . .

Michelle Stiles has stayed one step ahead of her stepfather and his devious plans by hiding out at Zane Hart's ranch. Zane has his own problems, having discovered a gold mine on his property that would risk a gold rush if he were to harvest it. But soon danger finds both of them, and they realize their troubles have only just begun.

Inventions of the Heart
THE LUMBER BARON'S DAUGHTERS #2

After learning their stepfather plans to marry them off, Laura Stiles and her sisters escape to find better matches and claim their father's lumber dynasty. Laura sees potential in the local minister of the poor town they settle in, but when secrets buried in his past and the land surface, it will take all they have to keep trouble at bay.

The Element of Love
THE LUMBER BARON'S DAUGHTERS #1

When Gwendolyn Brinley accepted a paid companion position for the Newport season, she never imagined she'd be expected to take over responsibilities as an assistant matchmaker. Tasked with finding the season's catch, Walter Townsend, a wife, her assignment becomes increasingly difficult when she realizes his perfect match might be . . . her.

A Match in the Making by Jen Turano
THE MATCHMAKERS #1
jenturano.com

⬧ BETHANYHOUSE

More from Bethany House

Ruth Anniston survived an injury that left her physically scarred. Now, she hides away from curious eyes as a kitchen and dining room supervisor at the El Tovar Hotel. When money begins to disappear from the hotel, she works together with the handsome head chef to save the El Tovar and forge a new path for the future.

A Mark of Grace by Kimberley Woodhouse
SECRETS OF THE CANYON #3
kimberleywoodhouse.com

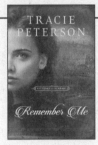

Haunted by heartbreak and betrayal, Addie Bryant escapes her terrible circumstances with the hope she can forever hide her past and with the belief she will never have the future she's always dreamed of. When she's reunited with her lost love, Addie must decide whether to run or to face her wounds to embrace her life, her future, and her hope in God.

Remember Me by Tracie Peterson
PICTURES OF THE HEART #1
traciepeterson.com

When midwife Catherine Remington is accused of a murder she didn't commit, she flees to Colorado to honor a patient's dying wish to deliver a newborn to his father. But what she doesn't bargain for is how easily she'll fall for the charming sheriff, or how quickly her past will catch up with her and put their love and lives in danger.

The Last Chance Cowboy by Jody Hedlund
COLORADO COWBOYS #5
jodyhedlund.com

BETHANYHOUSE